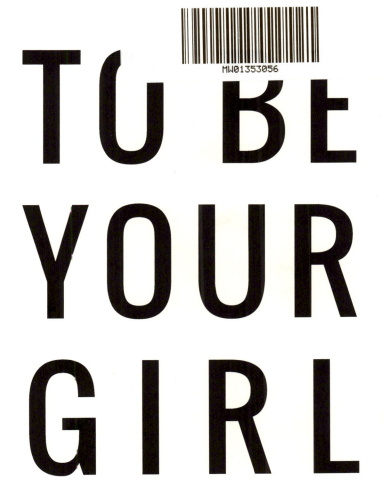

Copyright © 2019 by Rae Kennedy

All rights reserved. No part of this book may be reproduced or used in any manner without written permission of the copyright owner except for the use of quotations in a book review. For more information, address: raekennedystudio@gmail.com

FIRST EDITION
RAKE Publishing

www.raekennedyauthor.com

978-1-7333189-1-4

To Be Your Girl

CHAPTER 1

"THE FUCK?" HIS VOICE IS ROUGH.

And annoyed.

He steps out from the darkened doorway and into the tiny hallway, wearing only tight black boxer briefs. He is also literally standing a foot in front of me. I try to back up a bit but I don't have anywhere to go. Did I mention the hall is minuscule? I'm trying not to stare but the fixture in the ceiling puts out an impressive amount of light and every bulge and indent under his taut skin is illuminated—perfectly highlighting the clearly defined V just above the waistband of his boxers.

Don't stare at his crotch!

I gaze up his body, over his smooth abs and muscular chest. Then I see his arms. His broad shoulders and lean, cut arms are covered in full-sleeve tattoos.

He looks up, still acclimating to the light, one eye closed and the other squinting in my direction. His jaw is angular and defined, his mouth full with just-right pink lips. His dark blond hair is short on the sides and quite a bit longer on top, mussed all over. Fuck, he is gorgeous.

I'm going to be living with…this?

Tuck comes up behind me, placing his large warm hand on my shoulder. "Hey, looks like you already met. Great." He looks happily between us. "Haley, this is my roommate, Cade. Cade, this is Haley. She's moving in with us, remember?"

I stick my hand out and notice it shake a little. Wow, I need to get a grip on myself. He's just a human man—just the sexiest one I've ever seen in real life.

And he's mostly naked.

He looks at my hand then back up to Tuck. "Right," he says as a skinny blonde in a hot pink dress steps out of his room, carrying her shoes, her hair disheveled and makeup slightly smeared.

She doesn't seem to notice us standing there, or me with my arm still outstretched like a total moron.

"I had fun, Cade. Call me later?"

"Don't have your number." He yawns, eyes still half-shut, and steps back into his room, closing the door on the three of us.

Um...okay.

The blonde doesn't seem particularly dismayed, nor does she acknowledge us. She just turns and walks down the hall then out the front door. I turn to Tuck.

"What the hell was that?"

His face scrunches. "Sorry...but you'll probably have to get used to that. It's kind of a recurring thing."

"Maybe I should have looked into the on-campus housing."

"Stop being a baby. This makes way more sense. We're only five minutes from campus, you won't have to pay rent, and as an added bonus, I get to keep an eye out on my kid sister." His grin is easy and infectious. I have missed it. All I can do is roll my eyes and swat him across the arm.

"Ouch!" he says, rubbing his bicep. "You've become violent since I moved out."

"Well then, guess I can look out for myself."

Tuck humphs in disagreement. "Let's go get the rest of your bags."

He practically sprints down to his truck. I take more care going down the old concrete steps, which are cracked and buckled from the large maple trees in the yard.

When I reach the street, Tuck has already managed to sling all four of my bags over his shoulders, the straps haphazardly crisscrossing his torso. Balancing on one foot, he stretches his long arm across the passenger seat. The bags all shift to the left and he stumbles for a second before retrieving my purse. He turns around triumphantly, his big smile revealing the deep dimples in his cheeks.

"Are you going to let me carry anything?"

He tosses over my purse.

I roll my eyes at him. "Seriously?"

"I got this." He starts waddling up the steps, covered in my luggage.

If he wants to be my pack mule, I guess I'll let him.

I look up at the house, my home for the next two years. It's a one-story bungalow with shingles painted some earthy color that I can't quite make out in the dark—maybe a green? The lit front porch is painted all white with thick square columns. It is adorable—not at all how I had pictured Tuck's bachelor pad.

The warm August breeze sweeps through my hair and rustles the trees overhead as I follow Tuck up to the front door.

In the entryway, a few pairs of boots and sneakers are

lined along the thick baseboard. A black leather jacket and set of keys hang on the wall above a small bench.

Around the corner is a modest kitchen with cream-colored cabinets which look like they have been painted over a hundred times. I don't see a dishwasher, but the kitchen is bright and clean and smells faintly of oranges. It opens to the living room where there is one charcoal gray sofa, a flat screen television that takes up half the wall, and a worn, cognac-colored leather club chair in the corner.

The wood floor squeaks as Tuck emerges from the hallway.

"Hey, all of your stuff is in the room. Want a tour?"

"I think I just took it."

He returns my smile. "Yeah, it's not much, but it works. Here…" He ushers me down the hallway and points to the first door on the left. "I'm sure you gathered this is Cade's room." He points across the hall. "And this is yours. Next door is the bathroom and the last door down there is my room."

"Only one bathroom?" Shit.

"No, there's one attached to my room, so you'll be sharing with Cade." The look on my face must convey my horror because he adds quickly, "But you can always come use mine. Just…knock first."

"You're just as gross as you were at thirteen."

He winks at me. "Thanks, sis. Why don't we get some sleep? Cade and I'll both be at work in the morning but afterward, I'll show you around town a little and then to campus. Okay?"

"Sure."

"Night, Hale."

"Night, Tuck."

I shut the door to my new room behind me. It is small, of course, but very clean. A full-sized bed sits in the middle with just enough room for a nightstand on each side, right between the light blue-gray walls and lacy white duvet. A worn-out dresser stands across from the bed. I'm afraid to open the closet and decide to wait until tomorrow to be disappointed. The windows, however, are large and stretch from floor-to-ceiling with a deep sill where I can definitely sit and read or study, and the thick white moldings are everywhere and beautiful. I can work with this.

Being in Tuck's house feels weird. Leave it to me to be almost done with my Bachelor's then decide to transfer universities. Probably should have stuck it out, but I just didn't love the school and didn't click with any of the students in my program. Tucker had been ecstatic when I told him I'd applied to his alma mater. He is the main reason I'd decided on it. I've missed him since he moved out when he was eighteen.

Sheesh, that was over eight years ago.

I fall across the bed and let the pent-up stress from the move and the car ride dissolve into the soft mattress. The bedding smells like fresh laundry and the warmth envelopes me. I climb in without even taking off my clothes.

* * *

I awake early the next moring with soft light filtering through the lush green leaves of the trees outside my window. On the street, Tuck's truck is already gone. The house is quiet.

I take a lingering shower—the hot water doesn't die out after five minutes like at my last apartment and I feel like testing the limits. I dry my dark brown hair and let it hang in loose waves down my back. The waves aren't tight enough to be called curls so I usually just straighten my hair, but the straightener is still packed and I don't feel like fishing for it.

Back in my room, I put on some cute little briefs. They are white with yellow polka dots and yellow lace around the edges. I put on a tank top and then look around for my gray sweats. Three bags later I still haven't found them. Shit.

I give up and stalk out to the kitchen. What-the-fuck-ever. I'm starving.

There seems to be plenty of food in the house—lots of produce and dried pasta, but not much ready-to-eat. No cereal. Hmm. I bend over, searching the fridge. Guess I can make eggs or something.

"Whoa!" An unfamiliar deep voice is right behind me.

I yelp and jump back, hitting my head on a fridge shelf. Cade is standing in the kitchen, fully dressed, his blond hair brushed back smoothly on top of his head, shaved short on the sides. He has a wide, mischievous grin on his face. His eyes flicker quickly down to my undies then back up to my face.

Holy fuck.

I can completely freak out right now or I can keep calm and act like it's nothing. I'm cool. I don't care that this stranger is staring at me in my underwear—it covers more than my swimsuit. No big deal. We're going to live together. I should just get over it. I steady my expression and put on a nonchalant smile.

"Hi. Um...you startled me."

"I should say so." His eyes go to my bare legs again, not so subtly this time. "Haley, right?"

"Yeah."

His smirk is devious. He puts his hand out to me.

"It's nice to officially meet you," he says.

I take his hand and shake it firmly. His warm fingers curl around mine with equal insistence and a shiver runs up the inside of my arm.

I am being silly. Let's get this over with. I place my hand on my hip and put my little polka-dotted undies on full display.

"Well, it's only fair after I met you in your underwear that you get to meet me in mine."

Cade bursts out a hard laugh, slapping the counter as he looks back up at me. "Fair enough," he agrees, his smile showing through his eyes and it seems much warmer and more relaxed than it had just a moment ago. Of all the things I saw last night, I hadn't noticed his eyes. They are so blue.

He moves around me easily to grab an apple off the counter. "You won't find me complaining about it. Tuck might have a different opinion though…"

His gaze is definitely lingering on my panties, then up to my tank top. Am I wearing a bra? No. The refrigerator is still open behind me and my skin has gone prickly and my nipples are stiffening. That is my cue to go.

"Uh, I'll catch you later." I haul ass out of there. I can hear him chuckling from the kitchen behind me. Nice.

* * *

Tuck and I head out so I can get to know my new town and school a little bit. Class will start in just a few days and I am a bit nervous, but the campus is beautiful with huge oak trees standing out against a backdrop of stately brick buildings all laid out on rich green expanses of lawn.

The small downtown is also cute. It's packed with students and intellectuals looking around the shops and boutiques, sketching on benches, and playing street music. The excitement of a new school year is palpable.

We arrive home after grabbing a quick slice of gooey, greasy pizza for dinner. I have just walked in the front door, left sandal still in hand when a half-naked girl tears around the corner. Awesome.

"You are such a jerk, Cade. I never want to see you again!" She fumbles to get her heels on and stomps toward the door.

"That was sort of the point of the conversation we were just having." A shirtless Cade emerges after her, his face completely unaffected as he shrugs her off and turns back toward the living room. Poor clueless girl looks even more upset than before as she runs past me and out the door.

Yep, and I am just standing here holding my shoe. I have a feeling this is going to get old. On the plus side, I note that he never seems to let them overstay their welcome, so at least I won't have to try and pretend to get along with any of these girls over breakfast or something. That would be awkward. I decide I will just ignore them as they seem to do me and not worry about it.

But I can't ignore the smug look on Cade's face, who has slung himself over the couch, still sans shirt.

I walk over to him. "So…you're kind of a dick."

Cade's eyebrows rise incredulously and he opens his mouth as if to say something but then abruptly shuts it. His eyes narrow and he cocks his head to the left, studying me before a smile creeps upon his face. It is similar to the mischievous one he gave me when ogling my underwear.

"Was that a question?"

"Nope. Just an observation."

"Well. You've got me figured out then, don't you?"

Tuck walks in behind me. "Who's got what figured out?"

"Oh, Haley here's got me pegged. Called me a dick."

Tuck unsuccessfully stifles his laughter. "I'm guessing this has to do with the girl who passed me on the way out? Sorry, man. She's pretty good about calling out bullshit."

"Oh, I got it." Cade nods. "There are some perks to living with a chick though, aren't there, Dots?" He turns toward me, that stupid smile on his stupid pretty face.

"Dots?" Tuck looks confused.

"Never mind," I say, and then turn to go to my room, hoping neither of them notices the heat going to my cheeks.

Yep, he's a dick. Nailed it.

CHAPTER 2

The first week of class is uneventful. The second week, however, is when I meet him.

He sits next to me just after the professor has started the lecture.

"Do you suppose he wears the same pants every day or that he has multiple pairs he rotates?" he whispers, hunched down all sneaky.

I look at our professor. Milt Trobaugh does indeed seem to wear the same pair of itchy-looking pea-green wool pants every day. He pairs them with about three different cardigans he cycles through, all in different shades of brown.

I can't help the grin that turns up the corners of my mouth as I whisper from behind my notebook like a third grader.

"I think it's the same pair, but that he washes them every night—with his one cardigan and one pair of socks."

Then he smiles at me. A big, gorgeous smile with perfectly straight white teeth. They stand out against his tan skin. He has beautiful, big dark brown eyes with dark hair that just curls at his ears. His nose is straight, his features sharp and masculine. The spark in his eyes is playful, friendly, even child-like. His cologne is maybe a little heavy, but it smells amazing.

"I'm Adam."

"Haley."

"Haley. That's a pretty name. Perfect for a very pretty girl." His appreciation is so sincere I can't help but go all giddy googly-eyed at him. I may have also giggled.

Professor Trobaugh clears his throat and begins talking a little louder—definitely giving us the evil eye. Adam and I try hard to stifle our snickers. He opens his hand to me under the table.

"Nice to meet you, Haley." His voice sounds so sensual when he whispers my name.

"You too."

His thumb strokes the back of my hand just once before we let go. Wow.

When we get up to leave, his arm brushes mine and we exchange silly grins again.

"Hey, I'll see you around."

"Yeah, definitely," I agree.

I have to wait until Thursday to see him again. He sits in the same spot next to me like it is no big deal. We muse about Professor Trobaugh's lazy eye and how he got it through some crazy professoring accident, no doubt. An unlikely Indiana Jones.

On the way out of class, I don't see Adam, even though I am totally looking. He must be lost in the sea of coeds all rushing to get the hell out of here. I am halfway to the quad when he catches up to me.

"Hey!" he says, a little out of breath.

"Hi." I slow so he can walk with me.

"I was wondering if you wanted to… I don't know, get some coffee or something? Sometime?" He looks hopeful but a little nervous.

"Of course!" Too eager. "I mean, yeah, I'd like that." The joy on his face is boyish and heartwarming.

"I have a couple hours until my next class. Are you free now?"

Now? Yes, please. "Sure. I'm done for the day."

We walk over to a little coffee shop just off the edge of campus. It is cramped but cozy. There are tiny teal side-tables and yellow stools surrounded by mismatched chairs and cushions in varying shades of red, orange, and pink. Students are huddled in groups, reading and chatting and working on laptops. It is all grandma-friendly and hipster-cool at the same time. We go up to the counter and I am hit with warm aromas of cinnamon and butter, coffee and vanilla. The pastries in the display look like flaky, glazed-over heaven.

I order a caramel macchiato and decide to forgo the pastry. He doesn't need to see me drool this early on—best to leave a little mystery. When I reach for my purse to pay, Adam puts his hand over mine. It is soft and warm and covers mine perfectly.

"Let me get it."

"Oh, no that's fine, but thanks."

"I want to get it for you."

Is this a date? He really wants to purchase my coffee. So I let him. He leads me to a cute little table in the corner that is decoupaged with doilies. There are two rickety wood chairs with spindle legs that are all different colors and shapes—and lengths, I suspect, from the constant teetering back and forth.

"I've never noticed you around campus before this year. You're an anthropology major, right?"
I nod.
"We would have had some classes together before. I think I definitely would have noticed you."
"Yeah, I just moved here. It's my fourth year of college but I have a couple more to go since not all the credits from my old school transferred. I have to make up a few prerequisites and core classes, but I'm on track for the most part." I am totally babbling. But gratefully, he smiles and nods and doesn't act the least bit disinterested in my boringness. In fact, he seems enthralled by everything I talk about—even my addiction to Jane Austen and other classic novels.
"Oh, yes!" He feigns a British accent and fans his face. "That Mr. Darcy sure is handsome!"
I balk. He knows who Mr. Darcy is? *Pride and Prejudice* is my favorite. I am telling him this when he starts chuckling at me.
"You are just too cute. I'm glad I could surprise you. I haven't read the book but I've watched the movie like a million times with my mom."
A warm gleam shows in his eyes when he mentions his mom. Oh man. Sexy, smart, and treats his mother well— that is the trifecta. I am done for.
We talk for another hour about everything, it seems. He makes me laugh and is kind enough to laugh at my not-so-funny jokes. He somehow finds every opportunity to gently brush my arm, touch my hand, and lean close when he reaches to get some napkins.
Every time I can feel his warmth and smell his wonderful cologne, I am dizzy with his proximity. More than once I

have to stop myself from leaning over and smelling the spot right behind his ear above his neck. I do resist, though.

My macchiato is long gone but I don't want our time to end. He seems to be lingering as well. We get up to go and he holds the door open for me. The air outside is cool and crisp in contrast to the warm, embracing aroma in the coffee shop.

"Hey, so I can give you a ride home…if you want."

I'm glad he doesn't want to end it either. "Sure."

* * *

When he pulls up next to the house, I expect him to say goodbye, but he gets out and rushes around the front of the car to open my door. I don't think anyone has ever done that for me before. He takes my hand to help me out but doesn't let go as we walk up the path. My hand fits perfectly into his.

By the time we stop at the front porch, I feel giddy and my legs are like Jell-O. He sticks his hands in the pockets of his light, fitted jeans and looks at me through his lashes with a sheepish grin.

"I was wondering if I could get your number?"

He has the nerve to look uncertain of my answer as if we hadn't just had the best time together. He is standing there in his soft gray crewneck sweatshirt that perfectly complements his tan skin. He could have just walked out of a J. Crew catalog and onto my porch. What else am I going to say?

"Yes! Of course."

A smile lights up his face as he takes a step closer. I can feel his heat radiate toward me. He hands me his phone and I quickly enter my info then hand it back to him. He takes it, our fingers just barely grazing each other, sending a little jolt of electricity through my arm. Stepping closer, he leans in.

The smell of him is intoxicating. His face is just inches from mine. I tilt my head a fraction toward him. My heartbeat quickens and my hands feel clammy. He goes right in and brushes his lips softly against my cheek. When he pulls back, he has that cute boyish smile on his face again. Then he turns and walks down the steps.

* * *

I flutter in the door and twirl into the kitchen. In fact, I twirl right into Cade, who I don't see standing right in front of me.

I haven't seen much of him since I moved in, mostly just in passing. I can't quite figure out his work schedule and he is often out until the early morning hours. Whoring it up around town, I'm sure. Bumping into him and almost knocking myself into the counter is not ideal.

"Whoa, Haley. Apparently, we shouldn't meet in kitchens."

"Hmmm." I can't keep my grin down.

"You're beaming today." He looks me up and down.

"Yup." I glide past him to grab a pan. "And now I'm going to make dinner."

"Oh? I'll stay out of your way then." He moves around the bar and sits on a stool, looking at me intently. "What are we having tonight?"

"We?" He hasn't been home for dinner before.

"Duh." Cocky grin. "Do you want some help?"

"Uh, no. I think I can handle it. I'm just making some fettuccine alfredo." I start filling a large pot full of water for the pasta. I give him a look I'm sure reads as *you can't possibly be serious about helping me in the kitchen.* Growing up, my mom worked evenings, so Tuck and I learned to fend for ourselves early on. I cooked dinner most nights and am more than proficient in the kitchen.

"Okay. I'll just watch then."

I suddenly feel a little self-conscious as I begin melting the butter for the béchamel sauce. Is he going to sit there the whole time and stare at me?

He is.

With a smug-ass grin, I might add.

The alfredo sauce is almost done—it just needs to thicken up a little. I am stirring it when he interjects.

"You know what would make that even better? A pinch of grated nutmeg."

I look at him like he is fucking nuts. He is obviously fluent in facial expressions because he starts laughing at me.

"Seriously, just trust me."

I narrow my eyes at him, studying him for a second. His clear blue eyes are looking right into mine, relaxed. Fine. I turn and start rifling through the spice cabinet for the nutmeg.

"No, no." Cade gets up, walks over to the freezer, and retrieves a little baggy. Then he grabs a micro-planer from a drawer. They have some fancy cookware for two single guys. He comes over to where I am standing in front of the stove and playfully bumps me over with his hip.

"Fresh is always best." He grinds a couple dashes of fresh nutmeg into the white sauce and stirs it in. He gets a spoon from the drawer to his right without even looking and tastes a lick. "Needs salt." He adds some salt with one hand and stirs with his other. He has pushed up the sleeves of his shirt to his elbows, exposing the myriad of black and gray tattoos on his defined forearms.

I admire how his muscles flex under his tattooed skin as he works. This time when he tastes it, he gives a nod of approval. I am staring at him the whole time like he has just killed a kitten in front of me.

He glances over to me, that perfectly sexy smug smile on his face that kind of makes me melt and want to slap him at the same time. "Tuck hasn't told you anything about me, has he?"

"Um, no. Not really."

"Hmm. So you have no idea what I do?"

"No." Obviously.

"I'm a chef."

Well, shit. Now I look like a stuck-up bitch.

"Really?"

"Yeah. I'm the sous chef at *La Mer* downtown."

"Oh." I am a little lost as to how to respond to that.

"Oh?"

"I guess I figured you worked at like a tattoo shop or something."

"You know, I always thought that would be kind of fun—but then I have to remind myself that not everyone coming in for a tattoo is going to be a hot chick. There are a lot of sweaty guys you'd have to touch, too."

That is more like the Cade-response I expect.

"Is that all you guys think about?"

"Pretty much." He shrugs. "Hey, you know what would be great in this? Prosciutto. I just picked some up the other day. I'll make it."

He is like a giddy little boy getting ingredients out of the fridge—a very adept little boy who is seriously skilled with a knife and hot frying pans. I watch him render the prosciutto until it is crispy and smells amazing. He totally took over but I don't mind.

"You want some salad with this or something?" he asks.

"Uh, sure."

"There's some lettuce in the fridge. If you'll clean it and chop it up, I'll make some dressing. Caesar okay?"

"Yeah." I begin getting the salad ready. I have never been bossed around in the kitchen before but I'm not about to complain.

By this time, my stomach is rumbling. Cade whips up some dressing in a small food processor, blending in olive oil after adding the anchovies. Seriously? Who keeps anchovies lying around the house? A professional chef, I guess. Suddenly all the gourmet-quality equipment makes total sense.

* * *

BEST. DINNER. EVER.

We sit at the tiny bistro table situated in front of the bay window in the kitchen. Cade tells me about how he and Tuck met at a party his second year at the university. They were both trying to hook up with the same girl. Neither of them managed to close the deal. Apparently, she had a boyfriend. A big boyfriend—who was very jealous—but they did get matching black eyes.

Cade has an easy laugh that lights up his whole face. We are having such a nice time talking I almost forget he is a total dick. The food is delicious, and I decide I won't argue with him again about telling me what to do in the kitchen. Only in the kitchen, though.

"That was amazing, Cade. But you know now you'll have to make me dinner every night."

"Oh, that's how it works, is it?"

"Yup."

His smile is wide and gorgeous, but his eyes are devious. "That could probably be arranged—as long as you don't mind eating at weird times. I usually work the swing shift at the restaurant."

"I'm pretty flexible."

His eyes widen a fraction. Uh-oh. He definitely read more into that than I intended.

"I meant my schedule!"

"Of course you did." He sits back with a placating nod and licks his bottom lip. Oh shit.

My phone rings and I jump in my seat, forgetting what that sound is for a second. A phone? I don't understand. When I go to answer it, I don't recognize the number.

"Hello?"

"Hey, it's Adam."

Ahh!

"Oh, hey. How's it goin'?" Keeping it casual. Good call.

"Uhh, great. It's not too soon for me to call, is it?"

I'm sure my face lights up like a little girl just given a pony as I step away from the table and into the hall.

"No way." Pshaw, call me anytime you want.

"Good, because I was wondering if you would go to dinner with me tomorrow and I was hoping to catch you before you made other plans."

Plans? What the hell are those?

"No plans. I'd love to go to dinner with you." Embarrassing, jumping-up-and-down dance party in my head.

"Cool! Pick you up at seven?"

"Sounds great."

"See you then."

I am practically skipping when I come back out. Cade is at the sink rinsing off the dishes.

"Good call then?" he asks.

"Uh huh." I can't hold in my squeal. "I got a date for tomorrow!"

His face falls just a fraction. "Already backing out of our standing dinner arrangement?"

"I guess you'll just have to make me lunch or—no! Even better, breakfast!"

"Deal." He returns to laid-back Cade who is unaffected. "So, who's this date with?"

"A guy in one of my classes. We went out to coffee today. His name is Adam."

"Oh, so that's why you have that same shit-eating grin on your face as earlier."

"Hey!" I smack him across the shoulder. "Be nice. I like him."

"He sounds dreamy," he says, but the playfulness from before seems to be gone. After he finishes with the dishes, he rather abruptly walks toward the door, grabs the black jacket and leaves without a glance back or a goodbye.

Later that night, I figure out where he went when I hear him and someone in heels stumble down the hall and into his room. Followed by noises worthy of a porno.

Fucking fantastic.

CHAPTER 3

The next morning I forgo the shower and just put my hair up, throw on my most comfortable pair of thread-bare jeans and a zip-up hoodie. I only have two morning classes then I will be able to spend the rest of the day getting ready for my date.

As I round the corner from the hall, a savory scent wafts over from the kitchen and makes my mouth water. But the kitchen is empty. As I get closer and the aroma becomes richer and saltier, I know it is coming from the kitchen, but there is no food and, more noticeably, no Cade. I approach the counter and then see a note.

> *Had to leave early this morning but I never go back on a deal. Breakfast is in the oven.*
> *-Cade*

I open the barely warmed oven and sure enough, oh my good lord. Eggs Benedict. I split my fork down the center of the perfectly poached egg, the bright yellow yolk oozing out slowly. I don't usually like a runny yolk but this one is so smooth and creamy. The hollandaise sauce is rich and the perfect balance to the salty ham. I devour it. So quickly and unladylike that I am glad no one is here to witness it.

Before I leave for class, I scribble him back just under his note.

That was ridiculously delicious. Thank you. But if you keep this up it's definitely going to go straight to my butt.
   -Haley

* * *

My sociology professor announces the next assignment: group project. I'd rather slam my head against this table. It would be easy. If I hit my head hard enough, I might be excused from this assignment...

I look around the room. Everyone seems relaxed enough, chatting happily with smiles on their faces. The handful of people in my immediate vicinity have already paired up. I don't know anyone's name. Making new friends has never been my strong suit. Probably has something to do with my resting bitch-face. My heart beats faster. I fucking hate group projects.

"Haley!" A tall blonde comes over to me. She has a huge, toothy smile and bright blue eyes. In fact, her eyes are a little far apart for her face, but she is unusually pretty. "Do you want to partner up with me?" She sits in the seat next to me, her smile lights up her whole face. She has a small gap between her two front teeth and faint freckles on her nose. Her long hair is thick and straight, the light bounces off it like a halo.

I have no idea who this glow-y chick is.

I blink at her a couple times. "Uhh, sure."

TO BE YOUR GIRL

"Ohmygosh! How rude of me. I'm Court."

Court turns out to be a great partner. We have our project roughly outlined by the end of class, our respective parts to research over the weekend, and a plan to reconvene in class Monday.

"Hey, do you want to come out with me tonight? My roommates and I are going to go grab a few beers and watch the game."

Is it that obvious I haven't made any friends yet?

"That sounds like fun, but I have plans tonight."

"Next time then!" Court waves and heads off in the other direction.

* * *

When I get home from school I am exhausted. Cade is still gone and Tuck is at work. There is a huge merger going down at his firm and he has been going in early and working late every night. He also admitted to me that he is "sorta" seeing this girl named Ali. And for just "sorta" seeing this girl, she sure takes up a lot of his time.

I'm going to take a nap. Then I will be all well-rested for my date.

The nap is a good decision.

I spend way too long getting ready—much longer than normal. I style my hair with my iron to amplify its natural curl and then grapple back and forth about whether to leave it down or put it up. Maybe only half up? Everything I do only seems to make it worse so I just leave it down by default. I do a gray smoky eye with dark mascara that makes the gold flecks in my light brown eyes stand out.

I stare at the clothes hanging in my closet. I own exactly

four dresses, but I don't want to wear any of them. I need to go shopping. I go with the navy dress I wore to my cousin's wedding because it is sophisticated but still hugs my body in all the right places, showing off my slim waist, adequate cleavage, and flowing down just a few inches above my knees. I finish off the look with my silver four-inch heels that make my short legs look sexy and actually give me some height so I can walk amongst the normal-heighted people.

In the living room, I wait for Adam. I know the house is empty but I still feel all disappointed there is no one here to tell me how great I look. You know, just a little ego boost before the big date. Standing there alone all done-up, I suddenly feel incredibly nervous and jittery.

I need a drink. Wine.

There is some chardonnay in the fridge and I happily pour myself a glass. It is cold and crisp and goes to my head quickly. Wine usually doesn't make me so giddy, but then I remember how I slept through lunch. Figures.

As I finish the glass and prepare to pour myself another, I see the note on the counter. Cade has added to our running correspondence—he must have come and gone while I slept.

> *I can tell you from first-hand knowledge—you don't need to worry about your ass.*
>   *-Cade.*

It's just the wine that is making my cheeks so hot. Really. At the end, he has drawn a little winky face. Winky face? I find the dichotomy of tattoo-covered Cade drawing me a winky face inexplicably hilarious. The giggle emerging from my lips sounds foreign to me.

Wow, was that extra alcoholic wine? My absurd laughing fit is quickly interrupted by the doorbell.

* * *

Adam helps me out of his sporty red coupe with a warm and gentle hand.

"You really do look magnificent tonight."

"Thanks." I look down as my cheeks grow warm. "Again."

Don't get me wrong, I know I look fabulous. I spent half the afternoon making sure of it, but he's the one who looks devastatingly handsome. He's dressed in a soft charcoal gray sweater and dark jeans as he leads me to the restaurant. I laugh to myself when I look up and see where we are. *La Mer.*

He turns around when he hears me laugh and, God, is his face just perfect. Those deep brown eyes are lit up with his smile and I find myself staring at the little cleft in his chin.

"What?" he asks.

"Oh, nothing. I hear this is a good restaurant."

"It's pretty romantic." His cheeks flush. I swoon at embarrassed Adam.

We enter the restaurant and he is right. Everything is beautiful, serene, and very romantic. The tables are intimate with white tablecloths and little flickering candles that cast a warm glow over the space. Actually, there doesn't seem to be any lighting other than candlelight.

We are seated promptly for our 7:15 reservation and the server recites the evening's specials. They all sound so fancy. I am a little overwhelmed. Adam smiles his boyish smile at me, putting his hand over mine across the table.

"I think we could use just a moment." He is so freaking handsome, and he can't take his eyes off of me, even if he is sweetly amused by my obvious French-restaurant virginity. I order more wine right away.

Turns out I had no need for worry—everything set for us on the table is superb. By the time our dessert—a strawberry tartlet drizzled with decadent vanilla bean-infused crème fraiche—is set down I am pleasantly buzzed on wine and laughing uncontrollably at Adam's stories about getting stranded on a city bus in Brazil. He had fallen asleep and failed to get off at the stop with the rest of the Habitat for Humanity volunteers over last year's Spring Break.

He is charming and only reluctantly removes his hand from mine to eat. His gaze is altogether more heated as we take turns eating the sweet dessert from the same spoon.

After dinner, we walk out onto the sidewalk. It is dark and I can just make out the haze of the moon glowing behind the clouds. I should have brought a jacket but I'm not used to it getting cool this early in the year.

I am heading toward Adam's car when he reaches for my hand. I slow and turn to look at him as he laces his large fingers through mine. Suddenly I feel quite warm. He leans down and brushes his nose against my cheek. His breath is hot against my skin and his scent makes me inhale deeply.

"You want to take a walk with me for a little while?"

Dear God, yes.

I can only nod in response. And so we walk. He asks me some more questions about my hometown and what I was like in high school. But mostly we just walk. And look up at the stars. Adam releases my hand and wraps his whole arm around my shoulders, my body fits snuggly under his arm and I rest my head into his chest. One of the perks of being so short. I could sink into him right here—he is so warm and solid against me.

We stop at an intersection for the light to change. The air is breezy and I am more aware of my bare arms as we are motionless. Out of the corner of my eye, I see his head dip down as his hand sweeps over my arm. I turn my face up ever so slightly and it is all the cue he needs. He closes the space between us quickly and his lips are pressed against mine.

Despite the chills, his kiss is heated and he begins to move his mouth tenderly, coaxing it open to allow our tongues to massage one another. He tightens his arms around me, pulling me in against his body and I wrap my arms around his waist, running my hands up his back. We break the kiss but hold the embrace a few moments longer. Our noses and foreheads are together, lips just an inch apart.

"Ready to head back now?"

Not really.

"Sure."

The ride home is much too brief. I don't want to be anywhere else but here with him. His hand is resting lightly on my knee and he takes his eyes off the road to smile at me every few seconds. I am still blissfully drunk off our kiss—and let's face it, the wine too.

I've got a tight grip on his hand as we navigate the cracked steps up to the porch. *Please don't trip in front of Adam.* I probably shouldn't have ordered that last glass of wine.

He gives my hand a squeeze before releasing it when we reach the door. I look up at his dark brown eyes and he closes the space between us. His warm hand is on my cheek, then in my hair, holding my face to his. His lips meet mine gently at first. The kiss becomes wetter, more eager as his tongue maps my mouth. His breathing becomes erratic. He pulls me to him as my fingers grip his sweater. He pulls away too soon.

"I should probably let you go now."

What?

"Yeah." I smile as sweetly as I can. I want the smile to say, "I'm a good girl. I like you, and that was nice," instead of what I am actually thinking, which is, "I haven't gotten laid in forever and I would like to attack you while ripping all your clothes off."

"Bye, Haley." He leans down and kisses my cheek. "I'll call you later." And with his stunning smile, he turns and leaves. The scent of his cologne lingers around me.

* * *

As I breeze inside, Cade is just walking from the kitchen into the living room. He's carrying a big bowl and shoving his mouth full of popcorn when he sees me and freezes, hand still in mid-shove.

"Wow." A piece of popcorn totally falls out of his mouth. "You look great." He looks me up and down incredulously, lingering a bit too long at my boobs.

"I clean up nice, I guess." Clearly, I hadn't impressed him lounging around the house in my sweats over the last few weeks. Well, that is for the best because I certainly don't need Cade looking at me like that. The way he is currently looking at me. He nods his approval.

"I was just about to start a movie. You want to watch it with me?"

I am still too awake from the incredible kissing to go to bed.

"Sure. Just...give me a minute." I am not sitting next to Cade all evening in this dress.

He shrugs and plops on the couch, still eating the popcorn by the fistfuls. Okay, maybe he isn't that distracted by the dress. I still go and change into a light T-shirt and my most comfortable gray sweats. In the bathroom, I scrub my face clean and put my hair up into a bouncy ponytail.

When I come back out, he looks dramatically disappointed.

"No dress?"

"Um. No."

He has that devious panty-dropping smile on his face again. He looks at me like I am naked.

"That's all right. You looked nice in the dress, but not nearly as much as you do in polka-dots."

Heat rises to my ears and I can't think of a good retort. He motions for me to sit next to him.

"Sorry. It's just too easy to give you shit. I promise I'll be nice. I'll even share my popcorn." He holds up the bowl as a peace offering and I can't help but smile at the innocent look he so purposefully puts on his face.

I sit next to him and immediately swipe a handful of popcorn, giving him my best evil eye. Apparently, it is a pretty poor evil eye because it just makes his smile broaden. The movie is a ridiculous comedy from a few years ago. The jokes are juvenile, but I secretly love it.

We spend the first half of the movie intently

watching, laughing at every moronic joke and shtick while intermittently reaching for more popcorn. I try not to care when our hands brush against each other in the bowl, but it keeps happening and I swear he must think I am doing it on purpose.

More than once I realize my foot has wandered over to his side of the couch and is resting against his leg before I pull it away. He doesn't acknowledge our multiple accidental touches, but he doesn't move his leg either.

Near the bottom of the bowl of popcorn, I spot the perfect piece. It is huge and so unnaturally yellow I know it is going to be wonderfully buttery. Right as I reach for it, Cade snatches it. I reflexively smack his hand away. He drops the popcorn and looks at me, a little shocked. His astonishment quickly melts into his devious grin.

"What? You take up three-quarters of the couch and now you're going to hog the popcorn?"

"I am not taking up three-quarters of the couch!" I am not.

"Hey, you're the one who keeps touching me with your smelly feet." He is smirking at me. The jackass.

"My feet are not smelly!"

"Really? Let's see." He grabs for my foot. I kick and try to twist away from him but he is too fast and has my bare foot in his hand quickly. He pulls it up to his nose and scrunches up his face in an excessive display of distaste. "Whoa, super stinky."

I can tell he is joking, and I know my feet do not stink—oh god! Do my feet stink? Now he is full on laughing at me.

"You're an ass!" I grab for the popcorn and throw a few pieces right at his face. He is momentarily surprised then grabs a few pieces of his own and throws them at me, chuckling. He grabs my foot again and starts tickling the bottom of it.

Seriously? Apparently, I am six years old and I am laughing too hard to form any coherent sentences. I can only gasp out, "Stop!" in between sobs of laughter. I can't breathe. I am practically choking.

"Cade!" He's incessant. "Please...stop." I almost kick him trying to struggle away.

That was the first time.

The next time I actually do kick him in the face. A good hard heel right to the jaw. His teeth clank together when my heel connects.

"Ow! Fuck."

"Oh shit! I'm sorry, Cade!" I sit up toward him. "Are you all right?"

He has his hand to his face, massaging his open jaw. "I bit my tongue." He looks at me and abruptly seems less pissed and more pleased. "I think you made me bleed."

I can't control the giant smile that takes over my face.

"You're pretty happy with yourself, aren't you?"

"Well, you kind of deserved it."

Before he can retort—and I can tell it is going to be a good one—Tuck walks in the front door. I suddenly realize how close I am sitting to Cade. I scoot back to the other side of the couch. Cade straightens up a little too just as Tuck walks into the room.

He comes in, loosening his tie and collapses into the chair opposite the couch with a sigh.

"What are you guys watching? Oh, this movie sucks. Shit. You two have the same awful taste in movies. I'm going to bed." He gets up and moves toward the hall when Cade stands.

"Yeah, me too."

They both disappear into the hallway, two doors shutting behind them.

Really? Not even a "Goodnight, Haley." It is barely after midnight and I swear I have never heard Cade go to bed before two.

* * *

I climb into bed after finishing the last twenty minutes of the movie. I open my window just a sliver to let in the cool night air. My bed is soft and all-encompassing as I'm wrapped in my cozy blankets. I close my eyes and think over my day. The great first date. The moonlit walk. The first kiss. The second kiss.

Then I remember the mind-blowing breakfast. And the tickle fight.

My cell phone rings from under my pillow, jarring me from my thoughts. The screen is way too damn bright in my blackened room and it hurts my eyes.

It is Adam.

"Hi…" I am already smiling.

"I hope it's not too late to call. I just couldn't stop thinking about you."

Swoon.

"Me neither." That's mostly true.

"I guess I just wanted to hear your voice and tell you I can't wait to kiss you again."

Oh.

"Goodnight, Haley."

"Goodnight, Adam."

CHAPTER 4

Monday morning I am in the shower. You know, just showering. In the middle of shampooing my hair and humming some song stuck in my head when I hear the door open. *What the hell?*

"Hey!" I stick my head out of the shower, making sure to sort of wrap the curtain around me. Awkward, but functional. Cade is heading to the toilet, only wearing tight little boxer briefs. Red this time. As he walks away from me, I can make out his sinewy back muscles all heading down to two dimples just above his ass. It is pretty nice, definitely a firm little round butt in those snug briefs. Goddammit. "Get out of here!"

"Hey!" He turns to look at me, sleepy and...offended? "No looking. I need to piss."

"Excuse me? I'm naked in here!"

"Well, you're the one trying to sneak a look at my junk."

I swiftly retreat into the shower. "I was not."

"You keep telling yourself that." He is so infuriatingly good at flustering me.

"Fuck off."

"Feisty in the mornings. I like it."

I try not to, but I can completely hear him peeing. I scream just a tiny bit when the shower goes scalding hot and then ice cold after he flushes. I can hear him laughing as the sink runs. At least he is washing his hands.

I am especially glad to know he washed his hands when I come out and he is making breakfast. Actually, when it comes to the kitchen, at least, Cade is very neat and tidy. It is always spotless.

"Hungry?"

I eye him, not sure if I should act pissed about him interrupting my shower. But I have to be honest—I don't really mind seeing his almost naked, tattooed body. Considering the state in which I met him, I'm surprised I haven't seen him half-naked more often. I decide to play it off like I'm unaffected. Better not let him know I am still thinking about how great his ass looks.

"Whatcha making?"

"Smoked salmon frittata."

"Jesus."

He seems to enjoy that comment.

Tuck hurries into the kitchen, all suited up, and pours some coffee into a thermos.

"You having breakfast with us, man?" Cade asks him.

"Nah, I've got to run. I have a 10 AM deadline to meet. See you guys later."

I thought I'd see more of Tuck living with him.

The frittata is delicious. Damn. Now I really can't be mad at Cade.

"So, any requests for dinner? I have this evening off."

"Oh, sorry—I have plans tonight."

"Hmm. Same guy as this weekend?"

"Yep. Adam."

Cade looks at me sternly. He seems to be clenching his jaw too. Why is he being so judgmental? He hasn't even met Adam. Which reminds me—

"You'll get to meet him tonight when he comes over to study." We have a test tomorrow, but there's probably more than just studying on the agenda.

Cade doesn't seem very excited. "Super."

* * *

Adam looks all bashful, chinese takeout in hand, when I open the door to let him in. We settle on the living room floor, eating from the takeout boxes, our books and notes scattered around us.

We spend probably the first half an hour eating and snorting over Professor Trobaugh's newest cardigan in a rather fetching shade of mustard. Finally, we decide to start working. Adam is all cute and excited to show me the flash cards he has made.

I watch his large hands move as he cycles through them. They are very nice hands. His nails are short and clean, the fingers long and thick. I think about how I'd like to touch them or have them touch me...

"Ready?"

I wasn't paying attention. Oops.

I am recurrently distracted by him while he quizzes me. How his forearms flex when shuffling through the cards, how smooth and tan his skin looks against his light blue shirt, how his neck flexes when he laughs at my bizarre answers.

I swear I don't even hear half the questions—I am basically just throwing out related words arbitrarily. An hour later, my torture is finally over and he hands me the stack.

"Now you can test me."

"This isn't fair. Not only did you make these, but you've just gone through them twice." I'm a major complainer.

"Okay. How about you ask me anything you'd like. Make them as hard as you can."

"Let's do this." I grab my book and open it across my lap.

"But—let's make it a little more interesting."

I raise an eyebrow at him.

"Every time I get it right, I get something from you."

"Oh?" Now I'm intrigued.

"Yes. A kiss." His big brown eyes are too cute and wholesome to have such a scheming look in them. But sexy.

God, they are sexy.

"Accepted."

He gets the first question right. His face lights up. I lean forward and he is right there, giving me a very sweet kiss on the cheek. The next one is a quick, chaste kiss on the lips.

He misses the next few questions.

The third kiss lasts just a bit longer, his soft lips parting to allow our tongues to touch for the briefest of moments. He lingers there afterward. He smells like his delicious cologne and fried rice. It makes me smile.

I continue with the questions. I'm not going easy on him. Unfortunately, this means I haven't been kissed in the last ten minutes.

Change of strategy. I make sure he gets the last one right. I put my book down and crawl to him. As far as I am concerned, we're done studying. He grabs me eagerly and I yelp as he pulls me close and dips me toward the floor. Then his mouth is over mine, hot and firm, wanting. I let out a little moan of appreciation and he responds by intensifying the kiss, his tongue exploring my mouth deliberately with deep, slow movements. I have my arms wrapped around his neck as he holds me and I'm finding it hard to take regular breaths.

Then I hear a sound like someone clearing his throat behind me. Startled, Adam and I break the kiss. I am still out of breath when I turn to see Cade standing there.

"Oh! Hey, Cade." I shoot to my feet, smoothing my hair and straightening my shirt. I probably look a mess. "This is Adam." I motion to a more-than-confused-looking Adam as he gets up to stand next to me. "Adam, this is my roommate, Cade."

Now that introductions are complete, I realize I haven't told Adam about my living situation. They both eye each other suspiciously. Adam, obviously perplexed, is still the ever-polite man I have come to know and puts his hand out toward Cade.

"Nice to meet you, man."

Cade is looking at me instead of Adam.

"Sure." He turns and walks toward the front door without returning the handshake and leaves without another word. It is déjà vu. Maybe Cade has never actually been taught how introductions work.

"Your, uh, roommate there seems like a nice guy."

"Yeah, he can be kind of a dick sometimes."

Adam is clearly waiting for an explanation.

"He and my brother are best friends and they live here together. This is my brother's house and I just moved in at the beginning of the school year for convenience."

He seems generally appeased by that clarification. "I should probably get going. We should both get plenty of sleep before the test."

What!

"Guess you're right." Damn. But I can still be disappointed.

We gather his stuff and he leans in and gives me another nice kiss goodbye.

"See you in class."

"Night."

* * *

Over the next few weeks, my life falls into a nice routine. I get up and shower, inevitably to be interrupted by Cade's morning pee—which he simply "cannot fucking hold"—and then we eat breakfast together.

Sometimes Tuck joins us, but more often he is running out the door in the morning. Usually, breakfast is something easy and fast, like pancakes or eggs, but occasionally Cade surprises me with something absurdly elegant or involved, like homemade cinnamon rolls dripping with a spiced pecan caramel sauce. Thank goodness I am burning some calories riding my bike to and from campus.

After class most days I meet up with Adam. We often go to that little coffee shop where he first took me. Sometimes we sit out on one of the lawns, holding hands and just talking. We talk about growing up. What we were like in school. I immediately regret telling him I haven't had a boyfriend since high school, but he doesn't seem to care.

We are both from single-parent families. The way he

talks about her, Adam's mom must practically be a saint, whereas my mother is a bit more absent. Tuck and I had to stick together and watch out for one another after our father died twelve years ago. I was nine and he was fourteen. Tuck had to grow up much faster than me.

Adam listens attentively. He is a great listener. An even better kisser.

In the evenings, I go home and study, maybe watch some television while waiting for Cade to get home. He is off at irregular times, so we often have dinner at ten at night, but he comes home from cooking and running a kitchen all day, happy as can be to cook for me. He always gives me some simple task to do, usually chopping or stirring. Whatever assignment it is, he always insists it is incredibly important. Even these menial jobs incur his tutelage.

While chopping celery for the chicken pot pies one night, he comes up behind me. He has never been this close to me before. I can feel my ears go warm as my pulse quickens. He smells like fresh laundry and some type of great-smelling soap, the kind advertised specifically for guys. He wraps his arms around me and places his hands over mine. Are my hands clammy? Oh God. He guides the knife in my right hand and curls my fingers over on my left.

"Here, press your knuckles up against the knife like this." He proceeds to move the knife up and down slowly with his firm right hand over mine. I am fixated on the tattoos that end at his wrist in black scripted letters. I can't read what it says. If only he'd stop moving... "There. Now you can go faster and not worry about slicing your fingers off."

See, he is very helpful. He has also come up with this tantalizing habit of smacking me on my ass when dinner is just about done and telling me to go set the table. I can't help but squeal, flush, then giggle every time. It is so chauvinistic yet endearing at the same time. Is that possible?

During the week, the evenings are mine and Cade's. Adam is strict about not staying up late or going out on school nights. It is actually quite adorable. But on Fridays and Saturdays, he is at my door punctually at seven. Flowers in hand. I always feel a little embarrassed taking the flowers—it seems so over-the-top and formal.

Cade is still a total asshole whenever Adam comes to pick me up, but it doesn't matter too much. Adam is lovely enough to make up for it. He is just so...perfect. He's smart, handsome, funny, and the constant gentleman.

It is one of the best Septembers of my life.

* * *

The first Tuesday in October is perfectly ordinary until I walk into Professor Trobaugh's class. Adam isn't in his usual seat.

Then I look at my spot. On the table in front of it is a huge bouquet of red roses. Dozens of them in the most beautiful deep shade of crimson. As I walk up, I can clearly see the large name printed on the little card. I am painfully aware of everyone in the room watching me. I feel my face get hot as I take the card in a shaky hand. I am so overwhelmed and embarrassed I am surprised I'm not quivering all over. I already know who they are from.

Adam.
The card is corny. And sweet. And perfect.

Haley-

TO BE YOUR GIRL

I'm crazy about you. Will you do me the honor of letting everyone else know how crazy I am about you and be my girlfriend?
  Yours,
  Adam

Yours?

Then he is next to me. I sense his warmth and smell his magnificent scent before I turn around. He is there, big brown eyes looking at me questioningly. I am wordless. He is distressed.

"Yes." It is almost a whisper. But he hears.

He gives me the most breathtaking smile I've ever seen and scoops me up in a tight hug and spins us around. Right in the middle of class—until Professor Trobaugh comes in. I don't remember anything about that particular day's lecture except that mustard cardigan and how tight Adam squeezes my hand the entire hour.

* * *

The flowers take up our entire dining room table.

"Holy shit." Cade walks over, eyeing the bouquet. "You can tell Loverboy he doesn't have to try so fucking hard. Or has he never seen the goofy-ass smile you have when you talk about him?"

I roll my eyes. "Since you refuse to learn his name, you can just call him my boyfriend."

He raises his eyebrows, pressing his tongue against the inside of his cheek. "Well, I'm glad it worked for him. I would never give a girl roses."

"Never?" I cross my arms.

"Not roses. They're too cliché. And boring. They don't show any thought or originality. Plus, nobody's favorite flower is a rose. Fact."

"That sounds made up."

"What's your favorite flower?"

"I don't know. I guess I've never thought about it."

Then I see them swaying in my mind—the deep orange petals softly fluttering among the patches of icy snow not yet melted by the new sunshine, the grass still in its winter slumber.

"Orange tulips. There was a patch of them outside my window in the house we lived in before my dad died. They didn't bloom for long, but I was always so excited when they did because it meant Spring was finally coming."

"See." Cade tilts his head to me. "Not a rose."

CHAPTER 5

THE DATE IS PERFECT. AGAIN.

Adam and I are standing at my front door, the usual goodnights and shy smiles. He comes in close, his smile becoming lax and his eyes hooding over. I want it too. His lips are so soft and hot on mine. His smell is sweet but musky. His late-night stubble grazes my cheek as he moves down to kiss behind my ear. It sends shivers down the whole left side of my body. His breath sears against my neck as he kisses down to my collarbone. My heartbeat quickens and I'm lightheaded.

My arms are around his waist, holding him tight. I slip my hands under his shirt and slide them up his back. His skin is smooth and burning to the touch. His mouth is back to mine and the kiss is more urgent. I touch his hard stomach then move up to his chest. He groans into my mouth when I brush my thumbs over his taut nipples. He pulls away, out of breath. I am practically panting.

"Come inside," I beg.

He looks torn at my invitation. I can barely make out his deep brown eyes as he stands over me, silhouetted by the porch light.

"God Haley, I want to, but I can't."

Really? I'm here all worked up.

"I'm going home this weekend and I have to leave pretty early in the morning."

Oh. I guess he had mentioned something like that at dinner. Shit.

"I'll give you a call tomorrow. Goodnight."

"Night."

* * *

I am pissed. I shouldn't be, but I am. Not to mention horny. I slam the door behind me and just let it out.

"Fuck!"

"Whoa, Haley. You all right?" Cade is sitting on the couch, his usual spot, in his customary casual lounge position. "Everything okay with Loverboy?"

No way am I letting him think something is wrong with my relationship.

"No, he's still perfect." I need a lie quick. I take my high heels off. "My feet are just killing me."

"Come here and I'll massage them for you."

"Uhh…" That isn't the reaction I expected. "Thanks, but I'm fine."

"No, seriously. I'm pretty good at massages."

I'm sure you are. "Not necessary."

I pass him and head into the hallway when he seizes me around the waist and picks me up.

"Hey!" I flail around but he successfully carries me over and drops me on the couch.

"Sit your ass down and let me rub your smelly feet."

My feet do not smell.

TO BE YOUR GIRL

He sits on the end of the couch, grabs my feet and pulls them onto his lap, making me slide down onto my back. I stop resisting and just let the man give me a damn foot rub, if he is so insistent. I rest my head on the arm of the couch and close my eyes.

He starts with my left foot, gently rubbing my heel between his thumb and forefinger. His hands are warm and firm. It feels amazing.

Never turn down a foot massage, Haley. That's stupid.

He laces his fingers over the top of my foot with his thumbs on the bottom, making little circles first on my heel and then moving up the side of my foot. Then he deliberately rubs the spaces between my toes and massages each individual toe from joint to the tip of the pad.

I am a puddle on the couch by this point. I feel totally warm and like jelly all over. Then he moves to the balls of my feet, moving in larger, deeper circles. Cade is good at foot rubs. Like, really fucking good. The warm sensation in my foot oozes up into my leg, tingling on the way up to my inner thigh. He's being slow and thorough, and his hands are strong yet gentle with every touch. Cade is touching me. And I like it.

Shit.

His deft fingers move down to the arch of my foot. They are just slightly rough and calloused from use. They move up and down my arch, pressing into my foot, sending electric surges up to my pelvis and base of my spine. The insides of my thighs are buzzing and I feel like I need to press them together. My breathing becomes embarrassingly heavy and I let out a quiet moan of appreciation.

"Does it feel good?"

How the fuck can he ask me that?

"Ye...ah." I open my eyes to see him smiling coyly, but he isn't looking at my face. He is concentrating on my foot, thank God. I'm sure I am flushed all over.

He moves to my other foot and begins the process again. Rubbing my heel and ankle, up to my toes. The pressure is almost unbearable—it is becoming more of a throbbing between my legs and this time when he hits the tender spot, it sends a jolt right into my clitoris.

Ohmygod.

It pulses there and the sensation vibrates out into the pit of my stomach. The moan I let out is definitely louder this time. Is it obvious to him what is happening? Or can I just play them off as normal massage noises? I grab a pillow and throw it over my face, mumbling something about the light shining in my eyes.

I feel his hot hands moving slowly over my ankle and up to my calf. He starts massaging my calf muscle and it feels so heavenly.

I imagine him moving his hands up higher to my thigh. Maybe even higher than that.

I want him to—but he doesn't.

My lips are burning and starting to numb. A build-up gradually begins, causing my stomach to spasm. It spreads down to my sex, which clenches around emptiness, longing for something to be there. Something hard to fill it up.

My heart rate is speeding, and my blood is pumping at a furious pace in my ears and my center.

Jesus, I am coming.

Cade is making me come right here on the couch.

I stifle any sounds that come out with the pillow as I feel the final wave of pleasure surge through my body, my insides contracting violently around nothingness.

TO BE YOUR GIRL

The tension releases and I am finally able to breathe. My forehead has broken into a sweat. My legs feel like they are being pricked by thousands of pins and needles wherever Cade touches. And then he isn't touching them anymore.

"Hale?"

Shit. That requires some sort of response. I am not in the proper state to have a conversation. I slowly remove the pillow from my face, still avoiding eye contact.

"Yeah?"

"I thought maybe you fell asleep over there or something."

"No."

The temperature in the room seems to be coming back to normal and my breathing is much steadier.

"That was nice, Cade. Thanks." Maybe I can run to my room without him figuring out what he just did to me.

"No problem. The pleasure was all mine."

I sit up and look at him. He has that devious little snarky smile on again. Does he know? Because the pleasure was definitely all mine.

"Something's still bugging you, and it's not your feet right now. What's up?"

Right now? It's that a guy who is not my boyfriend just gave me an orgasm—without even touching me above the knee. I can't even be mad about it. It could have been Adam. Why wouldn't he give me this?

I blame my post-orgasm brain for what I blurt out next.

"My boyfriend won't have sex with me."

Cade's blue eyes become wide, his mouth slack with shock.

"What?"

That's just great. Now I must continue this discussion.

"Well, it's just that we've been seeing each other for over a month now and we haven't even gone to second base."

"Okay, first of all, he's a fucking idiot. Second of all, I'm sure he's just trying to take it slow and be respectful." That is pretty mature reassurance coming from Cade. "Trust me, he wants to put it in you." That's more like it.

"I'm not sure if I should be taking relationship advice from a man-whore." Oops, that may have been too far.

"Man-whore?" He smiles in amusement. "I don't think I can be classified as such by a virgin."

What?

"I'm not a virgin." I can tell he's incredulous. "What makes you think I am?"

He shrugs. "You just have a doe-eyed look about you. You look innocent, and definitely not like you've ever been properly fucked."

Heat blossoms on my cheeks and I realize my mouth is hanging open. I shut it and straighten. "I'm not sure how I'm supposed to look, but I'm not a virgin, it's just…been a while."

"Really?" He's humoring me. "How long is a while?"

Ugh. "That's not any of your business."

He gives me this look. The 'I'm not going to let it go' look.

"C'mon."

Fine. "Four years."

He only lets me see the surprise on his face briefly. "Wow—why?"

I don't know why I feel like I need to tell him.

"I don't know. With my first boyfriend… Neither of us knew what we were doing. We were seventeen. I knew the first time was going to hurt. I just figured it would get better from there. It didn't." I guess he was right about the being "properly fucked" part.

This is the first time I've seen Cade look so serious, even concerned. I haven't told anyone this before. Ever.

"What do you mean?"

"It just never felt right. It didn't feel good. It wasn't fun."

"Haley, I'm sorry."

"It's not a big deal. I just vowed that I would wait until it was with the right guy."

"Still, that's a long time."

"Yeah, well the classes at my last university were rigorous and extremely competitive. I had to focus on school to keep my scholarship. I didn't date or go to parties." I didn't make any real friends either. No wonder I was so miserable.

"Well, I hope that next guy treats you the way you deserve."

"Thanks."

Okay, this is getting way too weird and serious for me. I get up to leave when he grabs my elbow.

"Wait—" His sexy smirk is lopsided as he looks at me from under his lashes. "So, have you ever had an orgasm?"

I immediately feel the blood rush to my face. I am not answering that. I turn to leave but he still has my arm.

He looks up at me, completely sober. "Tell me."

"Only the ones I've given myself."

Plus the one you may have just given me a few minutes ago. But I'm never telling you about that one.

He seems genuinely satisfied with that answer. My ears are hot and my face is probably bright red at this point. I bolt to my room.

* * *

"Given yourself any orgasms lately?" Cade asks as he walks into the bathroom the next morning.

"Maybe you should give it a try sometime. You contract less STDs that way."

"Ow. Nice one. But I masturbate plenty and I don't have any STDs, so…"

"I don't want to know about how often you masturbate." I can't believe that just came out of my mouth without any hesitation.

"Really?"

"Really."

He chuckles at me then flushes. Scalding me again.

"Got plans for today?"

I can't think of anything to make up.

"No."

"Okay, get ready. You're coming out with me."

Apparently Cade's idea of "going out" is to the local farmer's market. It's an unseasonably warm morning for October. The light blue sky with the sun reflecting off all the brightly colored tents reminds me of being inside a kaleidoscope. The crowd is mellow, many families and people walking their dogs. Cade is in heaven, smelling all the produce and squeezing the fruit to test for ripeness. He grabs an armful of leeks and parsnips and apples and figs. I can see his mind working.

"All we need is some potatoes to mash up with the parsnips, and pork chops, definitely." He smiles at me, the sunlight just glinting off his thin lip ring. He only wears it occasionally, and I have never liked them on guys before, but it makes his full bottom lip look extra soft behind the metal. "Let's go."

He guides me through the crowd with his hand lightly at the small of my back. The touch is just enough to be distracting.

* * *

I am mesmerized as I watch him in the kitchen that night, preparing our meal.

Dinner is delicious, as usual. The savory pork chops are perfectly glazed with a fig reduction paired with the fresh apple chutney.

"I guess it's pretty easy to get laid when you cook like this."

"It is pretty easy for me to get laid, but I don't cook for girls."

"You cook for me."

"That's different. You're Tuck's sister. You're like the one I never had to tease and annoy."

Awesome. Glad to know that's how he thinks of me.

"You're not going out with your boyfriend tonight?"

Oh right, Adam. "No, he's out of town this weekend."

"Oh. If I'd known that I wouldn't have made plans."

Really?

He gets up and begins rinsing the dishes.

"Got a hot date or something?"

"I don't date."

I grab a clean towel and start drying the plates. "No? Just pick up random chicks at the bar?"

"I don't pick up chicks either. They pick me up."

"Bullshit."

He shrugs. "The college girls just want one thing from me, and I'm happy to oblige." He winks as he hands me the last fork to dry.

* * *

Thursday after class, Adam asks me if I'd like to go to dinner that evening. This is a break from our normal routine but I happily agree. I feel like we don't get enough time together. I want more. More of him. Sweet, warm, beautiful Adam.

I have a new dress for the occasion. It is tight and a deep crimson red. I match it with a rich shade of lipstick and nude pumps that make my legs look longer. I sweep my hair away from my face and fasten it in a low, loose side bun and leave my eye make-up bare—just some mascara on my long lashes that make my light brown eyes pop.

As I walk to the door, I feel Cade's eyes follow me from the kitchen. But I don't say anything, and neither does he.

At dinner, Adam tells me about his trip home the previous week. His younger sister won homecoming queen and he escorted her out to the football field before the announcement. She had been so excited. I imagine Adam at home with his family and it makes me happy.

Afterward, he pulls up to my house but he doesn't get out and open my door like usual. We sit there for a minute. Lingering.

"You look stunning tonight." His eyes dart down my body quickly, to my mouth then back up to my eyes. He licks his lips just enough to wet them. I know exactly what he wants. I want it too.

I lean toward him and he doesn't hesitate to kiss me. Eagerly. He smells delicious. His arms are wrapped around me instantly. His kisses are slow, getting deeper, harder, wetter. He wraps one hand behind my neck, holding me to him, while his other moves down to my hip, then further down to my bare thigh. He squeezes it with just enough force that I catch my breath.

He inches up my thigh, scrunching my tight dress up in the process. My black lace panties are entirely exposed as he pushes my dress up to my hips. He is kissing down my neck, breath scorching my skin. My heart drums in my chest and my stomach flutters as he moves his hand up under my dress to rest on my bare stomach. He is practically panting as his fingers slide over the lace, down to where the heat is radiating out. My head rests against the cold window but I am only focused on him.

Don't stop.

But he does.

"Dammit. I'm sorry." What is he talking about? "I don't want to feel you up in my car, and I don't want to push you. I want it to be special for you."

Doesn't he see I do not care where we are? I just want it. Does he think I am a virgin too? Probably.

"Don't be sorry. I don't mind. How about we go inside?"

He pulls down my dress to cover me back up. "I really can't tonight. I have a super early class tomorrow." He looks positively distraught.

Damn. "It's okay. You have all weekend to make it up to me."

"About this weekend..."

"What?"

"I have a party tomorrow night at the house. It's for a bunch of alumni. It's this big deal, and well...only Greek members are allowed to come."

Oh.

"I'm sorry. It will be boring anyway—you won't be missing anything. I wouldn't go if I didn't have to."

I'm not good at hiding emotion. I know he can see my disappointment. He is going to a party and I'm not allowed to go?

"Hey, I'll make it up to you Saturday night, all right? I promise."

* * *

Friday as I'm leaving sociology, I see a wild waving in my periphery.

"Haley!" Court catches up to me, her ponytail bouncing, two guys following close behind. "Hey, I'm glad I caught you. This is my roommate, Caleb."

She points to the taller one. He gives me a nod but doesn't smile. His black hair is shaved short and he has the most beautiful ebony skin I have ever seen.

"And this is our friend, Jake."

Jake is a few inches shorter with wavy blond hair and a duffle bag thrown over his shoulder.

"We are going to go play some volleyball at the Rec. You want to join?" Court asks, a hopeful smile on her face.

I chuckle before I can think of a response. "I don't think you want me playing with you. I have literally zero-percent athletic ability." Tuck got all those genes.

"Don't be silly. We'd love you to come with us."

"Next time, promise."

Court nods, her big smile never leaving her face. "You're coming to our Halloween party, right? It's going to be so fun."

TO BE YOUR GIRL

"I'll be there."
Crap.

* * *

I'm looking forward to a quiet Friday night. I lay on the couch, rereading *Persuasion*. I had just dozed off around nine—I know, I know, I am really getting out of hand—when I am startled awake by the sounds of the door opening and loud laughing. A high-pitched, annoying female laugh.

I sit up on the couch to see Cade walking in with hyena-girl stumbling in behind him. She is actually a very pretty brunette, but I can't get over the piercing sound coming from her mouth.

When Cade sees me sitting there he stops, his brows furrowed.

"Isn't it your date night with the boyfriend?"

"He's busy tonight."

Cade considers that for a moment, obviously still a little thrown. Does he want me to leave? Give him some privacy with his date?

"Huh." He seems to be saying it to himself. He turns to hyena-girl. "You can go home now."

She looks confused. Then mad.

"Are you fucking serious?" Her speaking voice is just as abrasive. Cade nods nonchalantly and opens the front door. She stands there for a second, seething. Then she walks out without another word but the look on her face is like murder. What the fuck is this about?

Cade walks over to the couch, not bothered a bit by the exchange, and plops down next to me.

"Rather hang out with you, anyway." He smiles so matter-of-factly at me I forgive him his rudeness immediately.

"She was kind of awful."

"Right?" He agrees as he chuckles. "Let's watch a movie."

"Okay."

"You go pick one and I'll get the popcorn and drinks."

"Deal."

The movie is one of my favorites. I've seen it a dozen times. It is a bit slow, dryly humorous, and understatedly romantic. Cade hasn't seen it before, but I can tell he likes it. He is just so easy, laughing at all the right times, even catching the more subtle comments. Two beers and two-thirds of the way through the movie, I am barely able to keep my eyes open as I sway on the couch. Cade notices.

"Tired?"

"Duh."

He seems to like me stealing his line. He cracks into a wide grin and snatches a pillow. "Come lie down." He places the pillow in his lap and motions me down. Right to his groin.

Um, no.

My hesitation makes him laugh harder.

"Oh, just come on already."

He gently puts his hand on my shoulder. I remind myself how he thinks of me as a little sister and let him guide me down to lay my head in his lap. The pillow is soft and my body immediately relaxes all over. He pulls down the blanket from the back of the couch and throws it over me.

He watches the movie as I close my eyes and drift languidly in and out of awareness. He bounces lightly under me when he laughs. I can smell the buttery popcorn and hear him take sips of his beer. His touch is soft as he brushes a strand of hair off my cheek, then I float away into sleep.

When I wake up I am too warm. And cramped. My limbs are jammed under me and I feel stiff all over. Something heavy is across my side. I open my eyes.

It's Cade.

He is lying next to me on the couch. His breathing is slow and deep, his arm is draped over my side and resting on my back.

I watch him sleep. He looks peaceful. I study his features. His skin is smooth and unblemished. He has a cute little bump in his nose. His full lips go into a small pout and a crease forms between his brows like he is dreaming about something distressing. I want to touch that little crease, smooth it out, like the rest of his skin. Then maybe just touch that skin too, down his cheek to the edge of his jaw...

The sudden clanking of keys at the front door alerts me. I slide out from under Cade's arm without waking him and scuttle to my room before I hear Tuck step onto the entryway tile.

CHAPTER 6

Adam is beautiful. Shirtless. He is leaned over me, pulsing, sweating, breathing strained, irregular. His face is serious but loving. He looks at me, dark brown eyes the warmest I've ever seen. "I love you Haley." Then he kisses me, his naked body coming down on mine, our wet skin rubbing together. Then I can just feel it, big and hard, moving inside me.

The buzz of my phone knocks me awake. Rude. I reach under my pillow and answer in a croaky voice.

"Hello?"

"Morning, beautiful."

"Hey babe, what's up?"

"Did I wake you?" I look at the clock. It is just after ten. Wow. I never sleep in this late. I had left Cade on the couch at about five o'clock. Guess I didn't get the best night's sleep there.

"Sorta." Plus you interrupted a hot dream.

"Sorry, I can call back later."

"No, I need to get up anyway."

"I missed you last night."

"Hmm…me too." He really is the best.

TO BE YOUR GIRL

"Pick you up tonight at seven?"
"Sure thing."
"Can't wait."

* * *

Adam is at my door at exactly seven—like always. But he doesn't take me to a fancy restaurant. He drives up to a nice apartment complex. The three-story buildings are large and surrounded by mature trees. I realize I have never been to Adam's place before. Is that weird? I am pleasantly surprised at a night in. He smiles a cute, slightly mischievous smile at me when he parks—like he knows something I don't.

He comes around, opening the door for me, and takes my hand and leads me up to the top floor of the farthest building. His hand always feels so nice wrapped around mine. I am suddenly nervous, but in the best way.

When he opens the door, all the lights are off but there are several candles on the table, the countertops, the coffee table, lining the shelves. The soft flickering light reminds me of our first date at *La Mer*. The whole place smells faintly of vanilla. Adam brings me into the dining room and pulls me out a chair. He is ridiculously excited. He goes into the kitchen and comes back holding a massive tray with two plates, glasses, a bottle of wine, and a large covered dish in the middle. He lays it on the table and hands me a plate and silverware. Then he pours me a generous glass of merlot.

"Beef stroganoff." He unveils the covered dish and serves me a heaping portion of the pasta with some salad. "It's sort of my specialty."

He is so proud of himself for this dish he made I don't have the heart to tell him it isn't that great. But hey, I have been pretty spoiled having Cade cook for me so often. His excitement is contagious. We talk about music and movies and school—and finish two bottles of wine.

We've been done eating for well over an hour when Adam gets up and comes over to me. He takes my hand and pulls me up to him. Without any hesitation, he wraps his arms around me tight and kisses me. He is all solid pressed up against me. Heat encompasses me along with his delicious scent. The wine makes me a little dizzy as the kiss intensifies. His hands are firm against my low back and I can feel him against my stomach. He is hard. And large.

Oh my. My insides turn to melting butter, sliding through me down to my toes. He tears away from my lips, his eyes hooded and glazed over.

"Want me to show you around my place?"

A one-room tour will work. "Sure."

He laces his fingers through mine and walks me around. Showing off the rooms with exaggerated enthusiasm.

"And here's the living room you've already seen"—using his hands to model next to the couch—"and then the kitchen. It's small, but perfect for stroganoff-making."

The first doorway in the hall is a small bedroom. His roommate moved out last semester and he'd decided not to get another one. The next room is the bathroom, complete with washer and dryer across from the toilet. Classy. The next is his bedroom. He opens the door and leads me in.

His bed is large and takes up most of the room. In the corner is a small desk and chair, piled high with books and a slim laptop. He has one lonely lamp in the corner. I can tell he had cleaned up for me. Nothing is on the freshly vacuumed floor, the bed is made, and it, too, smells like vanilla.

TO BE YOUR GIRL

"So, that's the tour. Want to go back out to the living room? Watch a movie or something?" He is so sweet, standing here with me in his room. Tall and dark in his black sweater and dark wash jeans, not expecting anything from me.

I shake my head, giving my best seductive smirk. I take the collar of his sweater and drag him toward me as I back up until the bed hits the back of my legs. He comes easily and finds my lips without protest.

His lips never leave mine as we lay on the bed. They become greedier. He moves his hands down the sides of my ribs, leaving behind a trail of heat. He grabs the hem of my shirt and smoothly pulls it over my head. Then he sits up over me and pulls his sweater off. His chest is glistening and smooth and tan and Jesus Christ, shirtless Adam in real life is way better than dream Adam. His arm muscles are all hard and ripple-y as he lowers himself on me. My nipples harden, straining against my confining bra. His mouth is on mine, tongue filling mine eagerly, wet. His breath is ragged.

"God, you're so sexy," he whispers.

Then he kisses down my neck to my collarbone. Every time he comes up after a kiss, his breath hits my damp skin and sends chills through my whole body. He begins kissing and licking down my chest and between the swell of my breasts. I am covered in goosebumps. My heart is pounding.

His warm fingers are on my stomach, sliding down to the button of my jeans. He undoes them smoothly and I lift my hips so he can pull them the rest of the way off. He tosses them on the floor then begins unzipping his jeans. I watch his large fingers slide the zipper down. His body is amazing, all toned and bulging. His pants are soon next to mine on the floor. Then he lies back down over me, kissing me hard.

His pelvis is up away from mine and his hands are busy. Is he taking his boxers off?

He is.

Okay, this is fast but I don't want to stop. Then his hands are on my hips, he slides his forefinger just under the elastic of my thong and begins to pull them down to my thighs.

Okay, apparently we are skipping second base altogether. That's all right. I like third.

With one hand, he continues pulling my underwear down while the other goes for his nightstand drawer. I hear the unmistakable crumple of a condom wrapper.

Whoa. I am not there yet. I need more foreplay. Are we going all the way already? My throat feels like it is seizing up on me. I can't get a full breath into my lungs. I feel lightheaded. This is too soon.

"Adam..."

"Yeah, babe." He is at my neck, his kisses becoming messier.

"I'm not sure..."

"Just relax."

Relax? I am practically hyperventilating. I sit up and scoot away from him into the headboard.

"No, I need to slow down. I'm not ready for this quite yet."

He is sitting there, naked. Gloriously naked. His cock sitting up between his legs is stiff, the tip dark red, stretched and shiny. He is ready.

"Are you fucking kidding me?" His voice is harsh.

I tear my eyes away from his erection at his abrupt words.

TO BE YOUR GIRL

His dark eyes bore into me, accusing. His mouth contorts. I have never seen him angry. "You pulled me on the bed with you! This was your idea!"

"I know. I'm sorry—"

"You're such a fucking tease. You cunt."

"What?" I can't believe he is saying this to me. I have never even heard him swear. His face is still twisted as he runs his hands violently through his dark hair. He is trying to calm himself down, but I am already off the bed grabbing my clothes.

"Haley, I didn't mean that—"

"No! I'm leaving." I pull on my jeans hastily, not even buttoning them. I throw my shirt on as I run down the hall. I can hear him behind me, tripping as he tries to dress. I grab my purse and shoes, fly out the front door, then slam it behind me.

I run down the stairs. I am on the second flight when I hear him call for me.

"Haley! Please, come back! I'm sorry."

"Fuck off!" I yell as I reach the bottom and run around the corner of the building.

I don't stop running until I pass the parking lot. My bare feet are cold and sting from slapping the pavement. It is dark out and he can't see which way I have gone.

I am alone.

I finally have a chance to catch my breath. My heart beats wildly against my ribs. What just happened? How had my perfect boyfriend suddenly turned into a jerk? The night has gone to shit. Then I realize how much so—not only am I unsure how to get home, I have no way to get there.

I check my phone. It is almost eleven. Tuck might be home. I call him. Voicemail.

"Tuck, I need your help right now. I'm not okay." I don't know what else to say. I hang up and sit down on the sidewalk.

The concrete is cold. My feet hurt as I put on my shoes and my fingers are stiff. I can feel warmth bubbling up in my eyelids, but I blink it away. I am not shedding any tears over this.

I sit there for a couple more minutes, watching my breath disappear into the black.

I don't know what to do.

My phone rings. I don't recognize the number.

"Hello?"

"Where are you?" Without warning, tears fall from both of my eyes.

Cade.

I tell him the cross streets.

"Stay there. I'm coming to get you."

CHAPTER 7

Cade is here in minutes. He pulls up fast in his black GTO. He jumps out of the car and runs around to me.

"Are you okay?" He pulls me up to my feet, both hands on my shoulders as he searches my eyes. He looks frightened.

"Yeah, I'm all right."

"Did he hurt you?"

"No—"

"I swear if he laid a fucking hand on you—"

"Cade, no. It's nothing like that."

He relaxes his grip on me a little and his face smooths out. "Good. Come on, let's go home."

He opens the door and I climb in.

My phone rings. Adam.

I ignore it. Then I get his text: *I'm sorry. Please call me.*

Cade gets in the driver's side, turns the key in the ignition, and puts his phone to his ear. "Yeah, I got her. She's fine. I'm taking her home. Of course, man." He hangs up and we pull out to the main street, Cade's arm thrown casually over my seat. "So...you gonna tell me what happened?"

"I don't want to talk about it. I'll just say that Adam and

I are over."

"Okay…" We stop at a red light and he taps his fingers on the steering wheel. "You know you scared the shit out of Tuck. He's over an hour away in the city and was freaking out."

I didn't think I could feel much worse. Wrong.

He looks at me sincerely. "Put my number in your phone. You can call if you need me. Whenever."

"Thanks." The light turns green, and he starts to turn left. "Cade—"

"Yeah?"

"I don't want to go home."

He looks at me, head slightly cocked. "No?"

"No. I need a drink. Or drinks."

He chuckles, the easiness back in his mood. His face is sexy. Especially when he smiles.

"Fair enough. I know exactly where to take you."

* * *

We arrive at a house on the other side of campus. The street is stacked with cars lined nose-to-end.

When we enter through the dimly lit living room, Cade takes my hand. He leads me through the tightly packed crowd of drunk and dancing partygoers to the kitchen. I am keenly aware he doesn't let go of my hand once we're through the mass of people. The kitchen is blindingly bright with a fluorescent light overhead that throws a strange neon glow over every surface and flickers every few seconds.

"Cade! Bro, how the hell are you?!" A large guy in a red T-shirt booms. He and Cade clasp fists then do that single back slap guy-hug thing. He lets go of my hand to do it. "I got some shots here with your name on them. And your girl." He looks over Cade's shoulder at me, eyebrows raised.

I blush at the idea of people thinking I am Cade's girl. Like he is a guy to ever have a girl.

But Cade corrects him. Too quickly. "Nah, this is Tuck's little sister, Haley."

Again with the sister thing. Fuck.

"Tuck's sister? Where is that motherfucker? Bring it here, girl." I don't even have a chance to comprehend what is happening before he pulls me in and swallows me up in a big bear hug.

"This is Zain," Cade tells me when I am released and able to take a breath. Zain clinks four shot glasses down on the counter in front of us and overflows them with whiskey.

"Two for each of you."

Shit. Let's do this.

"Cheers." Cade picks up a shot and hands it to me. I almost drop it when I take the alcohol-covered glass from his slippery fingers. He clanks his against mine and we tip them back fast. It burns going down my throat.

I need a chaser. No luck.

Zain slaps Cade hard on the back and they start talking about something. I turn to look back at the shots. I take a deep breath and down my second one quickly before I can lose my nerve. It is worse the second time. I feel the immediate urge to gag. But I don't.

When I look back over to the boys, Zain is gone. Cade is a little farther away, standing very close to a girl in a very short skirt. She is smiling up at him, his hands glued to her hips. Right. I roll my eyes. Cade brought me here to drink, not to actually hang out with me.

Guess I better drink then.

RAE KENNEDY

I pick up the third shot and swallow it without thinking. The third one is easier. I pour another. It goes down by far the easiest.

I leave Cade to entertain the new chick and find the mass of dancers in the living room very welcoming.

It's dimly lit and smells like sweat and beer. Everyone is moving in one giant pulse to the pumping music. I find the rhythm without difficulty as the beat and alcohol engulf me, melting me into a comforting oblivion. The alcohol goes to my head in no time. Other warm, intoxicated bodies rub up against me, the occasional hand on my back.

He smells like tequila. But he's cute. Full beard, white shirt. He is dancing near me when he sees me and comes over. He puts his hands on my hips and smiles at me. I am way too drunk.

"Wanna go find a room?" he whispers into my ear.

I shake my head at him.

The next guy to dance with me isn't so forward. He gets the hint and wanders off when I start dancing more away from him than toward him.

I'm dancing by myself in a blissful stupor when I feel him behind me.

I know from his scent right away, and the familiar warmth of his hands. But the way he touches me is not so familiar. I lean back into Cade's chest and we move together to the music. His hands leave a hot trail where he touches my skin, down my arms, over my ribs, and to my hips. He is so close I wonder if he can feel how hard my blood is pumping.

He splays his hands over my hip bones and presses me back against his pelvis. He is hard.

I suddenly have no air in my lungs. He holds me to him

TO BE YOUR GIRL

tightly as he bends with me, grinding up behind me. We are moving in unison to the beat. Thrusting. I arch against him. His face is right next to mine, mouth open, his breath hot against my cheek. I feel the pressure of his hand move from my hip down the front of my thigh then drag back up the inside of my leg. I am throbbing all over, sweating, panting.

He turns me around and I can see the lust in his eyes. Our legs intertwine, and his arousal is even more obvious against my thigh. The music is pounding. As we sway together, his eyes are on my mouth. His intake of breath is as rough as my heart thrashing in my chest. His lips part, glossy and swollen. I want those lips on me.

His hands are at my low back, holding me tight to him as we dip and rub our bodies against one another. He slides his hands down, slowly. They glide to my ass and rest there for a second lightly before they start applying some force against me, sending electricity down my legs. My clit pulses and I feel the wetness spreading in me. I ache for him. His touch is driving me crazy, and the alcohol is making me dizzy.

I have never been more aroused in my life. Not even an hour ago when I was lying naked on Adam's bed. My panties are soaked.

Is he as aware of my wetness as I am of his erection?

I rub against his leg, the friction of our jeans barely enough to subdue the excruciating ache of my little bud. My arms are wrapped around his neck. It feels like we are surrounded in fire—both covered in sweat. His eyes are closed, our noses almost touching. He bites his lip as he leans toward me. I can smell the whiskey on his breath. I tilt toward him, holding my own breath. I can just feel his bottom lip brush the top of mine when he opens his eyes.

He backs away from me instantly, breaking our embrace. He looks horrified, clutching his chest, hunching over. I just stand there. Still. My ears pounding with blood and music. He looks at me. I can't see the liquid blue of his eyes, but they are wide.

Then he turns and disappears through the crowd.

* * *

I look around for Cade but I can't find him. I do, however, find the bathroom. I sit in there for a little while. The room feels like it is turning over and a sourness is rising from my stomach. I stare into the open toilet, but nothing comes.

What the hell just happened? With Cade? The way our bodies moved together as we danced hadn't been friendly. It was sexual, and it had felt so natural. Just thinking about it makes me ache for him. But whatever physical reaction he had, he obviously doesn't feel that way about me. He'd practically sprinted away from me. Shit, I hope this doesn't totally ruin everything. I like having Cade as a friend. I rely on him.

I finally leave the bathroom after about the fifth time someone pounds on the door. A snarky-looking girl with frizzy red hair pushes past me as I wander out toward the living room. Still no Cade. I head to the kitchen and run into Zain in the hallway.

"Need another drink, girl?"

"Um, no thanks."

"Water?"

I give him an appreciative thumbs-up. He pours me a big glass of ice water. My head is already starting to pound. Tomorrow is not going to be fun.

TO BE YOUR GIRL

Zain has a concerned look on his previously jovial face. "You're not driving home are you?"

"No." Shit. I have no idea where Cade is. How am I getting home?

Then Cade comes up behind Zain, clapping him on the shoulder. "Don't you worry, sir. I'll be getting her home safe." Cade looks tired, worried, his hair still perfectly mussed, eyes clear blue. "You ready?"

He takes my hand and leads me to the car, not saying a word. The ride back to the house is equally silent.

He seems to be thinking. He is troubled. Is this about me? *Of course it is, Haley!* He freaked the fuck out after dancing—which was more like dry-humping, and after the almost-kiss...

Is it because he doesn't want me or because he doesn't think I want him? I do want him, but not in the way he normally gives himself to girls—the one-night-only kind of thing.

I haven't allowed myself to think about wanting Cade. Or if he wants me too. I am drunk enough, bold enough, to go for it. I need an answer.

* * *

When he closes the door behind us, I gather up my nerves and lunge at him. My plan is to land a good, solid kiss that will turn into a hot make out, which will inevitably lead to a marriage proposal.

I am so drunk.

He catches me by the shoulders before I am even close, stopping me with little effort.

"Haley, you are drunk."

Clearly.

It is at this moment I realize that he isn't. Not even close. And I look like a complete idiot. He is not even the least bit tempted by me. But my drunk brain isn't very quick at putting this together. I lunge at him again. Of course, he is still holding me back, so this attempt is thwarted as well.

This time he isn't at all amused.

"What the hell are you doing? Stop it."

He pushes me away from him and stalks off toward his bedroom. I follow like the stupid puppy I am. He turns around and glares at me.

"Seriously, get the fuck away from me!"

It feels like he just sucker-punched me and I have no air. I want to crumble to the floor. He has never looked at me with those eyes. That look of disgust. I retreat a few steps, afraid he might explode.

Suddenly, I don't know the person standing in front of me at all.

"You and me"—he points between us, a sneer on his face—"is not going to happen. I would never be with you. You're a naïve little girl."

With that he turns and goes into his room, slamming the door behind him.

I am frozen. I stand in the hallway alone for what seems like an hour. Shocked. At my behavior. At his. How has this night turned so wrong?

Steam fills the bathroom as I make the water in the shower as hot as it will go. The water beats down on my skin, turning it pink. It rains over my face and all the tension in my body melts with it. I allow the wave of emotion to come. Adam wanted too much, and Cade doesn't want me at all.

TO BE YOUR GIRL

The look on his face... It was like he hated me.
The tears running down my face only come out faster as I relive every moment. Then the sobs take over my whole body and I sink down to the tub and sit and cry.

CHAPTER 8

I don't talk to anyone the next day. There are eight missed calls and twelve texts from Adam when I wake up. I turn my phone off.

I stay in my room and do homework then take a nap, too exhausted and hung-over for anything else. I still can't figure out what happened last night. The one time I do leave my room to get something to eat, I don't run into anyone. Cade doesn't seem to be home.

I go to bed early.

Monday morning I wake up to the sound of the shower running. I've never heard Cade in the shower before me. Maybe I can get us back to our flirty, just-fun relationship we'd had before I went psycho and tried to kiss him. I get up and stride into the hall in just my little white tank top and pink panties. I feel confident until I am eye-to-eye with the bathroom door. Suddenly this seems like a bad idea

I push that thought from my head and walk in, convinced it will be an ice-breaker so we can put Saturday behind us. The bathroom is steamy, and it smells like that fantastic boy body wash. Like Cade.

"The fuck?" He sticks his head out of the curtain. Eyes

narrowed, jaw tight. Shit.

"Morning." I try to be as pleasant and nonchalant as possible. Not weird.

"Get out." His face is dead still.

I try not to let it show, but I know right then my face completely breaks.

He immediately becomes furious. "I said get the FUCK out!"

I can't stop the first tear from falling heavy to my cheek before I run out the door.

I don't want to believe how he is treating me. But then I realize I am just like any other girl he is done with. He doesn't give a shit about them or their feelings. He certainly doesn't give a shit about me.

* * *

After class I decide to walk home instead of bike. It is the first truly cold day of the year. The biting air at my cheeks and nose and the hissing wind through my too-thin jacket keeps me awake.

When I finally get home and walk inside, the warmth makes my face burn. I drop my things off in the entry and go to the living room. It is empty. The kitchen too. I open the fridge and then I see the cheese. Cheese has never made me cry before, but here I am staring at the fresh mozzarella and ricotta Cade and I bought at the specialty market on Saturday. We were going to make lasagna together tonight. But of course, we don't. I don't see Cade at all that night. I don't see him at all that week.

Tuesday, I skip Professor Trobaugh's class. I can't face Adam yet. Jesus, I have never been this much of a wreck before. I have never cried so much over boys—or let them interfere with schoolwork.

By Thursday I have convinced myself to go to class. I am an adult. I need to get over it. But when I walk into class, I realize I am so not over it. There, at my desk, is an enormous arrangement of roses. They are yellow, white, and pink—all in various states of bloom, packed tightly in a beautiful crystal vase. There must be three dozen. It is way too much.

I feel like turning around on the spot and running out of the classroom. But I don't. I walk up to my seat and sit in front of my ridiculously huge bouquet of roses. I look around the room, glad I don't see him. The card reads:

I'm so sorry.
  -Adam

I'm still not sure how to feel toward Adam. Or these flowers. But they are pretty. And I think I do feel a little better.

I spend that night alone at the house again. When Adam calls, I answer.

"I'm so glad you answered. This has been the worst week of my life."

I am silent.

"I know I don't deserve another chance, but I just need the chance to talk with you. To explain."

I still don't know what to say.

"Will you come to dinner with me tomorrow?"

My mouth is open, but I've not made a sound.

"Please?"

Still nothing.

"Haley? Are you there?"

I let out a breath. "Yes."

"Yes, you're there or yes, you'll have dinner with me?" He sounds so hopeful, just like the sweet Adam I know. I hate that he is cracking me.

"Well, obviously yes, I'm here." It feels good to be sarcastic again. "But yes, I will see you tomorrow too."

"You will?"

I can hear his smile over the phone.

* * *

Friday night I get ready in my room. I leave my hair down and put on my favorite pair of tight jeans and my brown leather riding boots. I wasn't planning on going for sexy, but I must admit my butt looks pretty good in these jeans. I am admiring the tight fit in the mirror when the doorbell rings. Adam is at least fifteen minutes early. That is very unlike him. I guess he is anxious to see me. That thought makes my heart flutter.

But when I skip out to the living room and around the corner to the front door, Cade has beaten me to it. I didn't even know Cade was home. He is standing there with the door open, Adam's on the porch, looking confused, and Cade is seething.

"What the fuck are you doing here?" He might as well have spat in Adam's face.

I speed past Cade to Adam's rescue. "He's here to pick me up." I smile at Adam, but I can feel Cade's eyes boring into the back of my skull.

"You've got to be shitting me. This jackass?"

I give Cade the steeliest look I can muster. "You're the

asshole here, Cade. Now stay the hell out of my business."

I turn and pull Adam with me down the walkway, facing straight ahead. I will not give Cade anything else. Adam seems oblivious about the exchange. He beams, puts his arm around me, and I immediately feel warm, relaxed, and safe. It feels right.

It also feels right in the car when he reaches over and offers me his hand. I hold it the whole ride, not saying anything. His thumb rubs the top of my hand. He looks serene, a smile in his cheeks. It is peaceful.

He brings me to a park curved over a hill, dotted with large rustling oak trees. We park near a group of weathered picnic tables. It is just getting dark outside and the cool blue blanket of the evening sky casts a somber air over Adam's normally cheerful face.

"We're not going to a restaurant?"

"Uh, no." He looks up at me, a little worried. "I really wanted to talk to you, and I thought we could use some privacy."

Oh. "Okay."

Two beams of light shoot into my eyes as another car pulls up next to us. Adam gets out and runs to meet the driver. I can't quite see what is happening, but it seems weird. Am I in the middle of a drug deal? I feel the need to bolt. But I'm too wishy-washy with the run-or-stay verdict and am still sitting in the seat when Adam gets back in the car, carrying a giant pizza box. My stomach rumbles as the cheesy aroma comes to me. The pizza guy is already pulling away and we are alone again.

"Do you want to eat outside? I brought some blankets. Or would you rather stay in here?"

It is freaking freezing outside. "Can we just stay in?"

His smile is gorgeous and comforting. "Definitely."

The pizza is hot and delicious, though the sauce burns the roof of my mouth. I didn't realize how hungry I am. Adam is a little over-zealous with his slice as well—he lost half of his toppings and a good portion of cheese to his lap. I can't stop laughing.

"Ah, man. That was like the perfect piece too."

Luckily, we have several napkins, Adam is quite cute, though, wiping up the mess, mumbling that he hopes it won't stain. It feels like I am back with the charming Adam I remember from that first day at the coffee shop. I eat my slice in the time it takes him to eat three. Afterward, he exhales and looks at me gravely.

"I guess I can't put it off any longer." Those big brown eyes of his are deep with sincerity. "I messed up. I don't even know how to start saying how sorry I am, or how to explain myself. I have no excuse. All I know is that I drank way too much wine and I wanted you so badly I couldn't see straight."

My throat constricts. I already know how I feel, and my answer to him. I know deep down he is a good guy. The right guy. I just can't get it out yet.

"I know I have no right to ask this of you, but if you'd forgive me and take me back, I promise I will do whatever it takes to make it up to you. To earn your trust back. And I swear I won't push you into anything you're not ready for."

I swallow hard at his words. A saltiness stings my eyelids. Dammit, a week ago I never cried.

"Will you give me another chance? I've been dying this last week. I...I'm... I think I'm falling in love with you."

At that, I pounce on him, wrapping my arms around his neck and planting kisses all over his cheeks and forehead and nose. Finally, I kiss his lips. He pulls me to him, encasing me in his arms. The kiss is slow and deep, full of relief and longing.

* * *

Adam walks me up to the door and kisses me goodnight. He doesn't need words. The smile he has had on his face all night says it all. I know I made the right choice. So, he isn't exactly the perfect guy I had built up in my head, but he is pretty terrific. And kind. And handsome. And he deserves a second chance.

I watch from the porch as he walks to his car. He gives me a goofy sideways smile and waves goodbye as he ducks into the driver's seat. And I know that he is the one I've been waiting for—a guy who truly cares about me. Someone who will treat me right. I am ready.

I bounce inside, humming on the way to get ready for bed. A tall girl with bad highlights storms out of the bathroom, ramming her shoulder in my chest, almost knocking me to the wall.

"Who the hell are you?" She glares down at me.

"Excuse me?" Who the fuck is she? And what the hell did I do?

Then Cade walks out of his bedroom, thankfully completely clothed.

"Come on. I'll take you home," he says with a sigh.

"What? No!"

He looks her dead in the eye. "Yes."

His eyes shift to me just briefly like he hadn't realized I was standing there. Still no emotion shows on his face. He turns abruptly and leaves, the tall girl follows.

TO BE YOUR GIRL

    I get ready for bed then crawl onto my fluffy mattress and under my cozy blankets. I ease to sleep and dream of cars and Adam and flowers.

    I have only a vague recollection of lasagna and cheese.

CHAPTER 9

I GROGGILY STAGGER INTO THE KITCHEN IN MY SWEATS, HAIR still in a messy bun when—surprise!

"Morning sleepy-head." Tuck is waiting for me at the kitchen table.

"Hey, I was beginning to think you didn't actually live here."

He smiles his big Tuck smile, all teeth and dimples. "I was thinking we could hang out today. You free?"

"Sure." I pour myself a large glass of orange juice and grab the box of cereal I'd bought—since I seem to be on my own for breakfast lately—and sit next to him. "What are we doing?"

"You up for a road trip?" Tuck has an adolescent gleam in his hazel eyes.

"Always."

Tuck doesn't tell me where we are going, but honestly, the drive is the best part. We stock up on junk food at the gas station and hit the road. We play the usual car games and argue over what kind of music to listen to. Tuck claims slow, soothing music will make the drive more relaxing and I insist that I will fall asleep if we don't have something upbeat to rock out to. Eventually, we turn the stereo off and just talk.

I like talking with Tuck. I am always reminded of how smart he is—how grown up he is. I have missed his stories, his advice.

"So, I hear you're dating some guy."

"Oh yeah? Where'd you hear that?"

"Cade."

Duh. "Some guy's name is Adam." I smile sweetly. I have a feeling he is going to go all protective big brother on me.

"Cade says he's a tool."

"Cade doesn't even know him. He's a great guy. I like him a lot."

"Is he good enough for you?"

"Why don't you send me a memo on the definition of 'Good Enough for Haley' and then I'll get back to you. I have a feeling no man would live up to it."

Tuck chuckles his deep, good-natured laugh. The corners of his eyes crinkle and he suddenly looks just like our dad.

"You're probably right. But you're my baby girl, Hale." And he looks at me, no condescension in his voice at all, only love. I should hug him more often.

"Well, I can assure you Adam is worthy. You'll have to meet him sometime. All you have to do is, I don't know, be at home like any evening."

"I'll have to take you up on that." His eyes are focused on the freeway. I haven't been paying attention to where we are going. "But seriously, I'm glad you have a boyfriend. I'm sure he is as wonderful as you say." He seems to be grappling with whether or not to continue. "Honestly, I'm just glad I don't have to worry about you dating...I don't know...Cade. I was a little worried about having you move in with us because of him. I mean, he's a great guy, just not if you have boobs."

I roll my eyes at him so hard. "I got that from the second I met him, Tuck. Trust me, you don't have to worry about him and me. We're not even really friends."

My voice shakes on that last part. That hadn't been true a week ago.

Tuck turns off onto an exit and I realize where we were going. Our dad's hometown. The town is more of a street with a few buildings on either side—a couple of restaurants, gas station, motel, a biker bar, and a school. Homes are scattered around the town center on large plots of land and the occasional cow can be seen wandering the hillsides. I haven't been here in years. Twelve years. Since we buried him.

Tuck pulls up to the cemetery, turns off the ignition, and just sits. I hardly even remember this place. He finally gets out of the truck and I follow him through the maze of graves, walking the paths of beaten-down grass and crunching leaves. Tuck stops in front of our dad's headstone. He touches the top and bows his head, breathing heavily.

"I just miss him," he says.

I have several pictures of my dad. I have his face memorized in all of them, the exact expression, his smile, his eyes. But when I try to picture him outside of those pictures, in real life memories, he is always blurry. It isn't that way for Tuck. His memories are clear. It is harder for him. I put my arm through his.

We stand there for a while. Silent, leaning on each other.

"Do you visit Dad often?" I didn't know he came at all.

"No. A couple times in the last few years. When I've been feeling a little lost."

"You feel lost?"

Tuck is my beacon. He is never lost. He sighs again.

"Work is crazy right now—all the hours, plus the hour commute into the city every day... Sometimes, I just don't know. I want to know I'm on the right track. That he would be proud of me."

"Of course he would be. You're amazing."

He looks over at me, shakes off his heaviness and grins. I love his effortless smile.

"I am pretty awesome."

I sock him in the shoulder.

"Damn, that was almost a real punch."

I put up my fist, threatening another but he just chuckles. Ego intact.

"Seriously though, I'm glad you're here with me." He hooks his arm around my neck and pulls me in for a half-hug, half-headlock. "One thing I know I'll never let him down on is watching out for you. I'll always be here for you, Hale."

Good thing he changed the subject quickly, I was starting to get weirded out by all the seriousness. It is just too unnatural.

"Let's go get something to eat."

Finally.

We go to the little diner in town. It feels vaguely familiar and smells like grease and pie. Our waitress's name is Cindy and she takes every opportunity she has to call me sugar, or punkin,' or honey-child. Tuck is cutie-pie and sweetie pants.

The food is as fatty as promised and delicious. My burger drips with cheese and my strawberry shake is too thick to drink through a straw. Tuck is in high spirits again all through the meal and the drive home. Or at least for the first half of the two-hour trip—I sort of fall asleep an hour in.

He wakes me up with a quick jab in the shoulder. I instinctively go to bat his hand away and grunt angrily. I crack my eyes open, we have just pulled into town and there is a weird buzzing noise in my ear.

"Hey, cranky—your phone is ringing. It's the boy."

I look at him still a little groggy and confused. Then I process the phone in his hand pointed at me. My phone. Oh. I snatch the phone from him. "It's Adam." What is with these boys not acknowledging his name?

"Hello?"

"Hey, gorgeous. What are you up to tonight?"

"Oh, nothing…" I am trying to be coy, but I can see Tuck out of the corner of my eye, head bobbing as he snickers. It's very distracting.

"Can I see you?"

I find a pen to throw at Tuck.

"I'd like that."

"Cool. Pick you up at seven."

* * *

Adam is right on time. Unfortunately, I am not. Tuck gets to the door before me, and I get there just in time to see the look on Adam's face when Tuck answers it. He isn't quite as surprised as when he met Cade, but Tuck is tall—much taller than Adam. And he did recently cut his light brown hair quite short. I always thought of Tuck as rather goofy, but I guess he could sort of look intimidating to someone who doesn't know him.

"Uh, hi. I'm Adam." He puts his hand out.

Tuck takes it, and I can tell he gives it an extra firm shake. "I'm Tucker."

"Oh! You're Haley's brother."

I slide past Tuck. "Yup."

They both seem taken aback by my sudden appearance, obviously unaware I had witnessed their exchange. I've wanted Tuck to meet Adam for so long, maybe even all have dinner together or something, but something about the vibe Tuck is giving off has me on alert. He's probably been talking to Cade, sharing in their mutual hatred of my boyfriend neither of them knows.

"See you later, Tuck." I grab Adam's hand and start walking toward his car.

"Nice to meet you, Adam," Tuck says dryly as we walk away. To the untrained ear, it might have even sounded polite.

Adam nods back in reply as I pull him away. I am ready to get out of here.

We go to dinner and a movie. The movie is basically one big action scene. Not my favorite, but I have a nice time, anyway. Really, I love going anywhere with Adam.

"Do you have plans for Halloween next weekend?" He looks super excited.

I am about to say no when I realize I do. "Actually, yes. I promised my friend Court I'd go to her Halloween party."

"Oh, I know about that party. I have to make an appearance at the frat's party, but I can meet you there later."

"Sure." Now I just have to figure out a costume. Always the worst part.

* * *

The following week I am so busy with school I still haven't thought of a costume. Midterms are coming up and it seems all the professors have decided to jam in an extra chapter or two of new material we need to know before the test. I am studying every night. Plus, I have two papers due.

By the time Friday night and the party rolls around, I am scrambling.

I run to the costume shop after class which, of course, is practically picked clean. I decide to go for something easy—just wear a skimpy dress and add an accessory. It looks like they have cat ears, a halo with wings, and devil horns. Not very creative. Oh well, that's what I get for waiting until the last minute. I don't want to be a cat—that would require face makeup or something. The wings seem like they would just get in my way, and I already have a red dress, so the devil wins.

I make my hair extra big and curly, apply heavy black makeup around my eyes and a deep red lip to match my tight dress. I also put on the sky-high red pumps that I never wear. I will probably sprain my ankle at some point but I'll take that risk.

Court is kind enough to pick me up and I agree to help her finish setting up the decorations.

"You look sexy," Court says to me, gleaming from the driver's side of her white Jeep Wrangler. She has creamy white makeup over her porcelain skin. Big, dark lashes fan around her too-big blue eyes and there's a pop of red the shape of a heart just in the center of her lips. With her blonde hair in perfect ringlets around her face, she looks like the perfect living doll.

"Wow! You go all out." I slip into the passenger seat.

"I effing love Halloween." She flashes her pretty white teeth, grabs the gear shift, and peels out so fast I have to hold on.

We get to her apartment and set up the food table. She has already streamed the living room with fake cobwebs and various skeletons and skulls. Her roommates return with the dry ice for the jungle juice and with that final touch, it looks perfect. We turn up the music and test the jungle juice. It is pretty amazing. By the time all the party guests have arrived, I am sloshed.

Court goes off, mingling with her seemingly endless line of friends. I wonder if she notices she has at least three guys following her around like puppies.

A few hours have passed. I expected Adam would be here by now. Instead of continuing to pound drinks at the refreshment table, I decide to go dance.

The music is loud, but everyone is having a good time. A guy dressed as a Smurf keeps trying to dance up on me and I keep dancing away—he seems like a nice enough guy, but I don't want that blue body paint on me. He is irritatingly persistent, so I break away from the dance floor altogether. I stumble into the hallway, laughing and try to catch my breath. It is friggin' hot in here.

I step outside on the balcony to get some fresh air. The sky is black. Yellow streetlights shine in regular intervals down the road against bare tree branches, casting eerie shadows on the sidewalks. The breeze is cool, a slightly smoky scent in the fall air.

"Hey."

I turn around to see Cade behind me. He comes out

and leans against the railing, crossing his tattooed arms at me. I think this is the first time he has spoken to me nicely in almost two weeks.

"Hey yourself."

He looks relaxed in all black. He doesn't seem to be in costume. He has this half-grin on his face as he looks me up and down, lingering at my lips.

"A devil, huh? Tempting." He slurs his words so badly that I can't stop myself from bursting out laughing.

"You are drunk."

"Maybe a little." He moves a step closer to me.

I can sense his body heat and it gives me the chills. He's leaning in toward me, his blue eyes not quite focused but still burning into me. His perfectly soft lips are slightly parted, his breathing getting heavier.

"You want to dance with me?"

My heartbeat quickens immediately, and my face feels hot. My legs are already starting to tremble at the thought of him close to me again. My body is so easy to respond, and it is saying yes. God yes. I am surprised in my inebriated state that I am able to think straight.

"We better not. It didn't work out too well last time."

He takes a step back, the devious smile back on his lips. "Yeah, I wouldn't be able to keep my hands off you, anyway."

What? He licks his bottom lip. The strumming in my belly is at full force at the way his eyes are devouring me.

"Haley? There you are." I turn to see Adam. He looks wholesome as can be in his baseball uniform. I need to be rescued before my body completely betrays me. I run to him quickly.

"Hey! Let's go inside, I'm getting cold out here."

TO BE YOUR GIRL

We leave Cade on the balcony. Adam and I stay at the party for another hour or so, dancing and talking. He knows a ton of people here—laughing and carrying on conversations with a bunch of people I don't know. He doesn't introduce me, either.

Right now, Adam is exchanging stories with two other guys about this year's rush. The guy dressed as a banana keeps snorting and shifting in front of me until I am completely squeezed out of the circle. My red solo cup is still half full of the vodka-cran Court mixed for me. She made it so strong I'd almost think she was trying to get into my pants. I finish it in three large gulps.

Adam finally sticks his head out of the circle.

"Hey, you want to get out of here? Go to my place?" he asks.

I was beginning to think he'd forgotten about me.

"Sure."

* * *

As soon as we are inside his apartment, I jump on him. Our mouths connect and I wrap my legs around his waist and he carries me easily to the couch. He smells so good. I quickly begin unbuttoning his shirt. He removes my plastic devil horns and tosses them on the coffee table. Before I know it, my dress is hiked up to my waist and he is on top of me, kissing me hard. I squeeze him with my thighs and curl my fingers through his hair. He pulls back.

"Whoa, babe—you're pretty drunk." His lips are red and shiny and our breaths are still uneven and heavy.

I try to pull him down again but he holds himself up.

"Let's wait until you're sober. Okay?" Shit. I feel ready,

but he's right. "You want to watch a movie or something?"

"Sure." That sounds nice. I guess.

Adam gets me some water and puts on a boring war movie. Okay, it wasn't really boring—just not my thing. Is he trying to sober me up or put me to sleep? Adam doesn't seem that into it either. About half an hour in he is yawning something fierce. Lame.

"You mind if I just take you home? I'm tired and I've got a busy day tomorrow."

He always seems to be busy "tomorrow" but I do my best to hide my disappointment. "Yeah, no problem."

On the ride home I try to figure out if I am more disappointed that I don't get to stay with him or that he doesn't seem to want me to stay.

* * *

I shower when I get home. I feel much better, but when I crawl into bed I am restless. I'm anxious and unbelievably sexually frustrated. I can't turn my mind off. I'm seriously contemplating masturbation, but it just doesn't seem to do it for me lately. I lay there for several minutes, just still, trying not to think about Adam—or Cade.

I must have dozed off because I am pulled awake by loud whispering and giggling in the hallway. I am perturbed. Then it sounds like someone is stumbling, falling into the wall, immediately followed by more laughing and shushing.

"Cade!" More laughing. "Stop!" Her voice is clear. His response is too deep and just sounds like vibrations through the door. They close Cade's door and then it is quiet. I close my eyes again and try to find my way back to the dream I had been having.

Then I hear a moan. Barely audible. Then another one, soft. Then a deeper one—Cade.

I pull my pillow over my head to muffle the noises. But they start coming louder, turning into rough grunts. I can make out the distinct thumping of the headboard against the wall. And now she is spewing out-loud "Ohs" and "Yeses" and "Oh Gods." I can't take it anymore. I am practically suffocating myself with my pillow. I feel like kicking and screaming and throwing breakable objects at his door.

Did I just turn into the old lady yelling at the neighborhood kids to stop rough-housing on her lawn? I am getting crotchety. Here I am, alone in my bed on a Friday night while everyone else seems to be out having fun, having sex, living their carefree college lives—I want that too.

So I text Adam.

Me: *Will you come over?*

Adam: *It's really late*

Me: *I'm in bed and I'm sober* (that's mostly true) *Come join me*

He doesn't respond for a few minutes.

Adam: *K be there in 10*

I unlock the front door then run back to my room and put on the sexiest pair of black lace underwear I own and a matching black bra. I slide under the covers and wait for Adam, my heart pounding loudly.

The door cracks open slowly as he walks in. He closes it noiselessly behind him.

"Hey."

"Hey."

I sit up, letting the blankets fall to reveal my skimpy

bra. It barely holds in my ample breasts. He smiles as he removes his coat and peels his shirt off. He walks over to the side of the bed as he undoes his jeans and drops them to the floor. I haven't seen this smile before. It isn't sweet or shy—it is too confident. Maybe it is his lusty smile?

He crawls on the bed toward me. I swallow hard and my hands are sweaty. He kisses me, and I am sure he can feel my lips trembling against his. I am hyperaware of the heat of his body and his large arms on either side of my head, caging me under him. He pulls back the covers and looks up and down my body. I have always been proud of my slim-yet-curvy figure but suddenly I feel like I am about to sprout some hideous deformity and send him running.

I don't.

Instead, he removes his boxers releasing his erection. I think I might hyperventilate. He lays back over me, resuming our kiss. The kiss is getting more frantic, his tongue wet and sloppy over mine. He trails his fingers down my stomach and rubs them over the thin fabric of my panties.

"Oh, you're so ready."

I am?

Before I know it, he has swiped my underwear off and rolled the condom on. I close my eyes and wrap my arms around his shoulders as he shoves himself inside of me. I let out a small gasp from the feeling of being stretched and the sudden fullness.

I grip his back and he moves back out and in again. I am happy I don't have any pain or the discomfort sex has brought me in the past, but there is still a little too much friction. My body is putting up too much resistance.

His head is at the pillow above my head and his shoulder is smashed into my face, making it hard to breath.

His right hip bone is also digging into my leg with each drive and I keep trying to shift my bum over to ease the constant jabbing but his weight on me is too much. He starts speeding up, his thrusts becoming more erratic and I can't meet him with any type of rhythm.

He is obviously near the end of his enjoyment. Shouldn't I be screaming his name by now?

My mind drifts to the sounds that had come from Cade's room earlier. I wonder if she is still here, if he is awake. Maybe they are just resting for round two. Adam starts pounding into me even faster, his breathing is sporadic, and he is sweating. On me. He is literally sweating on me.

He finally shudders over me then collapses on top of me. His body is damp and heavy and hot. I suddenly feel like he is going to suffocate me. Thankfully, he rolls over onto his back, panting hard.

After his breathing quiets he kisses me quickly on the lips and stands up.

"I have an early study group in the morning. You don't mind if I head home, do you?"

Is he serious?

"Um. That's fine." It isn't.

He dresses even more hurriedly than he had undressed twenty minutes ago.

"I'll call you later," he says. Then he leaves, closing the door behind him and I am left sitting in my bed—naked, except for the black lacey bra he never attempted to remove. And alone.

CHAPTER 10

The next day I sleep in late and stay in my room studying all day. Midterms are going to kick my ass. Around dinnertime, I decide to take a shower and freshen up. I also realize I am famished. I put on my super soft pink sweats and a tight black tank top before heading to the kitchen.

Cade is in the kitchen, cooking.

Of course.

I open the fridge casually without making eye contact. I was hoping to find something quick to eat, but suddenly, under the pressure of Cade watching me, the full refrigerator literally has NOTHING in it.

I mean nothing. I am beginning to panic. I am obviously taking an unnaturally long time at the fridge. Then I realize I am standing with the door open and the coolness is making my nipples harden. Shit. I close the door and Cade is chuckling behind me.

"Everything all right over there?"

I turn on him and glare. "Yes."

"Looking for something in particular?"

"No."

He can tell I am flustered and being extremely short

with him. I just hope he doesn't notice my nipples at full attention. But he is looking at my face. He looks a little sad.

"Haley?"

"Yeah?"

"Hey, sorry if I was a jerk to you at the party yesterday."

"You were a jerk to me yesterday?"

He looks at me confused, nose scrunched, ring protruding from his bottom lip. I continue with an explanation.

"Because yesterday was probably the nicest you've been to me in a couple of weeks. You actually said words to me."

He looks at the stove and is silent for a while.

"You want a grilled cheese?" He lifts his baby blue eyes to me. My stomach grumbles. He breaks into a big smile, full of beautiful white teeth. "Yes, then?" His gorgeous face is perfect when he smiles.

"Sure."

He lights up. He starts pulling things out of the fridge and spewing out options. "We've got cheddar, provolone, pepper jack... Do you want ham or tuna with it? Or grilled onions or jalapenos?" He looks at me expectantly, arms full of cheese.

My mouth is agape, and I am a little overwhelmed.

"What am I doing?" He smacks himself on the forehead. "First, we need to choose what kind of bread. Let's see... We have whole wheat, sourdough or rye." He looks at me again in question.

I am finally able to speak. "I had no idea a grilled cheese could be so complicated."

He bites his lip, tugging on his thin silver ring. "You're right. Ham and cheddar on sourdough sound good?"

"Sounds great."

I sit on a stool at the counter and watch him make us two identical sandwiches. His arms, covered in black ink, flex as he slices and butters the bread then places them on the skillet with a sizzle. It smells delicious. He moves fluidly around the kitchen, putting things away as he goes. He flips the sandwiches with no hesitation and they are perfectly golden brown.

We eat at the small bistro table across from one another. The first bite is amazing with the melty cheese oozing from between the buttery-crisp slices of bread. I hum my appreciation.

"So how's the boyfriend?"

Boyfriend? I suddenly realize it is almost eight o'clock and Adam hasn't called me yet. That is unusual.

 "He's great."

"No plans with him tonight?"

I guess not. "Nope."

I look at Cade as he eats. His jaw taut under his smooth skin while chewing, his long lashes against his cheeks, his dark blond hair all pushed up to the top of his head.

I become very curious. "It's Saturday night. Why aren't you out?"

He looks up at me an amused smile. "I got so shitfaced last night I decided to give myself a night to recover."

"So you're staying here?"

"Yup. You?"

"Uh huh."

* * *

After we eat, I help Cade do the dishes. He washes and I

dry. I remind myself next time to be the washer as he takes every opportunity to splash me with the soapy water.

When we are finished I saunter into my room where my phone is charging. I check it. Still no call from Adam. He is really anal about schoolwork—he probably just got caught up studying. I decide to just call him myself and see how he is doing.

It goes to voicemail. Oh well. I don't leave a message. He will see that I called and that is enough.

I go back out to Cade, who is still in the kitchen. Glass bowls are strewn on the counter and he has a big scoop in his hand.

"You look like you could use some ice cream." He raises his eyebrows suggestively at me.

I walk up to the counter. He has bowls filled with toppings: little candies, sprinkles, whipped cream, and a hot fudge sauce simmering on the stovetop.

"Shit, Cade. You discovered my weakness."

"Oh yeah, what's that?"

"Anything smothered in steaming chocolate."

"I'll have to remember that." A smirk tugs at his lips.

He scoops me way too much ice cream and I proceed to cover it with way too many toppings.

"This is going to go straight to my ass," I say looking at my heaping bowl.

"This ass?" He smacks me hard right across my bum as he leaves the kitchen, carrying his equally massive bowl of ice cream. "Looks fine to me," he calls over his shoulder.

I join him on the couch and we watch an old sitcom marathon. Maybe it is the sugar rush or just Cade's silly laugh but the show seems much funnier than I remember. At one point, Cade is doubled over laughing, hand clutching at his belly until the laugh becomes silent and I can only make out a wheezing sound. He is trying to catch his breath as he wipes a tear from his eye and it's contagious. I can't help but laugh back at him. By the end of our laughing fit over nothing, my stomach aches and my cheeks are sore. I can't remember laughing like this in forever.

When I finish my ice cream, I am stuffed, and suddenly freezing. Cade notices my shivering and pulls the blanket down over us. We are on each arm of the couch, our feet meeting in the middle.

"Damn, your feet are freezing! Get away from me with those things," he teases.

"Warm them up for me." I smash my cold feet up to his and rub them up against as much of his skin as I can.

"Stop! Your feet are like weapons. First the smell and now they're like icicles."

"Oh shut up! What's with you and my feet? You're like obsessed."

"I am?" Then he looks genuinely confused and I remember the infamous foot-rub-orgasm. I feel my cheeks get hot. Maybe I am the one obsessed.

"Never mind. I'll go get some socks."

"No, it's fine. They are practically warm now after stealing all my heat. Guess that's what I get for being so hot."

I swat him on the shoulder.

"Abusive!"

"Shut up."

We laugh to several more episodes together, his warm toes against my feet the entire time.

My eyelids are beginning to encroach on my vision. When my eyes start to glaze over, I lay my head on the couch pillow and doze off easily.

Suddenly, the support drops out from under me and I am aware of arms around me. I am just disturbed enough to realize Cade has lifted me off the couch. I am able to wrap my arms around his neck and my head falls heavy to his chest.

I am still too out of it to form any sounds or open my eyes as he carries me down the hall. He smells like the air after it rains. Then he is lowering me and the softness of my mattress comes up to greet my tired back. The warmth of his body is no longer around me.

I want to open my eyes. I can still feel him standing near me. I want to hug him to me.

Then I feel his hands on my hips. His fingers are between my sweatpants and my underwear. Then he slowly slides my pants down to my ankles before removing them completely.

The chilly air hits my legs and I squirm as chills run up from my toes. It's just enough to wake me to the point that I realize Cade is undressing me. Cade. My Cade. I'm not sure if I should try to stop him or beg him to keep going. Then the thick blankets are over my body. He tucks them up under my chin and down my sides. I can't remember the last time I was tucked in like this.

I can smell him. His breath is warm and sweet on my face. I desperately want to open my eyes. I try but I can't. His lips are soft as he lightly touches them to my forehead. He lingers there for a few seconds as he takes a full breath.

"Night, Hale."

* * *

RAE KENNEDY

The next few days I am consumed with studying for my three midterm exams and writing two huge midterm papers. I am too busy to do much of anything else. I do get in a shower here and there. Luckily, Cade has started making me breakfast again so I'm not going totally hungry. I'm also still up studying when he gets home at all hours of the night, so when I hear him come in, I take a break and watch him cook. Sometimes I will help, but mostly I like to watch. I look forward to that time of the day more and more.

It is the longest I have gone without hearing from Adam. On Tuesday, I am surprised I don't see him in class for the test. It is a large class but that still seems odd. I figure he is just as swamped as I am with school. Even more so actually—I know he is taking seven more credits than I am. I tell myself that I am too busy for any type of social life this week, anyway. I decide to not worry about it until after the week is over.

Thursday afternoon, I turn in both of my papers and have only one exam left the next morning. I am studied out. The small print in my textbook begins to blur into one large gray mass. That seems like a legit reason to call it quits. I need literally anything else to do for the evening.

I take a shower and do my hair for the first time in four days. I put on my light worn-out jeans with the holes in the pockets and strut into the living room.

Cade has just finished putting dishes away when he sees me.

"What are you up to tonight?"

I stretch across the couch. "I don't know. Hanging out with you."

"Oh really?" He saunters over and sits down on the

TO BE YOUR GIRL

floor with his back to the couch. He leans his head back against my leg.

"Yup," I confirm.

He chuckles at me when his phone rings.

"This is Cade... Okay... Hang on let me check." He puts his hand up to the receiver and looks at me. "Hey, do you mind going to the restaurant with me and hanging there for an hour or so?"

Really? "Sure."

His smile is warm as he turns back to his phone. "Yeah, I can come in and cover. I'll be there soon."

* * *

In the kitchen, Cade is the BOSS. I sit on a stainless steel table in the corner, swinging my legs. The kitchen at *La Mer* is spotless—every surface shiny. All the line cooks move at a frenzied pace but skillfully around one another like a choreographed dance. Servers rush in and out, balancing trays, yelling for orders and calling out their positions to avoid collisions. The clanks of metal ring around the room like an orchestra.

And Cade is there in his crisp white smock firmly commanding everyone—the Conductor. They all respond quickly with a "Yes, Chef," or a "Right away, Chef." He looks so professional in his neat white uniform, even with the sleeves rolled up and his tattoo-covered arms exposed. I watch his face as he supervises all of the dishes being made, sending plates back that don't meet his standards. Every once in a while, I catch his eye and he smiles and nods over at me.

He brings me a small plate with several different things

on it—a scallop, some shrimp, some angel hair pasta tossed in a light creamy broth, and a little salad with large shaves of fresh parmesan. It is all delicious.

He comes back over, a sexy smile on his lips.

"Here, try this." He holds up a small, cocoa-dusted ball to my lips. I open my mouth and he puts it right on my tongue. The chocolate is rich and dark. It melts almost instantly and disintegrates with tiny bubbles. I close my eyes and hum with delight.

"It's our specialty dark chocolate truffle with champagne."

"How come you never make these for me?"

"Woman. I cook for you all the damn time!"

I chuckle back at his wicked smile.

He unbuttons his smock. "You about ready to go?"

"Yeah."

"I'm just going to go put my things away. I'll meet you out front."

As I walk out through the dining room, I hear his laugh. Adam.

I glance to my right and see the familiar brown hair that curls just over his ears. Adam's back and broad shoulders are barely visible behind a massive column. Why is he at La Mer? On a Thursday? I walk over to him and as he comes into view, so does the pretty girl sitting at the table with him. She has smooth tan skin, wide, dark eyes and black hair. I have never seen her before, but then I realize that I haven't actually met any of Adam's friends. I go up and stand next to him.

"Hi."

He looks at me without an ounce of recognition on his face.

"Adam, who is this?" the pretty girl asks.

"Who am I? I'm his girlfriend."

She shoots him an accusing look.

Adam's face is smooth and his voice steady as he tells her, "I don't have a girlfriend." He turns to me. "I think you're confused."

What the fuck? I suddenly can't think straight. I feel lightheaded like the room is toppling over. I am confused. What's happening? Why is he talking to me like he doesn't know me? Why is he looking at me like I'm crazy?

"What's going on here, Adam?"

"Yes. What is going on here?" Cade steps up behind me, placing his hand on the small of my back.

I'm cold and sickness pools in my stomach. "Is this how you're breaking up with me?"

The pretty girl stands abruptly and throws her napkin at Adam. "I'm leaving."

After she clicks away, Adam turns on me. The sneer on his face is hideous.

"Thanks for ruining my evening. She was a sure thing, too. Unlike you."

I feel tears wobbling in my eyes. *Don't do it. Don't cry.*

"You better watch your fucking mouth," Cade growls. I can feel the tension in his body and the heat radiating off him as he moves closer to me.

Adam turns to him like he has just realized he is there. "Hey man, it's not my fault your girl here is a lousy lay."

I don't even see Cade move from behind me but his fist connects with Adam's face. Adam immediately brings his hands over his nose as blood starts gushing between his fingers. Cade stands rigid at my side. He puts his hand on my waist and steers me toward the doors.

CHAPTER 11

Cade is driving fast. I am looking out the window, trying to concentrate on anything but the tears streaming down my face. The sky is heavy and gray.

What the fuck just happened? Adam had only ever looked at me with adoration. Today he'd looked at me like I was nothing. I grab my purse and search frantically through it for something to wipe my wet face. Nothing. Fucking perfect. Somehow staring into my purse, not finding even a receipt with which to dry my tears, makes me feel completely defeated. That's it. I start to break down. My body shudders with sobs. Then Cade's hand is in front of me, with a napkin.

"I'm sorry…" Sob. "…I'm such a mess." I feel so stupid.

"Are you kidding me? You're the last person in this situation who needs to apologize."

"Maybe he's right. I'm awful in bed." I begin bawling into my hands even harder.

"Look at me," Cade says. I keep my head down. "Fuck!"

He slams on the breaks, takes my chin in his hand and turns me toward him. His light blue eyes dig right into mine, his face close.

"Trust me. It's not you."

I stare into his face. He does not falter for one second.

"Believe me?"

I give a slight nod and he releases my chin. He drives forward, looking at me while still trying to keep an eye on the road.

He looks pained. "Haley?"

I hiccup in response.

"So you did actually sleep with him?"

I make eye contact with him for just a second and nod, then look away quickly. I can't stand the disappointment on his face. I feel so ashamed. The sobs are now wracking my entire body. I am full-on ugly crying in front of Cade. I want to die. He puts his hand lightly on my shoulder and squeezes reassuringly. He is trying to figure out how to calm me down without any success.

After a few minutes, my shaking subsides and I am able to catch my breath.

"Was the sex really that bad?"

Why is he asking this?

I don't want to talk about it. But I am able to answer shakily between cries.

"I don't know. I mean, it didn't hurt."

"It didn't hurt? Fuck." He hits the steering wheel with his palm. "It should be so much more than that." The muscles tick under his jaw. "I swear to fucking God, if it was any other restaurant I would go back there and beat the living shit out of him."

I shake my head at him. "He's not worth it."

He really isn't.

"You're right." But his knuckles are still white as he grips the wheel.

* * *

When we get home, I feel like a zombie. I miss the hook when I go to hang up my coat and it falls to the floor. This makes me cry again. Cade hurries in behind me. He hangs up my coat then wraps his arms around me. My hands are balled up under my chin, my head against his chest, getting his shirt wet. I lean into him. I feel like I might collapse but he holds me up.

We stand there in that embrace for a long time. No words, just an understanding that he is going to hold me as long as I need him to. He's warm and his arms are solid. He rests his chin on my head and I take a big calming breath, inhaling his scent as I do. He smells like fresh laundry. My cries disintegrate into the occasional hiccup and he walks me to my bedroom.

I immediately crawl on my bed and coil into a ball. I am surprised when I feel the bed dip behind me under Cade's weight. He curls around me and we lay cuddled on top of the covers for over an hour.

I watch the sky outside my window go from a hazy slate to a deep midnight blue. My eyelids are swollen and sore. My actual eyeballs ache. Is that possible? I close them and then all I am aware of is the soft velvety blanket under my skin and Cade's body heat against me—his slow breathing on my neck and his hands clasped over mine, holding tight to my chest.

"You should probably get changed and go to sleep," he whispers.

Suddenly I am freezing as he moves to get off the bed. I sit up and watch him walk toward the door. He is leaving. I

TO BE YOUR GIRL

feel my chest lurch forward, my body begging to be near his again. I feel more tears fill my eyes. I can't find my breath. Or words. All I want is to plead with him to stay.

When he reaches the door, he turns to look at me, his beautiful blue eyes so calm until he sees my face.

"You change and get ready for bed. I'll be right back. Promise."

He thinks I am still crying over Adam. I'm not. Adam made me feel like a total idiot. But in this moment, I don't even miss him. It is the thought of Cade leaving that frightens me. I want him to stay. To be with me.

I change and pee and brush my teeth. I think about keeping my sweats on, but they always get bunched up to my knees and make me too hot if I sleep in them, so I slide them off and get under the covers in just my underwear and sleep tank. It is cold between the sheets.

Cade comes in a few minutes later in short white boxer briefs, his chiseled chest gloriously bare. He turns off the light and walks over to me slowly. Only a hint of light from the window glints off his pecs and over the tattoos on his shoulders. My heart is suddenly beating forcefully against my chest as he pulls the covers back and gets into bed with me.

Without even asking, he pulls me to him. I nuzzle my face into the crook of his neck. His hands are firm against my back and our bare legs are instantly entwined. I squeeze my arms around his waist—his skin is perfectly smooth against mine.

"Are you feeling better now?" he whispers.

"Yes," I breathe back. I hope that doesn't mean he is going to leave again.

He doesn't.

We stay wrapped around each other. He slowly slides his hand up to the back of my neck and squeezes it gently. I don't even realize I exhale a quivering moan until it happens.

"You're so tight."

Apparently.

He begins rubbing his thumb and middle finger in small circles on either side of my neck at the base of my skull. It feels amazing. My lips are parted and I am breathing heavily against his collarbone. He brings his other hand up and begins kneading down my neck to my shoulders. I can feel the tension leaving my body and my head falls limply down, my forehead pressing hard against his chest.

"Wow, you really need this. Turn over and I'll give you a real massage."

I don't even think about protesting. I turn to my stomach and nestle my face in the pillows. Cade reaches over and rubs some of the lotion I have on my nightstand between his hands. Then he comes back over, straddling me. His fingers slide easily around my neck, his thumbs moving up and down in long, slow strokes. The lotion is sweet and smells like almonds.

He rubs down my shoulders, his thumbs moving in deep circles. The pressure is agonizingly pleasurable. He massages all up and down my arms and then down to my hands, massaging each individual finger to the tip. I have never felt so soothed or relaxed in my life. Cade might give the best massages in the known universe.

He inches the bottom of my shirt up just a little and begins kneading my low back, just above the rim of my panties. The excruciating ache in my groin is instantaneous. I press my thighs together as the tingling begins to spread. I squirm and he asks if I am all right. Shit. I mumble, "Yes" into

the pillow. I want him to continue. I decide to make it easier for him and without thinking I reach for my shirt and strip it off over my head. The air is chilly against my bare back but my breasts are safely pressed against the mattress.
 I feel him freeze over me. He is hesitating. Balls. I hope I didn't just ruin this.
 I hear him dispense some more lotion and then his hands are back on me. He works up and down my whole back, kneading with his knuckles hard then rubbing over again soothingly with his palms. His long fingers massage down the sides of my ribs and slide back up, grazing the edges of my breasts. A zing of electricity shoots down the backs of my thighs and puddles behind my knees.
 Cade's hands are strong and warm, moving over my bare skin, applying pressure in all the right spots. I am completely peaceful and I can feel the temptation of sleep tugging at my limbs. I don't want it to end, but before I know it I am out.

* * *

When I wake, I am still on my stomach, the covers tucked up to my chin. The room is all white with the soft morning light filtering in through the window. As my eyes absorb the light, Cade's face comes into focus on the pillow next to me. He is awake. And looking right at me.
 "Morning." He looks blissful.
 "You haven't been watching me all night, right? Because that would be creepy."
 I am glad I can make him laugh.
 "No, I swear. You just finally looked so peaceful while you were sleeping, it's beautiful to watch." Beautiful? "And

RAE KENNEDY

I wanted to make sure you were all right. I care about you."

"You care about me?" Yeah, like a little sister, remember?

"Of course I do." His small shy smile appears. Is he blushing? He's making my stomach flutter and it gives me a sudden hope.

I have to ask. "You mean you care about me like a big brother." Right?

He looks at me, completely earnest. "No. My feelings for you are nothing like a brother's."

Feelings? Holy shit. Suddenly my heart is in my throat, I can feel the pulse of my blood moving to the surface of all of my skin. All of it.

Cade has non-brother-like feelings for me? The words are in my head and then they just pour out of my mouth.

"Do you like me?"
He swallows hard, the little crease appearing over his nose. "Isn't it obvious?"

Honestly, the signals I have been getting are kinda mixed. He moves like he is going to reach for me, but then stops. Maybe remembering I'm practically naked. And so is he.

Does he like me in that way? I have to know.

"Do you want me?" I'm not even thinking when I say it.

"Fuck."

"Well?"

We stare at each other for a moment.

He is so clearly being torn to pieces, but I need to know. This may be my only shot.

"Do you want me or not?"

He looks at me fiercely, jaw clenched. Is he going to reject me again?

I can't stop myself. "Because, Cade—you can have me."

TO BE YOUR GIRL

He closes his eyes, his face contorts in pain. He is. He is going to say no. He doesn't want me. I am mortified. He lets out a long sigh and opens his eyes. My eyes lock on his clear blue ones just for a second before he reaches his hand to my face and pulls me to him.

"I want you."

Then our lips crash together and he is kissing me, hard. Hard but his lips are so soft, his skin smells so clean and his mouth tastes so sweet.

He slides his hands down my bare back and crushes me against him. I am intensely aware that my naked breasts are pressed against his smooth chest and I cling to him. His fingertips glide up my spine, stopping to wrap behind my neck, his thumb stroking my cheek. His mouth is devouring mine.

Gradually, I can feel his control come back as his soft lips press slow and deliberately against mine. He pulls away, sucking my bottom lip just long enough for me to catch a breath before his lips are back over mine, his tongue confidently sweeping into my mouth. Holding me firmly, he rolls me onto my back, his hard body covering mine. The weight of him and his hot skin touching mine is glorious.

When he pulls away this time, he bites my bottom lip. The hint of pain is exquisite. Our faces are just an inch apart. My chest is heaving as I try to steady my breathing. He sweeps a piece of hair from my forehead as he looks into my eyes.

"Hale, I've wanted you since the second I saw you. Standing there in the hall, you were the cutest little thing I'd ever seen. And off limits. Tuck made sure I knew just how off limits you were."

Tuck told him I was off limits? That sounds about right.

"Then you smiled at me and I was wrong. You weren't cute—you were gorgeous. Then the next day in the kitchen in your underwear—fuck. I had a hard-on all morning."

I'm smiling big.

He smiles back at me, a heart-breaking smile, as he continues. "I was surprised at how much I liked you, just being around you, and how much I wanted to protect you. And I knew I needed to protect you from me. Then all of a sudden you had a boyfriend, and I was so mad that he got to be with you and I didn't. I didn't realize how much I wanted you until we danced, and I almost kissed you... I thought if I pushed you away, I could keep my promise to Tuck. But I missed you too much."

I don't have any words. So I kiss him, holding his face in my hands I can feel the stubble along his jaw. I feel his body melt against mine as our lips meet.

A door shuts in the hallway. Tuck's footsteps are unmistakable as they pass my room.

"Shit. I should go." Cade moves away but I hold tight to him.

"I don't care what Tuck thinks."

He chuckles quietly. "Yeah, well, you're his sister. He won't murder you. Just... Not like this at least."

"Okay," I agree.

He squeezes his eyes shut when he kisses my lips quickly then I let him go. After he leaves, my tiny bed suddenly feels enormous.

* * *

I get dressed and ready for class. I have one more test this morning that I—surprise!—haven't studied at all for but I'm not even thinking about that. When I get to the kitchen, Tuck and Cade are sitting at the table with a heaping plate of fluffy yellow scrambled eggs and a pile of steaming pancakes. Normally, I would be ecstatic that Tuck is having breakfast with us—today, all I want is to get Cade alone again.

As Tuck talks about the merger at his firm and his date with Ali that night, I feel a nudge against my foot. I glance over to Cade. He is smiling wickedly at me. A smile takes over my whole face. I kick him back under the table and try to steady my expression as Tuck looks at me. He is asking me a question about how my classes are going but it is hard to concentrate and act normal at the same time Cade is rubbing his foot up and down my calf.

After breakfast, Cade and I do the dishes as Tuck gets dressed for work. I wash this time. I am scrubbing the last soapy plate when Cade grabs me around the waist and kisses me fully on the mouth. He smells like maple syrup. He pulls away with a satisfied grin just as Tuck comes around the corner, still fixing his tie. I stand stock straight and finish cleaning the dish, praying Tuck won't notice how flushed I am.

When Tuck leaves, it is already time for me to go to class and for Cade to head to the restaurant. Before he steps out the door, Cade gives me one more quick kiss.

"I'll see you tonight?" He is smiling against my lips.

"Yeah."

Then he walks out the front door.

I sigh and grab my book bag when the door swings open and Cade bursts back in. He reaches me in two strides and literally pushes me up against the wall, kissing me passionately, his tongue desperately seeking mine. Our breaths are becoming ragged as our lips melt into each other. He unpins me from the wall, his lips red and swollen.

"Fuck. I've really got to go now."

He turns and leaves a second time. I am left needing more.

CHAPTER 12

I GET HOME AFTER CLASS AND THE HOUSE IS EMPTY. I AM antsy. Cade is working through the dinner shift and won't be home until ten or eleven. I don't know what to do with myself. All I want to do is be with him, and touch him, and kiss him, and oh jeez. I get in the shower, taking extra care to shave my legs and trim all my lady parts. I curl my hair, put on just enough mascara to highlight my golden-brown eyes and some gloss to make my lips look extra pouty. I decide to just wear jeans and a pretty floral flowy top. I cannot wait for Cade to get home.

A slow creaking of the front door at six o'clock has me running for the door.

"Well, that's a nice welcome home!" Tuck is beaming at me. I think I recover my disappointed face quickly enough he doesn't notice. I keep running toward him and give him a big hug.

Right, this was my plan all along, Tuck.

"How was your day?" I ask, trying to continue the charade of being interested in Tuck at the moment. Am I a bad sister?

"Oh, it was all right. About to get much better though.

I'm going out tonight."

"Yeah?"

"Yeah?" He gives me a quizzical look. "I told you all about it this morning."

Gah!

"Oh, I remember now, sorry! Midterms have my brain fried this week." Solid recovery, Haley.

"But they're done now, right?"

"Yes."

"Sweet." He walks past me, toward the hall to his bedroom. "Hey, don't wait up for me tonight. I'll be home late...or not at all." He does the creeper double eyebrow raise at me.

"Gross! I don't want to know about your sex life!"

But he disappears down the hallway, laughing before I can find something to throw in his direction.

* * *

After Tuck leaves, I find myself posing in various spots around the living room and kitchen, trying to figure out how to best appear sexy but nonchalant, and not at all like I am waiting around for Cade to get home. Nothing I do feels natural. By the time he gets home at ten-fifteen, I am practically asleep on the couch with some lame made-for-television movie on.

I sit up instantly.

"Hey." He nods at me as he passes me and goes down the hall to his bedroom.

What the fuck? Is he already over it? I hear the shower running and I throw myself back down on the couch. So far my plan of Cade immediately grabbing me, throwing me down on his bed and having his way with me isn't progressing as I had hoped.

He comes out a few minutes later in a worn pair of jeans that hang from his narrow hips and a short-sleeved band T-shirt, his hair still damp and perfectly tousled.

He sits next to me as I inch myself up against the armrest.

"What are we watching?" He looks at the television screen.

"Nothing."

"Good."

He has me by the hips and pulls me down the couch toward him in one smooth motion. Then he is over me, his body pressing me to the cushions as he lies between my legs. His lips are soft and sweet as they part mine to allow him inside. His tongue is greedy. I intertwine my fingers in his hair, holding his mouth firmly to mine. His hands trail down my ribs to my hips, then up under my shirt, setting my skin on fire.

The pull between my legs is beginning to build and I squeeze him between my thighs as his fingers reach my bra. His burning palms skim over the thin lace and my nipples become instantly hard. I arch up into his grip, wanting more sensation. My breath becomes strained. I've thought of nothing but having Cade all day and now he is here, and I can tell he wants me just as much.

Our kisses grow more lustful as his fingers go around my back and nimbly unhook my bra. I want him to touch me so much—I am practically quivering beneath him. Then he moves his hands slowly up beneath the underwire to cup my breasts, his thumbs press firmly on my nipples and send shocks down my spine.

All I can feel are his eager lips, his large hands stimulating my tips, and his leg grinding heavily against my groin. The friction is just enough to satiate my pulsating bud. I rake my hands slowly down his chest to his firm stomach, rocking against him.

Cade massages my breasts as I drag my hands further down his body until I feel him. Even through his pants, I can tell he is rock hard. He groans over me, gripping my hips tightly as I stroke up and down his length over his jeans. His fingers dig into my flesh, and we hungrily lick and nip at each other's lips. I feel blissfully aroused. I'm practically melting in my panties.

I kiss his neck. His smell is like sweat and rain. When he can't take any more, he slides his hands to the top button of my jeans and starts to undo them. I reach for his waistband and undo the button. Then I pull down the zipper.

There is a loud stomping noise outside the front door. Fuckity fuck!

We sit up quickly, straightening and buttoning up our clothes when Tuck comes bursting through the door, slamming it behind him.

"Fucking bullshit!"

"Whoa, you all right man?" Cade asks.

"No."

Tuck looks extremely upset as he collapses on the chair across from us. He sighs heavily and closes his eyes as he throws his head back. My cheeks feel hot and I can tell my lips are swollen. Cade's hair is completely disheveled. I wonder if I have enough time to re-hook my bra without Tuck noticing.

"Ali and I broke up."

"Oh Tuck, I'm sorry."

"Sorry, bro. You want a beer?" Cade gets up to get some drinks from the fridge, and uses the opportunity to adjust himself, I notice.

"I'll be fine." He doesn't look very fine. "What are you guys watching?"

"Uhh…" Cade looks at me from the kitchen for help. Sorry. I shrug. I have no clue either.

"Just some silly TV movie. Let's watch something else," I offer.

"No, we can finish this." Tuck looks like he wants to do anything other than talk about Ali.

So, we watch the second half of the ridiculous movie that is on. This movie makes no sense. I guess we missed some key parts from the beginning. But Cade comes to sit next to me and he throws the blanket over our legs. I don't think Tuck is watching the movie—he is way too absorbed in his thoughts. He doesn't notice Cade rubbing my leg or us holding hands under the blanket the entire time, either.

* * *

I am lying in bed staring at the ceiling, watching as the occasional passing car washes light across the surface and then fades away. The rustling of the dried leaves outside is a constant soothing whisper. I look at the clock.

It is 2:42. I still haven't fallen asleep. I can't shut off my mind. I can't stop thinking about Cade. The way he smelled, the weight of his body on top of mine, the feel of his lips on my skin, his firm massaging of my breasts…

I can't stifle how awake my body is or trick it into forgetting he is just across the hall.

I give up.

RAE KENNEDY

It is cold outside of the covers. I tiptoe across the hall in just my thin white tank top and purple silky underwear and close Cade's door behind me as quietly as I can. I can just make out the shape of Cade's body, his bare chest rising and falling in the slow, steady rhythm of someone deep in sleep.

I lift the covers just enough to slide in. I straddle him and pull the covers down over both of us as I plant a soft kiss on his lips. His brow furrows as he blinks awake.

As soon as his eyes open and he sees me, his face brightens into a big sleepy grin. He crosses his arms around my back and pulls me in tight as our mouths meet again. His lips are full and soft, massaging against mine, parting them to taste me. He pulls back for just a second, sucking on my bottom lip then biting it gently.

I can barely concentrate on the kissing because his hands are burning a pathway down my sides to my hips, resting on the bare strip of skin between my panties and shirt. His thumbs and forefingers slide just barely up under my shirt. They feel strong and decisive, yet tender. Meanwhile, the kiss is getting rougher.

My breathing is so erratic I think I might get a little lightheaded. I can hear my pulse pounding in my head. Then he starts making little circles on my skin, his thumbs dipping just below the top of my underwear, then around and up under my shirt. It's driving me crazy. His hands slide farther up my back, pushing my shirt up to my waist. He runs his fingers lightly across my back, leaving goosebumps all over.

I end our kiss and sit up to catch my breath. As I do, Cade lets out a faint whimper and tightens his grip on my hips. His lips are shiny and swollen, his eyes hooded and lust-filled. As I straddle him, I can feel his erection hard against the sensitivity of my aching heat. I move just slightly against him, and the friction against my silky panties is spectacular. Cade responds by letting out a deep breath and closing his eyes as he caresses my uncovered skin.

"God, you drive me crazy."

I smile down at him. "Yeah?"

He nods. "I always have a hard-on for you."

I pull my top over my head and toss it to the floor. I let my long hair fall down my back, exposing my naked breasts. Cade immediately sits up, wrapping his arms as far around me as they will go.

"You are so gorgeous, baby." He leans forward and kisses my neck firmly down to my collarbone then just to the tops of the swells of my chest. He leans back and brings both hands up to cup my breasts. They feel heavy, perfectly filling his hands. He looks at me, his completely sexy devious smirk on his face. "And these tits are even better than I imagined them." Then he lowers his lips to my rigid little pink nipple and kisses it softly. It's so soft it almost tickles and leaves me aching for more. More pressure. "Really, these are spectacular."

I giggle at his appreciation of my boobs. I was blessed with nice perky, round full breasts. He licks his thumb and places it over one nipple as he closes his mouth over the other, moving his thumb and tongue in mirroring circles. I let out a soft moan and rock against him. Each broad stroke of his tongue over my nipple sends pulses of energy down my spine and makes my sex throb. I'm gripping his back, fingers digging in deeper and deeper as waves of pleasure surge through me. He lifts his face and finds my mouth again, restraining my moans.

His hands move across my skin, down to my behind, squeezing softly. He slips the tips of his fingers just under the edge of my panties. My pussy is suddenly tingling all over and aching for his touch. I lift my hips up just enough so he can slide his hand down over my underwear to where my clit thrums for him.

"Fuck, Hale, you're soaked."

By this time I am panting and can only gasp out a weak "Uh huh."

He slides one finger inside my panties, finding my slippery folds then moving up to put the wickedest pressure on my stiff little bud, sending a bolt of electricity to my toes and causing me to gasp in his ear. I can feel his smile against my cheek as he moves back to take my lips. His kissing is slow, sensual, mimicking the slow circling of his finger on my clit. Then he slides his finger down and enters me in one smooth motion and I can't help but cry out.

"Jesus, baby, you're so tight."

I'm focused on my breathing and the feeling of newness and the fullness of his thick finger inside me when he pulls it away.

"You okay?"

I look at him, a little confused. "Yes." Why wouldn't I be?

"You seem a little tense."

I don't feel tense.

"Come lay down with me."

He lowers me next to him on my back and lays close to me, propped up on his side. He touches my face, rubbing my cheek with his thumb then down my neck between my breasts and down to my navel, where he splays his hand out to rest on my stomach.

"Just relax," he says.

I think I am relaxed until I realize his hand is practically bouncing from the fluttering in my tummy. My body is all wound up and anxious. I look at his hand, following it up his tattooed muscular arms to his defined shoulders and finally to his face. He is smiling serenely, beautiful and calm. And he is looking at me. He leans down and kisses me softly behind the ear, then on the cheek, forehead, nose, and then on the lips. I finally feel the trembling in my stomach ease up. He gazes at me adoringly, our noses just touching.

"Do you trust me?"

I nod.

Some of the lust returns to his eyes as he hovers over me. He puts both hands on my hips and hooks his fingers inside my waistband. Then he slowly pulls my panties down. I lift my pelvis to help him. Okay, now I'm completely naked. In front of Cade. For the first time.

He lies next to me, placing his hand on my lower abdomen again.

"You all right?"

I nod again. I am starting to drown in how gentle he is being with me. He just screams too much sex to be going so slow. But it is nice.

"I promise I will listen to your body's responses, okay? Just relax."

I smile at him and his smile back is so sweet, and so sexy. He kisses me again, slow and tender. He smells like a rainstorm and just a little bit of salt. Our tongues meet and he licks the inside of my upper lip.

I run my fingers through his hair, tugging just a little as the kiss deepens. I never imagined being with Cade would be like this. He's in no hurry.

His hand inches down to my swollen pussy. My clitoris is fully engorged and as soon as his fingers trace over it, sharp jolts of ecstasy pulsate through my core and out to my extremities. His lips never leave mine as his fingers continue to stroke through my folds, going down to my entrance and trailing the wetness back up and around my stiff clit, alternating between maddeningly tight circles and long broad sweeps.

I lace my fingers through his hair, clinging to him, moaning into his mouth with every breath. I feel my thighs ease and my legs spread for him, urging him further. I can sense his grin widen against my lips and then he begins to kiss down to my breasts, stops to suck on each nipple, then continues down to my belly button.

I close my eyes and focus on the pressure of his lips and the heat of his breath against my skin. Then he is lower. I know he is right at my pussy, looking at it completely spread out before him.

I feel his hot breath first, then his lips right where I want him as his fingers nudge at my entrance. He flicks his tongue briefly against the sensitive bud and my body responds with a buck. He licks it again with a more deliberate stroke as he slides one finger inside me. I cry out in surprise, in pleasure.

His mouth is massaging me, soaking me as he pulls his finger out and, more forcefully, drives it back into the hilt, over and over. I've never had a guy spend so much time giving me pleasure. I am writhing under him, my body wracking with waves of intensity with each stroke of his tongue and touch. My stomach is tightening and my lips are tingling with numbness. Then he slips a second finger inside of me and I feel my body compress around him.

"Come for me, baby."

His words send me right to the edge. Then he closes his lips around my clit and sucks gently and I am over, convulsing around him, crying out his name.

I am still trying to catch my breath and find my bearings when Cade comes up to lie on top of me. My tummy is still pleasantly spasming and my lips are so numb they feel like they are twitching when I try to smile back at him. His face is right up to mine. He looks so happy—triumphant, but happy.

"Wow." I am still too dizzy to say more.

"For me, too." He presses his lips softly to mine just for a second, closing his eyes as he does. When he opens them, they are gleaming. His bare chest and stomach are hot against my skin. He shifts to an elbow so all of his weight isn't on me, eyes locked on mine. He brushes hair from my face, and I run my fingers up and down his smooth back. I have never felt so content before—so safe. I want him so badly, like this always. I don't even think about what I breathe into his ear next.

"Cade, I want you inside me."

His eyes roll back in his head and he bites his bottom lip. Hard. "Oh God, I want that too, babe." He lets out a restrained breath. "More than anything. But not tonight."

He looks at me with pained eyes, pleading for me not to ask again. I can tell it is taking all of his willpower to stop himself.

"I need to make sure I get it right with you." He moves to sit up. "I'm just going to go to the bathroom. Stay here." As he bends and stands, he is clearly in physical discomfort. I can see his enormous erection straining against his inadequate boxer briefs.

"Hey, stop. At least let me return the favor." I eye his crotch giving him my best seductive smile.

He looks down at his raging hard-on. "I'm fine. Really, Hale."

"Cade! Get your ass over here." I haven't had a ton of sex or any mind-blowing orgasms like the one he just gave me, but I sure know how to go down on a guy—and I am damn good at it. I made sure of it. I gave my first boyfriend head to get out of having sex so often. I actually enjoyed it.

Cade can tell I am serious and doesn't need much convincing. He jumps back on the bed, his smile big and wicked.

I push him down on his back. He puts his hands up behind his head and looks up at me, intrigued and aroused. He is laid out before me and my gaze greedily devours every inch of him. His legs are muscular like a runner's. His stomach is hard, his abs and chest clearly defined under his smooth skin. I run my nose down his stomach to the deep cuts above his hips. He smells wonderful. I kiss him just there and feel the muscles in his stomach contract. I slide my fingers under his waistband. The skin there is soft and burning hot. I pull his briefs down and he kicks them off quickly.

There he is, naked and glorious. His cock is long and thick, the skin pulled tight against its painfully engorged state. I lean over him, my lips almost touching that soft shiny tip. My breath is heavy against him. I look up and our eyes meet. His are erupting with lust and longing but he looks like he is holding his breath. I keep my eyes on his as I softly kiss the tip of his aching prick, then lick him in one solid stroke from base to tip. I watch as he throws his head back, eyes closed before I take him fully in my mouth. He mouths something that looks like, "Fuck."

Cinching my forefinger and thumb around the base, I work him in and out of my mouth, pumping him up and down with my lubricated hand. I press my tongue all around his length, sucking gently on my way up before plunging him back in all the way down, deep into my throat. I keep a steady rhythm, then quicken my pace as I hear him quietly groan into his pillow. He is surrendered completely to me.

I feel his hand in my hair, his fingers digging and massaging into my scalp. I move up and down faster, sucking harder. I keep up the pace as he starts rocking his hips, thrusting into my mouth.

"Fuck, Hale... I'm going to come... You should stop if you don't want me to..."

I feel his erection swell and pulsate. He grips my hair tightly as his abs flex and he releases in my mouth, warm and sweet. I milk his throbbing cock a couple more times and suck the last drops of cum off the sensitive tip, making him whimper. I like this side of Cade. Vulnerable and completely mine.

He lays there for a few moments, entirely spent. "Jesus, where did you learn to do that?"

"I don't know what you could be talking about," I say in my most innocent voice.

"A girl hasn't gotten me off with a blow job since I was a teenager. They usually get tired before I'm even close. I guess I just wasn't expecting... I mean...you're such a good girl, and that was...really great."

"So a good girl can't be good at head?"

He is surprised by my words. I am secretly thrilled. He is lying before me naked, a sheen of sweat over his body, the sheets rumpled all around him, and he is satiated, mesmerized—by me.

"No. I mean she can, but it's more than that. You…you liked it. I mean really liked it."

I look at him sheepishly and nod. I am thankful it is too dark for him to see me blush.

"Fuck. You are dangerous for me," he says, panting.

I have never been called that before.

"You ready to go to bed?" he asks.

"Yeah." I slide off the bed, find my panties on the floor and put them on quietly before stepping toward the door.

"Where are you going?"

I look back at him, a little confused. "Um, to bed?"

"Yeah. With me." He throws the covers back and motions me over.

"I thought you had a rule or something against letting girls stay the night with you."

"Trust me, I have no rules when it comes to you." He is dead serious, his angular jaw clenching before the playfulness creeps back into his eyes. "Now do I have to come fucking get you or what?"

I run back to the bed, jumping into his arms as he wraps us up in the covers. He cradles me to his chest and kisses my forehead.

"Night, Hale."

I snuggle up closer to him, tightening my hold. I fall asleep almost immediately.

CHAPTER 13

I WAKE TO THE SOUNDS OF CADE BREATHING SOFTLY INTO HIS pillow. His arm is draped heavily over my stomach. I need to pee like a mother.

I slide out from under him, careful not to wake him. I find my shirt crumpled in the corner. How the hell did it get all the way over here? I guess I was a little over-zealous last night. I tiptoe into the hall and close the door silently behind me. Just as I turn around for the bathroom, Tuck comes out of his bedroom, heading down the hall toward me.

Shit. I take a couple of steps toward the bathroom and when he gets to me, he doesn't seem to notice which door I had come from.

"Mornin'." He offers me his sweet Tuck smile, but he still looks like crap. I wonder if he got any sleep last night. Hope he didn't hear us.

"Hey, how are you doing?"

He rolls his eyes at me. "Don't worry about me." He clasps my shoulder as he passes. "I've been through worse. Just heading into work."

"On a Saturday? Again?"

"Yep."

"Hey, Tuck?"

"Yeah?" He stops a few feet past me and turns. His eyes look too old.

"Can we talk, uh...later?"

"Sure thing, sis. Everything all right? Is it the boy? Haven't seen him around in a while."

"No, that's not it. I mean...well kind of, but—that's over."

"Oh?" He crinkles his forehead and frowns. He is going to go into protective mode and hug me or something.

"Yeah, but it's good. He was a jerk. I'm fine with it. Really. Actually, I'm great." I'm beyond great.

He smiles and nods, but doesn't quite believe me. "Some advice? At twenty-one, they're all jerks. Trust me—I used to be one of them."

* * *

I hop in the shower. The water is scalding hot against my skin. I love it. I stand in the water for a long time, thinking about the night before. Cade's hands on me, in me, his mouth, his tongue... I have tingles just thinking about it.

Then the door bursts open and Cade comes in and promptly takes a piss.

"I'm glad to see you're still kind of a dick," I tease him.

"Yup."

I turn and jump, startled when I see his head sticking in the shower curtain.

"Hey! Get out of here!" I splash water at him, successfully getting him to retreat.

Outside of the curtain, he hollers, "You do realize I saw you very naked like six hours ago, right?"

"Yeah, but it was dark." I turn and almost slip and fall on my butt. His damn hot-as-fuck face is at the other end of the shower curtain, looking at me.

"You're right. This is so much better. And you're all... wet." His smile is maddeningly sexy. He's looking at me like he wants to eat me.

"Get out!" But I am laughing and he doesn't budge.

"Can I at least get a kiss?"

He looks at me so sweetly it makes my stomach flip. I step toward him, my wet lips meet his. Then his hands are on both sides of my face and I am moving backward as he steps over the tub to press me against the tile. Our mouths are locked together the entire time, the hot water streaming over both of us, getting in our mouths, making my breasts slide easily across his chest. I move my hands down his wet back to his soaked boxer-briefs, hook my thumbs in the waistband, and start to shimmy them down when he drops both of his hands and holds them firmly at his hips.

"These stay on. They're the only thing keeping me from fucking you senseless right now."

"And why aren't you again?" I breathe between lapping up his kisses.

"Fuck if I know." We are all slippery lips and tongues and hands. "Don't ask me when you've got me hard. I can't think straight."

He stops kissing me, our lips still touching. I am gasping for air so heavily I inhale mostly water.

"I can't wait to be inside you, but when it happens, I want you to be ready for it," he says against my mouth.

I feel pretty ready right at this moment. He gives my bare ass a squeeze, then steps out of the shower. He turns around before closing the curtain, dripping all over the floor.

"What do you want for breakfast?"

"I'm not really hungry."

"Me neither."

* * *

"You have to come shopping with me."

Court's invitation is a welcome distraction from thinking about Cade. I can't keep my mind from wandering to him even while deep into the bargain racks at the mall.

"You seem happy today," Court comments from between two scandalously short dresses. I just smile and nod. Court holds up the two dresses, shaking them toward me. "Black sequins or blue jersey?"

"Black."

"Okay." She throws it on top of the stack of dresses she has compiled over the last hour. "It needs to be perfect."

"Why is that again?"

"It's a blind date, so if he ends up being amazing, I need to look hot. And if he ends up being boring, then at least I got a fabulous dress out of the deal."

"Good thinking."

"Right?" She bobs along the store, her long blonde hair tied in a knot on top of her head. Even dressed casually, she looks elegant with a pop of red on her lips. She turns her light eyes toward me as we make our way to the dressing room. "Tell me why you are grinning so goofily today!" Her smile is big and white and impossible to refuse. She hauls her armful of dresses in the dressing room as I sit on a pink bench outside the door. "Is it Adam?" she calls over the partition.

"Um. No." I'm not sure how to explain that one. "That's definitely done."

"Oh good!" She comes out wearing a little metallic dress, hands on her hips. "You were already so smitten with him by the time we met I was hoping you would figure out he was an asshole before I had to tell you and then you hated me for it."

How did she know?

"You're right. I probably wouldn't have believed you."

"Yup. 'Cause us girls are bitches."

"Totally."

"So?" She twirls around in the shiny number. "Yea or nay?"

"Nah."

With a firm nod of the head, she is back behind the door. "So if it's not Adam, who's the boy?"

"Who says it's a boy?"

She comes out in a tight yellow dress that clings to her legs. "I say it's a boy because you keep getting all far-off and day-dreamy."

"Okay, it's a boy."

She jumps up and down, practically squealing. "Spill it! But first—what do you think?" She spins around again.

"That one's okay."

Her face falls a little. "But my butt looks good in it, right?"

"As always."

She perks up and goes back in the room. "So who is it?"

I hesitate to tell her. Why? "Uh...my brother's roommate, Cade Renner."

Silence.

That isn't like Court.

I roll my eyes. This is why I didn't want to tell her. "Go ahead and say it."

She steps out of the dressing room hesitantly, wearing a cream lace dress. "I won't say anything. I just need to know that you know what you're getting into. If Adam's frat has some rumors around campus, Cade has a reputation the whole town knows about."

"I'm well aware of his reputation—and the truths behind it. I live across the hall from him."

She looks suddenly very worried. "Have you slept with him?"

"Not exactly."

"That's good. Those kinds of guys tend to get bored and move on if you give it up too soon."

I know that is Cade's MO, but he isn't going to do that with me. Right? He isn't going to move on after we have sex.

Like Adam did. Shit. Panic starts to strangle my chest.

"I know it sounds stupid, but I really think this is different." I try to put as much conviction in my voice as possible. Her face clearly says she doesn't believe me, but she doesn't say anything.

I'm about to defend Cade when—wait, what?

"Hold on. What rumors about Adam's frat?"

"Oh. Shit. I shouldn't have said anything about it. Really, it might not even be true—"

"Court. Tell. Me." My serious face—getting shit done for twenty-one years.

One thing I've learned about Court is she never says anything bad about anyone. Like Ever. She looks tortured to tell me this.

"Well, the rumor is that several guys in the frat bet on the girls they can bed. There's apparently a whole point system and they get more money if the girl is a virgin or not in a sorority or hard to get, things like that. And I've heard the money put up is big."

I'm in shock. "What?"

"I don't know for sure if Adam is involved, but he's the biggest trust fund baby of them all, so I'd be surprised otherwise."

"Trust fund?"

"Didn't you know? Adam's dad is a big-time CFO for some investment firm in the city."

His dad? He'd told me he'd been raised by his single mom. Was anything he told me real? Was it all just a game? How can I trust anything a guy ever tells me again?

"I did not. He was a good liar."

"Fuck 'em."

"Ha! Now, that was something he was not good at."

Court giggles from behind the door then steps out in an intricate cream lace dress.

"That's the one," I say.

She scrunches up her nose as she nods, her smile showing off the cute little freckles on her high cheekbones. "I think so too."

* * *

By the time Court drops me off at home, it is almost dinnertime and after our talk I have convinced myself that I should hold off with Cade. Make sure it is something real before I let him into my pants.

I walk into the living room and Cade is standing there.

All gorgeous in dark jeans and a black button-up shirt that fits snugly across his broad shoulders, the sleeves rolled up to his elbows, showing off his intricate tats. I am taken aback by the sight of him. He is waiting for me. Me. My body responds immediately—my heart racing in my throat, my hands sweaty, and my skin heated. My plan of no sex might be very short-lived.

"Hey." He smiles as he steps over to me, his eyes flickering down to my lips as he brings his hand to my cheek. "I missed you today."

My knees are like jelly at his words and I lift my face to meet his. His lips are warm and soft, gently moving against mine. I slide my arms around his neck, holding him to me to deepen the kiss but he pulls away too soon. He runs his thumb over my bottom lip, making my breath catch.

"I thought maybe I could take you out tonight."

Like a date? "Yeah." I am still breathless. Going out will be good. I'm less likely to jump him in public. Right?

He smiles wide, his perfect smile that makes him look so happy, younger. "Do I need to give you time to get ready?" He is closing the space between us again and it's giving me chills. The memory of lying naked with him last night is suddenly all-consuming. I nod, looking him right in his bright blue eyes, trying not to let him know how much his closeness affects me.

"I could help you out of these clothes if you like." The glint in his eye is devious. He tightens his hands around my waist.

I slap his forearm and wiggle away from him. "I thought you were going to be all gentlemanly tonight."

He backs away, hands up in surrender. "I'll be anything you want, Haley." But his eyes are still eating me alive.

TO BE YOUR GIRL

I run to my room before I make any bad decisions.

I am staring at my closet in my matching peach panties and bra, cursing the fact that I hadn't bought a new dress while I was out shopping today. I finally settle on my tight jeans, boots, and a burgundy sweater that clings just right to my curves.

When I go out to the living room, I expect to see Cade sitting there with a huge grin on his face. Instead, I see Tuck. He claps his hands then rubs them together, obviously excited.

"Where are we going tonight, sis?"

Uhh... I don't know how to respond. The only words that pop in my head are *but...Cade...date...*

Then Cade comes out from the kitchen behind Tuck, the look on his face clearly expresses all the emotions going on inside me. His jaw is tight and angular as he speaks.

"Looks like we're all going out tonight." Then he forces a large smile.

Dammit.

"This is going to be epic." Tuck grabs me around the waist, smooshing my face into his chest as he pulls Cade in around his neck. "My favorite girl and my wingman."

My face is close to Cade's and I see his eyes widen at the wingman comment. He mouths the words *I'm sorry*.

All I can do is laugh. First date officially thwarted.

* * *

The bar is full of laughter, rowdy guys around pool tables, and Irish rock music. Tuck slams three more huge beers down on our shiny table, spilling foam over the rims of the mugs. He is already drunk. Cade squeezes my knee under the table before releasing it as Tuck sits.

"Cade, let's do some shots!"

"Ah, no man. I think you've had enough."

"You are no fun right now, bro."

A couple of girls walk up to our table. The one with her boobs practically pouring from her shirt puts her hand on Cade's shoulder and then smoothes it all the way down his arm. She leans into him, pressing her chest right up against him. I want to claw her hair out. But I don't. I sit there like a lady. And guzzle my drink.

"Hey, baby, you wanna dance?" Boobs asks. Her lips are too close to Cade's ear. Her voice is thick like she's purring.

Don't fucking call him baby.

Cade totally just looked at her tits. She bats her eyes at him, sort of pouting her lips. His eyes flash toward me, he looks a little...panicked? Embarrassed? He is definitely turning red. I can't help but let go of my anger and smile at him.

"No, thanks. I'm just hanging with my friends tonight."

The girl visibly scoffs at him but he doesn't see it. He turns away from her too fast to give me a wink across the table. The girl stomps off along with her friend—who apparently had been giving Tuck some attention.

"What the fuck, man? What kind of wingman move was that?"

"Sorry, I just wasn't into that girl."

"No shit. You know that's not how being a wingman works. You take one for the team. Come on! How many times have I done that for you?"

Cade goes a little red again. Does he think I don't know he's a man-slut?

Tuck gets up from the table and rubs the back of his

neck. "I'm getting some shots." He heads for the bar.

Cade puts his warm hand over mine and leans in close. "I'm sorry about that."

"About what? The girl hitting on you or for checking her out?"

His blue eyes go wide, his mouth slack.

I burst out laughing. "I'm just kidding, Cade. It's fine."

The distress in his face softens but doesn't go away completely. "You sure you're not mad? Jealous?"

"I'm not mad. And I never said I wasn't jealous."

He laces his fingers through mine. His smile is heart-stopping. It's like I am the only other person in the room. The touch of his hand is innocent, but still intimate, promising so much more. But after an instant, we part again. Tuck sloshes over to the table with three shots. Cade and I just kind of sit there.

"Don't make me drink all these. You two need to catch up. I've already had two at the bar."

I have never seen Tuck this wasted. I'm surprised he is still forming coherent sentences. Shit, I'm surprised he is still standing.

"I'm going to the restroom. I'll be right back," I say.

I head for the back where there is a huge line of women waiting. Sweet. The buzz in my back pocket tickles. I take out my phone. It's a text from Court.

Call me in five minutes.

A few minutes later I dial her number.

"Hello?" she answers.

"How's the date going?"

"Oh my god! That's awful!" She says it with such conviction I almost believe I have just given her the most dreadful news.

"That good, huh?"

"Where are you?" She sounds so worried. I have to keep from laughing too loud. She is a good actress.

"We're at Flanagan's downtown."

"I'll be right there!" She promptly hangs up.

* * *

When I get back to our table, the shot glasses are empty but we have apparently gained a few more skanks. One girl is rubbing her hand through Tuck's thick hair while the other two hang all over Cade. The bleach blonde looks like she is whispering in his ear and the other one is clearly trying to sit on his lap. I roll my eyes as I pull out my stool. This is going to get old real fucking fast.

Cade straightens when he sees me, flinging the lap-dancer to the floor on her butt. That makes me smile. She gets to her feet, cursing. The other girl doesn't seem to notice. Cade is looking at me, clearly exasperated. He stands. "I gotta take a leak."

Ear girl wraps her fingers around his collar and smiles up at him. "Want company?"

Seriously? In a bar bathroom? Is this real life? I'm starting to get mad again.

He pries her fingers from his shirt. "I think I can manage on my own."

She crosses her arms and sticks out her chin. Dear God. Cade leaves quickly.

The girl from the floor is by her side and they turn toward Tuck. "Let's go, Tiffany."

They scoff away and Tuck slams his fist down on the table when Cade strides back over. "Dammit! What's with you tonight, man?"

Cade doesn't know what to say—obviously him turning girls away all night is a novelty. So I speak up.

"You know what, it's probably me. How are you supposed to pick up chicks with me hanging around? I'll just leave and let you boys have fun." Cade's jaw tics under his skin. "My friend, Court, is coming in a minute. She can take me home."

Cade looks like he is about to protest but Tuck chimes in.

"Your friend Court, eh? Would I like her?"

Yes, probably. "No."

Cade doesn't look happy. "Haley, you don't have to do that."

But before he can say any more, Court runs over to our table.

"Hey!" She looks gorgeous, her cheeks flushed from the cold outside as she takes off her coat and scarf. "Thanks for saving me, Haley." She gives me a big hug.

"No problem. Court, this is Cade."

They shake hands over the table and she flashes him a stunning smile.

"Hi, Cade. We've sort of met before."

"Uh yeah..." He returns her smile but I can tell he doesn't recognize her at all.

"And this is my brother, Tuck." I motion over to the incredibly drunk one across from me.

"Hey, gorgeous." Tuck grabs her hand while completely eye-fondling her entire body. I want to face plant on the table.

"Nice to meet you, Tuck." If she is offended by his inebriation or blatant ogling, she doesn't show it. She smiles

just as wide for him as Cade—maybe wider.
"You want to get out of here?" I ask her.
She breaks her gaze with Tuck to look at me. "Are you kidding? I just got here. I'm ready to drink!"
"Oh, hell yes!" Tuck jumps up enthusiastically. "What'll you have?"
"Anything with tequila," Court replies.
Tuck clasps both hands over his chest. "I just fell in love."

* * *

Cade continues to decline girls' attention throughout the night, but Tuck doesn't seem to mind—he and Court are preoccupied taking tequila shots. Cade leans over to me, his lips brushing my ear and his warm breath sending shivers down my neck.
"Dance with me."
I know that is a bad idea. "Okay."
We try to stay at a friendly distance on the dance floor, but it is crowded and guys with hard, pointy elbows keep bumping into me. Cade has no choice, really, but to pull me into his arms. His body is strong and solid against mine, but also yielding to my every curve and movement. He moves right along with me, our rhythm the same. His hands softly slide down my back to grip my hips. He feels so good wrapped around me. My arms are locked around his neck, our faces very close.
"God, I've wanted to touch you all night." He looks at me, breathing gone ragged and licks his lips. Those beautiful full lips. I want those lips on me so badly.
"Yeah?" Now I am out of breath.

His hands dig into my hips. He bites his lower lip. "I always want you." His beautiful eyes devour me and I feel heat drip all the way down. He rips his gaze away and buries his face into the crook of my neck. I can feel him actually growling against my skin.

"We can just tell my brother, you know."

"Yeah, I know. But we should probably do it when he's sober."

He's right about that.

"Hey, guys?" Court pushes her way to us, interrupting the moment. When I look over at her, she is directing an approving smile toward Cade but then she makes a face with the cutest little crinkle above her nose. "I think Tuck needs to go home."

She is correct. When we get to the table Tuck is passed out, face-down, beer still in his hand. Classy.

* * *

Cade and I are sitting toe-to-toe in the bathroom, Tuck is passed out by the toilet after having emptied his stomach only four times. Cade nudges my foot over with his and I push back. The innocent if a flirtatious game of footsie quickly morphs into very suggestive toe rubbing.

"Ready to put him to bed?"

"Yeah." I try to hide my yawn when I say it, but he catches me.

He just smiles his sexy half-sleepy smile at me as we get up and walk Tuck to his room, each of us under an arm. Let's be real, Cade is doing most of the lifting. Tuck falls face-first onto his bed without even a sound. Still out. I take off his shoes and Cade manages to get the comforter over him.

We leave Tuck to sleep it off. As soon as we close his bedroom door, I feel nervous. Nervous that I won't be able to turn Cade down, we'll have sex, and my worst fears will be confirmed. That I really am horrible in the sack and, like Adam, he will dump me.

This is irrational. Doesn't stop me from feeling it.

Cade puts his arm around my shoulders and pulls me to his chest. "Sorry we didn't get to have an evening together."

"Me too."

"You okay?"

"Yeah."

He gives me a knowing look.

"I'm just tired." *Gather your courage, Haley.* "Can we just go to sleep tonight?"

I don't know what reaction I expect. Disappointment? Frustration? But it isn't what I get. He looks into my eyes warmly and smiles.

"Babe, just sleeping with you will be the highlight of my whole fucking day."

We brush our teeth side-by-side at the sink in just our underwear. It feels so ordinary but affirming, like we are a real...couple.

I try to spit out the toothpaste as discretely as possible—turns out that's incredibly hard to do. I look over at him in the mirror. Even brushing his teeth he looks sexy.

"You don't have to work for it, do you?"

He spits.

"What do you mean?"

I rinse my brush. "The girls."

He washes out his mouth.

"Oh." He looks down, a little shy even. "I guess not. Not

for those types of girls, anyway."

He puts his toothbrush away.

We climb into his bed. I snuggle up to him, laying my head on his bare chest, just under the swell of his shoulder.

"How many girls?" I regret asking as soon as the words are out.

"Definitely not answering that."

"Are you...uh...safe with all of them?"

"Every single one, I swear." His arm is wrapped around me, resting at the small of my back. His other hand is over mine, holding it firmly to his chest. I can feel his heart beating under my palm. "Are you worried about that?"

I want to act like I'm not, but—

"No, don't answer that. You have every right to worry about that. I'm not offended. If it makes you feel more at ease, I get tested every couple of months when I donate blood. I'm clean."

"You donate blood?" I had no idea.

"Yeah, it's important to me. I mean, I'm O-Negative—that's the universal donor so...I just feel like if I can donate I should. That's actually the reason I haven't gotten any tattoos in a while." The conviction in his voice makes me feel there is more to it than that, but I don't want to pry.

He kisses the top of my head.

"Night, baby."

I sink into him and he holds me through the night.

CHAPTER 14

All day Sunday, Tuck is here.

At breakfast: he keeps complaining of his splitting headache. I give him a couple painkillers with water and suggest he go back to bed. He insists he will be fine once he eats. Then he proceeds to cover his eggs in hot sauce and eats every bite. Cade and I can only exchange secret glimpses and smiles across the table.

Rest of the morning: Tuck announces we should all hang out before he leaves for his business trip Monday morning. So we do the dishes. Together. Then Tuck and Cade start playing this macho video game. They try to get me to join but I kindly decline and excuse myself to go shower and do some homework. Lame.

At lunch: we go to our favorite pizza place that sells these enormous pieces by the slice. Tuck pulls up a chair and wedges himself between me and Cade. Literally. Like, I have to screech my chair over.

All freaking afternoon: it seems like I can't get away from Tuck and his big goofy, clueless grin. At the grocery store, Cade just gently touches the ends of his fingers along the back of my arm but then Tuck keeps turning around

TO BE YOUR GIRL

to ask asinine questions like *should we get the can with meatballs or franks*. Always meatballs, Tuck, always. Every time I feel the warmth of Cade's hand on my back or the brush of my arm against his, it is short-lived because Tuck. Is. Still. There.

At dinner: Even though Cade and I usually cook dinner alone together, today, Tuck wants to help. Cade has him chop the vegetables. That is usually my task. I stare at Tuck chopping all haphazardly and completely uneven. I don't even realize I am grimacing at him until I catch Cade in the corner, snickering at me behind his fist. I try to relax. Tuck is leaving soon for a whole week—he's my brother, I love him, I can handle this night. But then while he eats his food, he chews really effing loud.

After fucking dinner: Tuck finally goes into his room. Cade grabs me by the waist and pulls me tightly to him, his strong arms around my shoulders, and his lips at my cheek.

"Have I told you how crazy you've been making me all day?"

His words make me smile.

"No, but I'm listening." I draw a line with my finger across his chest, down his taut abs to just above his belt buckle. I hear the hitch in his breath as he leans in to kiss my lips.

"Hey, guys! Want to watch a movie?" Tuck calls from the hall. We step away from each other before he rounds the corner. Just before.

"Every fucking time!" Cade curses under his breath, his fists balled at his sides.

After the movie—another action flick—I am hopeful the day of Tuck is over.

"Which one next?" Tuck holds up two more movies, his

face entirely lit.

"Don't you have to get up early tomorrow?" I'm grasping here. It's only 9:30.

"Psh. I'm wide awake."

I don't want to watch either action flick B or C, so I get up.

"Well, I'm exhausted. I'm going to bed."

"Okay, sis, see you tomorrow." Tuck turns his over-eager attention to Cade. "You pick, man."

Cade watches as I walk away behind Tuck, obviously conflicted. He chooses movie C. As I enter my room, my phone buzzes.

Cade: *Will you come to my bed later, after Tuck's asleep?*

Oh, God yes.

Me: *Definitely*

When I slide into bed, I really do feel exhausted.

* * *

I am awoken by a draft of cold air on my spine. Then comes the hard chest at my back and the warm arms wrapping around my waist. His lips brush lightly at my neck.

"I couldn't wait for you any longer."

"I fell asleep."

"Then go back to sleep." He kisses me just behind the ear and I press back against him as he squeezes me tighter. I drift into a dreamless sleep.

The clock reads 7:02. Blue is just starting to creep into the dark morning sky. When I roll over, Cade is there. Serene and beautiful. I can just make out the slow pulse in his neck. I nuzzle up next to him, rubbing my hands into his back and breathing him in. Then I kiss him just there on the neck. His skin is warm and smooth and smells just like a summer afternoon storm. It smells like Cade. A low grumble rolls through his chest.

"I didn't mean to wake—"

The brush of his thumb over my nipple through my thin cotton shirt sends a shudder through my body and out my throat.

"We have to be quiet, baby. Tuck's awake." His whisper is warm against my cheek. "I want you naked."

Done. He helps pull my top over my head and I wiggle my panties down as he kicks off his boxers to lie somewhere under the covers.

Then he is over me, body hot and pressing against my skin. His fingers grip around the back of my neck and into my hair as he lowers his lips to mine. His kiss is soft but needy. *You're not having sex with Cade yet, remember?* My resolve may be weakening. I rake my fingers down his naked back and then curl them around the firm curve of his butt. He has such a nice little booty. He hums his appreciation as he sinks his tongue into my mouth.

I want him so badly.

I am completely lost in him—his scorching tongue, the press of his palm against my breast, his skin grinding against mine. The heat is sinking into my belly and the familiar ache is building between my thighs. All I can do is rub them together to get some relief, squirming under him, feeling so...empty.

But then I can't even do that.

"Spread your legs for me."

He slides his hand down my stomach, but he doesn't touch me—he grips himself. Then the unmistakable press of the end of his cock at my entrance is all I can focus on—

even though our mouths are still frantically pulling at one another. Is he going to put it in me? My body is eager for it, opening to him. But I am a little nervous at the thought of him inside me. Cade. My Cade.

But he doesn't push in. The broad head of his prick is sliding up and down, spreading my wetness, teasing every sensitive fold as it passes.

"You're so wet and swollen. I'm going to come just thinking about it."

"Cade…please…" is all I can pant out before that blunt head strokes up to my throbbing little bead and the wave that crashes through me is so overwhelming, it is almost excruciating. I let out a breathy moan.

"Shh, babe." Leaning on his elbow, he puts his other hand over my mouth. "Bite down if you have to."

His broad tip is moving silkily through my pussy and up again to rub against my painfully erect clitoris and my eyes roll back.

"Keep your eyes open, baby. Look at me."

I'm doing my best to focus back on him, his parted lips, the panting of his breath, his eyes locked onto mine.

"I want to see you when you come."

My legs are starting to shake against his hips. The rubbing of his cock against all my wetness is too much.

Every time it moves down to my entrance, I can feel my inner muscles contract, willing him to go deeper, to relieve the constant swell inside. To fill me. But he doesn't. He just drags it back up to nudge my thrumming clit, sending new ripples of pleasure through my body. I can't get enough air through my nose and I keep trying to gasp through my mouth which is still covered by his palm. He is looking at me the whole time with those beautiful blue eyes, the faintest smile on his lips, looking entirely too sweet to be doing the filthy thing he is doing to me. When his erection slides back down, I can feel my pussy clench, pulling him in, just the tip.

It catches us both by surprise.

"Do you have a condom in here?" His voice is raspy.

I don't.

I can only shake my head in response. I want to tell him I am on the pill and to just shove inside me already but I keep silent.

"Fuck, you're going to get me just like this."

He pulls out the tip of his cock and rubs it in furious little circles over my excruciatingly sensitive button and I am gone. I bite down hard on the heel of his hand as I shatter under him, my knees falling to the bed. I see him grab his discarded boxers and empty himself into them with a couple of shudders.

My cheeks are flushed and hot, aftershocks still vibrating through my stomach as he comes down and replaces his bitten hand with his soft lips, kissing me until I come back to earth.

"You coming may be the most beautiful thing I've ever seen." He strokes a piece of hair from my face. My forehead is damp with sweat and I'm pretty sure I look more a mess than beautiful, but I feel wonderful.

"Don't stop next time."

"You're sure?" He is so earnest in the question.

"Yes." I pull his head down to my chest and hold him to the soft swells of my breasts, massaging my fingers through his hair.

He lays still on me and his breathing slows. I close my eyes and just feel his smooth, heated skin against me and his heart beating soft under it. He is amazing. I have the sudden urge to tell him I love him—but it is definitely too soon for that. Verging on crazy.

That's bat-shit, Haley.

The knock at my door is loud. I sit bolt upright.

"Hale, you still driving me to the airport?" Dammit, Tuck.

"Yeah…" Shit. "Uhh…" Fuck. "Let me get dressed. I'll be right out," I finally spit out.

I jump out of bed to the closet, tossing clothes out of my hamper in a frenzy to find my favorite jeans. Cade is chuckling quietly at me from the bed. There he is—gloriously naked, all lean muscle on display not even trying to stay covered, relaxed—and here I am, shaking as I pull on my socks.

"I'm going to go put my bags in the truck," Tuck calls through the door as he leaves.

I feel better when I'm dressed. Cade has gotten up. He comes up to me as I reach the door, sexy smirk on his lips and whispers in my ear.

"I can't wait to have you all to myself this week."

Oh boy. I don't know if it is the thought of being alone with Cade, the heat of his breath on my neck, or the lust in his voice that sends goosebumps prickling all down my side.

Then he kisses me. My hands are tangled in all his sexy bedhead and his hands are on my butt, holding me against him. My lungs feel empty when I pull away.

* * *

The whole ride I think about Cade. My stomach is flittering and flipping and I can't keep the grin off my face.

Tuck glances over at me, the corner of his mouth turned up. "You seem really…I don't know." His brows knit together as he takes the off-ramp toward the airport. "Happy." His smile at me is big and real and all Tuck.

My big brother, the one person I know will always be there for me. He only wants me to be happy. He will understand about Cade. I want to tell him so badly. The words are in my throat, but they don't come out.

"I guess you're handling your break-up better than I'm handling mine." He taps his thumb against the wheel.

"I was just able to figure out I was better off without him rather quickly. That happens when you break up while he's on a date with someone else."

He turns his head to me in slow motion, eyes bulging out of their sockets. "What?"

"Don't worry. Cade already punched him in the face for it."

He seems to appreciate that.

"Wait. Cade?"

Shut up, Haley.

"Yeah. It happened at his restaurant." I try to play it off as lightly as possible. He seems confused, but thankfully he drops it.

We park at departures and I run around to the driver's side of the truck as Tuck retrieves his suitcase. "Thanks for the ride. See you Saturday."

Tuck gives me a quick hug and waves to me before he turns and goes through the sliding glass doors. He is really leaving. My hands feel clammy sliding against the steering wheel on the drive home.

As I drive up our little street, I can see the house getting closer, closer to where Cade is. The twisting in my stomach is now a thick knot. I am freaking nervous but also so excited. I feel like I'm going to pee my pants as I run up the steps to the front door.

But when I get inside Cade isn't there. Not in the kitchen, living room, his room, or the bathroom. Well, sonofabitch. I fish through my purse for my phone.

Cade: *Sorry babe, got called in early to work. Be ready for me tonight.*

CHAPTER 15

Class is boring. When Cade finally comes home, I am more than ready for him. As soon as he walks through the door, I can hear my heart pounding into my ribs and his face lights up when he sees me. He is all pretty blue eyes and straight white teeth as he sweeps me up into a hug and kisses me.

"I'm going to go change. You hungry?"

"Yes."

He comes out in a tight red tee and straight jeans that hug his butt. He extends his hand to me. "You ready?"

I take his hand and we walk to his car.

We go to a new restaurant that just opened. Bad idea.

My soup is cold and Cade's salad is drenched in dressing.

The server kind of fumbles all over herself but she is very sweet and apologetic about it.

When my medium-well steak arrives, I swear it is still bleeding. Cade notices me poking at it and insists we send it back to get one that has been cooked properly, though we are wondering if that's even a possibility here. Meanwhile, Cade laments that his tenderloin has absolutely no seasoning and there's not even a sauce to save it. By the time my second, very well done, steak arrives, we are over it. Cade gets the check and we leave, barely having touched the food.

The breeze is unusually warm as we walk down the sidewalk. The sky is a light misty gray and it still smells like leaves, even though they have long fallen from the trees. Cade takes my hand in his and rubs the back of it with his warm thumb.

He takes me to a gallery I wouldn't have even known existed by looking at it from the outside.

"The university just got this exhibit on loan from the History Museum in the city. It opened last week," Cade tells me.

I look around the expansive square white room covered with the most beautiful old black and white photographs. In the middle of the room are several large pieces of metal machinery enclosed by clear glass cases. How had I not heard about this?

"I thought you might like it. You said one day you'd like to work at a museum, right?"

I look at him in awe. How did he know that? I don't remember ever telling him that.

I walk around the room, looking at every photograph carefully. They are stunning. The whole exhibit is about the Industrial Revolution with pictures of laborers building the first skyscrapers, and workers in factories. I can see the dirt under their fingernails and practically hear the inner cogs grinding in the machines. It's so fascinating to me.

"You like the photographs?" Cade asks from behind. He's been so quiet, following me around the room that I almost forgot he is still with me.

"Oh yes. Photography is my favorite. My father was a

photographer."

"Oh yeah? I think Tuck mentioned something like that before."

"When I was little, I used to love him taking pictures of me. I loved it even more when he would let me take the pictures. He would always tell me about things like aperture and focal length, even though they went way over my head." Cade is focused intently on me as I speak.

A flash of my Dad's smile, complete with a five o'clock shadow and a dimple in his left cheek, fills my vision. Tuck has his dimples.

I am brought back to the present as someone walks past us. "A photograph is a snapshot into someone's world. Unmoving forever in time. I think that's where my interest in anthropology comes from. You can learn so much about a person's life from a single item. A photo. Photographs of my dad are the most treasured things I own. All I have of him now are artifacts."

Cade holds my hand, our fingers clasped together tightly as we walk through the rest of the exhibit.

* * *

As we walk back toward the car I smell the most divine savory saltiness. Right then my stomach growls. Cade chuckles.

"Hungry?"

"Starving."

"Me too."

We stop by the hot dog stand. The guy is closing up for the night, but we manage to snag a couple of dogs. We load them up high with toppings: caramelized onions, sauerkraut (which I don't even like), mustard, and melty cheese. It's the best damn hotdog I've ever had. Cade and I huddle under a nearby awning and devour them hastily.

When we are done, Cade wipes some mustard off my chin with his thumb and then sucks his thumb clean.

"Let's do something fun," he says.

"Aren't we having fun already?"

"Play a game with me." He looks mischievous.

"Okay…"

"Truth or Dare."

"No way!"

"C'mon. I'll even go first. Dare."

I narrow my eyes at him. "Fine." I cross my arms, trying to think of something good. "You have to yell penis as loud as you can. Right here."

He stops abruptly and cocks an eyebrow at me.

"Girl"—an evil smile spreads across his face—"this is going to embarrass you way more than it will me."

And then he does it. Arms out in the air, his face to the sky he screams, "PEEENISSS!" just as an older lady with a small dog walks by.

He was right. I am horrified. I'm sure my face is deep purple, and he just looks down at me and smirks. He even has the gall to be all sexy about it. "Your turn."

Shit.

"Truth."

He doesn't even take a minute to think of it. "Did I get you off when I gave you that foot rub?"

I am shocked. I'm pretty sure my face goes completely white, my eyes wide.

He just chuckles at me. "I thought so."

If I was uncomfortable before, I am mortified now. He

pulls me to him and hugs me tight. He kisses the top of my head and whispers in my ear.

"Do you know how much knowing that turns me on?"

A smile tugs on my lips at the thought and I relax into the hug a little.

"It's your turn."

"Okay," he says, "truth."

I look up at him. The heavy clouds in the evening sky reflected in his eyes are kind of mesmerizing. The air around us is thick, warmer than normal. It feels like little bubbles of mist are softly breaking against my face.

"Have you ever been in love?" I ask.

He looks off thoughtfully for a second.

"No." Then his blue eyes are back on mine, his arms tighten around my waist. "I thought I was once, but now I don't know. So probably not, right?"

"Probably."

"Have you ever been in love?"

"Hey, you can't ask me that. I haven't said Truth or Dare yet."

"You're right. Your turn."

"Dare."

That mischievous grin is back. Uh oh. He points across the way to a playground. "I dare you to go take off your underwear and leave them in the playground."

"What?" These are one of my favorite pair. "Not happening." I also think that may actually be a crime that would land me on the national sex offender registry.

He has a devious look in his eyes. He throws me over his shoulder and runs to the playground. All I can see is the ground moving fast below me. I'm flailing my legs and beating his back with my fists, begging him to put me down.

My escape attempts are weak at best, and he knows it. The mist has turned into a light sprinkle by the time the grass turns into heaps of bark.

When he sets me down, he is not even out of breath and that devilish look in his eyes has only intensified. I turn and run and he chases me around the swings. I'm screaming and giggling the whole way. I elude him through the bright red and blue jungle gym, but he catches up to me as I'm climbing the ladder. I manage to slip from his grasp and slide down the huge slide. As soon as I reach the bottom, he is already upon me, tackling me to the ground.

My heart is racing. The rain is starting to come down heavier, but I hardly notice. His smile is amazing as he takes my face with both of his hands and kisses me. Right in front of the yellow spiral slide.

His mouth is warm and his teeth just barely nip at my bottom lip. I slide my hands under the warmth of his jacket and he envelopes me in his arms. With his body heat against me, I don't even mind when the raindrops turn fat and heavy.

A deep rumble of thunder sounds in the distance. Cade and I pull apart just as the dark clouds above decide to dump a constant stream of water on us. Cade is laughing as he takes my hand and we start running toward his car.

By the time we get to the car, we are drenched. My hair is plastered to the side of my face. He opens the door for me, and I sink to the leather seat then shrug out of my dripping jacket. Cade slides into the driver's seat and blasts the heat.

I am shivering. He takes both of my hands into his, rubbing them warm. The raindrops hitting the roof sound off like hundreds of drums. The outside world is obscured by the solid wall of rippling water sheeting against the windows.

Cade leans in to kiss me on the lips and a drop of water falls from his hair onto my nose. "Home?"

"Home."

* * *

As soon as the door closes behind us, Cade has me up against the wall. Our mouths are devouring one another.

He grips my butt and thighs and my fingers are in his still wet hair. I'll never be able to forget the scent of the rain on him. He pulls me with him toward the hallway as he kicks off his shoes. I slip out of my shoes, almost tripping but he has a hold of me. His teeth tug at my bottom lip as he starts to undo my jeans. I fumble for the button of his and we stumble out of our wet jeans with some difficulty. He falls against the wall, breaking our kiss and we laugh at the way our pants awkwardly cling to our ankles. We finally get them off and then he removes his shirt and I pull off mine before his mouth is back on me and he is pushing me back toward his bedroom.

When we get to the door, he lifts me up. My legs instantly wrap around his waist and he kisses my neck. Our frenzy has me too excited to think. I fall to the bed, bouncing and he crawls over me, his hot hands on my still damp skin.

"Babe, you're freezing."

"Not really."

He rubs up and down my arms and covers us in the blankets. He is lying on top of me, our noses almost touching. My heart is pounding but I try to steady my breathing. His skin is perfectly smooth, his eyes so beautiful and clear, his lips full and slightly parted. I reach out to touch his cheek and draw my thumb across his bottom lip. I notice him swallow hard.

"I can't believe you're really with me like this. That I get to have you," he whispers to me.

There goes my heart punching in my chest again.

I take his head in both of my hands. "Then you obviously don't see what I see." And we kiss.

Sliding my fingers down the taut skin of his back, I find the dimples just above his ass. His knees wedge between my legs, spreading them farther apart. I can feel the crest of his rigid penis through the thin fabric of his boxers against my thigh. He's hard for me. Just the thought makes my toes curl.

I try to catch my breath in between kisses and sucking his reddened lips. His hands are sure and warm as they travel across my body, over my hips, and up my stomach to the sheer fabric of my bra. He removes my bra quickly and massages my breasts, pulling my nipples gently. I arch against him and breathe out a small "ah" as the torture sends a molten heat through my core and down to my toes. He gives every inch of my body attention before moving on to the next, and I've never felt so appreciated.

I want to feel this way all the time.

I run my fingers over his chest, squeezing his nipple between my thumb and forefinger before sliding them down his stomach to his hips to trace over the delicious 'V' cut just above his shorts. Then I slip inside his waistband and take him fully in my hand. His erection is heavy and firm as I massage it. Cade groans and digs his fingers deeper into my hips as he sucks on my breast.

I can already feel the slickness against my panties and my center aching with heat. His fingers curl under the hem of my panties and I instinctively lift my pelvis so he can slide them off easily.

He lifts one of my legs to his lips and kisses the back of my knee. He trails his lips down my inner thigh until he reaches the apex.

His breath is against my pussy, which I can tell is all wet and engorged before him. He runs two fingers between my slippery folds and spreads them.

"I'm going to make you come now."

I try to say yes but it only comes out as a whimper.

He licks me in one firm stroke as he sinks both fingers inside of me.

"Oh, baby, you don't even need this. You're so wet."

He scissors his fingers inside me, stretching me wide as he continues taking me in his mouth. His tongue flickers quickly against my clit then he goes slower so he can suck on it. I can't take the pressure building inside me or the tingling in my toes and buttocks. I'm panting and gasping and I'm pretty sure moaning embarrassing things like "God" and "yeah" and "oh" and "fuck." All the while his fingers push in and out of me, faster. Then he hits that perfect spot inside me and I lose it. I squeeze my eyes shut and fist the sheets. My thighs squeeze his head as I come hard on him.

"God, you feel so good and tight when you come on my fingers, baby. I can only imagine how good that's going to feel on my cock."

"Yes." I'm still panting.

"Yes?" He looks up at me, lips wet and parted, his eyes dangerous.

"Please." I'm writhing underneath him. My insides are

still painfully contracting, the orgasm rippling through my belly.

He removes his underwear and reaches for a packet from his nightstand. "Promise you'll tell me if anything doesn't feel right, or if it hurts. I'm going to try, but God, I think once I get started I'm not going to be able to hold back."

"Don't hold back. I want you."

I watch as he puts on the condom. Then he lays back over me, covering us with the blankets. The faint light from the window just falls on his beautiful face, his messy hair and the perfect bump in his nose. His forehead rests against mine and he looks at me with the faintest smile of pure happiness is on his lips. I can only hear the pumping of blood in my ears and the soft spattering of rain against the window outside.

He closes his eyes and kisses me so softly, taking in a deep breath as he does it. His hands hold my face and my fingers are digging into his shoulder blades. I can't hold him close enough to me. I feel the blunt tip of his cock nudge at my entrance and I realize my legs are shaking at his sides.

"Sure you still want this? We don't have to rush."

"Yes." I really do.

He puts his hand to my cheek and kisses my lips again, lingering there. My chest collapses as I let out a breath and we are still for a moment.

And then he slides inside me. Slowly. Easily. Inch by inch he fills me up, stretching me. When he finally fills me completely and stills, all the air has poured from my lungs. I hear a low rumble from his chest as I struggle to breathe again, then his face is back to mine, his breath hot and quick.

"You all right?"

I nod, our swollen lips brushing against each other.

"You feel so good." He takes an unsteady breath and licks his lips. "I'm not going to stop now."

Please don't.

As he pulls out of me, I can feel every bulge and ridge of him drag against my inner walls. He slides out slowly. Exquisitely slow. All the friction and sensation is both unbearable and perfect. He pulls almost all of the way out before pushing back inside me, deeper. I can't help but arch up into him and gasp out an "oh," clutching at his shoulders as he kisses me again. He swallows my moan and sucks on my tongue and tugs at my lip with his teeth. His kiss is urgent but he pulls out of me slowly, then steadily thrusts back in, creating a slow and torturous rhythm.

Cade pulls my thigh up, opening me wide for him. This time he pushes fast and hard into me. And deep. It sends a jolt through my pelvis to my spine. He begins to move in and out a little faster. I'm tingly all over. His breathing becomes more labored at my ear. A thin layer of sweat forms between our bodies and across his back where my fingernails are digging in.

All I can smell is our rain-soaked skin. Then, lifting up, he puts my knee over his shoulder and this time when he slams into me, it knocks the air out of my lungs as I cry out loudly. He is now pumping into me repeatedly, and hard. It feels so good—I want more of him. I lift my hips to meet his pace, urging him into me, my pussy squeezing him tighter. He buries his head into my neck and I can feel his low grunts against my skin.

He is still hitting just the right spot every time he thrusts and before I realize it my insides are contracting tightly around his hardness and I'm getting lightheaded. My eyes roll into the back of my head as I convulse with my orgasm, my insides twisting in knots. I'm overheated, out of breath, and out of control. I feel like I'm floating outside my body, weightless and euphoric. It's never felt like this—I've never felt like this. And I can't imagine wanting anything—or anyone else ever again.

Cade's hand is in my hair and he pulls me back to him as he whispers in my ear.

"I'm going to come with you, baby." His voice is jerky but he pumps into me steadily. I don't think the pressure can build anymore but it does and my orgasm finds a crest and breaks under him. I'm lost in it. He is over me, hot and damp. He holds me tight to him when he stills and whimpers as he empties inside me, almost trembling with the overwhelming climax.

We lie still for a few moments, his body heavy on mine. There is only breathing, our hearts trying to steady themselves, and Cade's hand under my head and his lips at my neck.

"I'll be right back." He kisses my jaw as he slides out of me. It feels painfully tender. I might have just winced a little.

His smile, replete with happiness, falls. "Are you okay? Shit, did I hurt you?"

"No, that was..." I can't even form words. "...how I've always wished it would be."

His mouth is in a line and he looks serious.

Suddenly a panicked thought stabs through me. "Was it okay, I mean, was I okay...for you?"

"Are you kidding me? Okay? That was fucking amazing."

I try to keep down my smile. I fail. "So...you want to do

it with me again?"

His sexy smirk creeps over his lips. "You up for round two?"

"Give me a minute."

He chuckles and kisses me on the forehead. "Anything for you." Then he leaves the room.

When he comes back, he's naked, and the condom has been disposed of. He slides in next to me under the covers and his skin is freezing. I shriek and try to wiggle away from him but he grabs me and pulls me to him.

"Warm me up."

He's so freaking cold. "I kind of hate you right now."

"I don't think so."

He's right. He's not nearly as cold now and I sink against him, letting out a deep sigh. My eyes won't stay open. I'm too relaxed. Satisfied. Blissful.

His breath is tickling my neck and his voice is low and deep. "So you dodged the question earlier, but I want to know. Have you ever been in love?"

"No."

"So not even a little bit? Not even close?"

"The closest I've ever been to 'in love' is right now." My breath stops as I realize I just said that out loud.

He strokes his hand through my hair, nuzzles at my cheek, and whispers just audibly, "Me too."

CHAPTER 16

It is maybe one of the first times I haven't woken before my alarm goes off. The sound has never been so irritating. I want to smash it for interrupting the perfect dream I was having. I breathe in deeply as I stretch my legs all the way to my toes. The pillow smells like him. Then I realize I hadn't dreamed it. I am in Cade's bed. It was real. And it was perfect.

I have, unfortunately, been neglecting my homework over the last several days. I think spending time with Cade is a perfectly valid excuse, but I don't think dull Professor Trobaugh will accept it in exchange for a paper on how the dwellings of early American Nomads differ by region. So I trek balls early to the library and knock out the whole damn thing with twenty minutes to spare before class. Probably not my best work.

When I get out of class, I have a text.
Cade: *Can't stop thinking about you*
Me: *when will you be home tonight?*
Cade: *way too fucking late*
Me: *Boo*

When I open the doors to leave the building, I am

practically sucked outside by a sweep of wind. I would not have believed it was the middle of the day if I did not know it absolutely was. The sky is the darkest shade of blue-gray it can get before it turns black. The clouds are thick and rolling onto themselves, devouring each other as they grow. Cannibal clouds equals scary.

A deep rumble vibrates from a distance and I can smell rain in the air even though it is not raining. I make it to the bike rack around the back of the building. The rack is old and slanted. Rust is growing in the patches where the black finish has chipped off. It rattles as I fumble with my lock and I feel a large, cool drop on my hand. The air is unusually warm and eerily still as I start to pedal home. Rain patters my handlebars and nose. The clouds sag above me with the weight of their load. I ride as fast as I can—it is only a matter of time before they break.

And they do. Just as I turn the corner onto our street and I can see the white craftsman porch, a powerful blow of air hits my face, followed by the shock of a solid sheet of water cascading over my entire body like a ton of concrete.

When I finally reach the door, I am like a melting ice cube. This storm system is much worse than last night. When I get inside, I can't stop shivering and my clothes are dripping along the floor.

I turn the heat up in the hall and jump in the hottest shower I can stand. I still can't seem to get warm enough. When the water starts to cool down, I concede and get out. Dammit, I'm still frickin' cold. I dry my hair and dress in the fuzziest pair of socks I can find, my cozy sweats, and like three sweatshirts. I grab my phone and head to the living room.

Cade: *Are you home yet?*

Me: *yeah*

Cade: *I left something for you in the oven, to make up for the horrible dinner last night*

I open the oven door and there is a perfectly browned and bubbly lasagna.

Me: *Jesus. Are you for real?*

Cade: *All for you babe*

Me: *Is this real life? Or am I actually schizophrenic and you are a very elaborate figment of my imagination?*

Cade: *I'm not sure what to say to convince you I'm not, that a very elaborate figment of your imagination wouldn't also say...there's an excellent Chianti in the cupboard to go with it*

I'm elated at the sight of the pretty dark bottle. I'm going to drink that entire thing.

Me: *I wish you were here to help me drink it, and maybe keep me warm*

Cade: *Cold?*

Me: *Yes! Even with a bazillion layers. I look homeless*

Cade: *Doubt it*

I snap a picture of my old sweats and my hair all wild and frizzed out and send it to him.

Me: *See?*

I dish myself some lasagna and pour a large glass of wine. Let's be real—I fill a 16 oz. drinking glass full of wine. Outside, it is still pouring and the wind gusts with a far-off whistle. No reply from Cade. I conclude he is probably just busy working. But in the back of my mind, I hope I didn't totally turn him off with my hasty selfie.

I have finished eating and am rinsing my dish when my phone buzzes.

Cade: *OMG. Take it off.*

Cade: *Seriously though. You're still sexy as hell.*

I settle on the couch with the remainder of the bottle of wine in my glass. I blame my next move on drinking half a bottle in thirty minutes. Completely. But he did ask me to take it off. I take a picture in my sheer bra. The wine has warmed me up on the inside, but apparently not on the outside because while obscured, my erect little nipples are still very much in view.

No response from Cade. It's seven o'clock. Dinner rush is in full speed. I cuddle back under some blankets on the couch and open the book I've been dying to start reading since summer. The loud crack of lightning shakes against the windows.

I wake around eleven. The rain is crashing against the roof. I should just go to bed. I take my phone with me.

Cade: *FUCKKK!!! You can't send that to me at work. Do you know how difficult it is to walk around with a raging hard-on? Shit I almost just left so I could come home and suck on those amazing tits of yours.*

I go directly to his bed.

* * *

It's still dark out. I can't hear the rain but I can here the melodic drips from the eaves to the damp ground. I'm wide awake but it is too early to get up. Cade's warm body is completely wrapped around me. His arms are crossed over my chest, holding me tightly to him, his legs and feet tangled in mine. I don't remember him getting into bed last night. He's passed out. His mouth is slightly open and his hair is an absolute mess but my heart leaps into my throat just looking at him.

There is just enough glow from the window to make

out the intricate drawings on his arm, all black and gray ink—a swirly tentacle coming down his bicep and a sharp knife on the underside of his forearm. I slide up to him, pressing our bare chests together to get a better look.

The octopus is huge on his shoulder. But it's not quite an octopus—it is a human skull morphing into tentacles that wrap around his arm down to the elbow with other sea creatures tucked in between. The knife is a huge chef's knife extending from the inside of his elbow to his wrist. It looks so real I go to touch it. I slide my finger along the blade. Then I notice a little tattoo, a tiny bag of flour near the crook of his elbow. Finally, I lean in to try to read the scrolly lettering at his wrist, but he rolls over.

His arms wrap around me and I burrow my face into the side of his neck. I instinctively hook my leg around his hip and I can feel his huge erection through his boxers against my open groin. It sends a jolt through my pelvis and I can't help but rub against it to soothe the itch in me. God, I'm already achy. And wet.

"Mornin'." His voice is full of sleep.

"Morning." My voice is barely a whisper and cracks.

He has me on my back instantly, our fingers laced together above my head. Our lips are nipping, pulling, sucking at each other. I'm already moaning into his mouth and have my legs locked around his waist.

He brushes his soft lips over my nipples.

"I've been thinking about these all night." And he sucks on my nipple. Hard. His mouth is hot as it pulls me. It is almost painful. All I can do is whimper.

I don't tell him to stop as he strips off his boxers and peels my underwear off next. When the cool air hits my wet pussy it makes me shiver, but I can't suppress my silly smile.

He releases my nipple as our mouths meet again and our tongues are hot and needy for one another. His hand is at my thigh, touching my wetness. He sinks two fingers into me slowly and I gasp as they slide in and out of me.

"God, Hale, I love how you want this as much as I do. Are you ready or do you want me to go down on you?" His light blue eyes are looking up at me expectantly. I can tell he won't be disappointed with either answer.

I shake my head. "I'm ready."

His super sexy smile spreads wide over his gorgeous face as he retrieves a condom from the drawer.

His mouth is back over mine and I grip his hair. He enters me smoothly and fast. He isn't holding back. It takes my breath away every time he pounds into me and my head keeps hitting the headboard but it only seems to add to the pleasure. I thrust my hips with his every motion and I am pushing with my hands against the headboard to equal his force. Our rhythm is perfectly in sync.

I try to stifle my screams every time we meet, but he keeps moving my hand away from my mouth. He likes it. He wants to hear me scream. He moans deep in his throat against my cheek. We are still thrusting together furiously, both out of breath and sweating. The slapping of our bodies resonates around the room. I can feel my sex clenching around his cock, squeezing tighter every time he pulls out. It's coming and I can't breathe, or see, or think. Then he pulls out completely and I am empty.

I'm panting here, giving him the what-the-fuck face and he smiles. That stupid, sexy as hell, infuriating smile of his. His breathing is as heavy as mine as he kisses me with soft lips, then flips me over onto my stomach. He is instantly over me, the slick smoothness of his chest sliding up my back as he enters me from behind and, oh God, it's so good. He sweeps my hair away and kisses my neck. He is sliding in and out of me hard, hitting just the right spot. My face is buried in the pillow and I can't take much more. The pressure is building again quickly. My toes curl as I contract around him and I scream into the pillow.

"God, it feels so good when you do that." His voice is raspy and ragged but he hasn't let up on his deliberate pace.

His fingers are intertwined with mine above my head, holding tight. I'm coming down from my orgasm and all I can comprehend are the spasms deep in my belly, the numbness in my toes, and Cade's heavy breathing just behind my ear. And of course, his hard cock rocking in and out of me, still sending waves of pleasure through my over-stimulated body.

I lift my hips to meet his thrusts. He is somehow going even deeper inside me, and faster, and harder. He squeezes my hands tight and sucks hard on my neck. He is shuddering over me and I know he is coming.

Even after his body stops quivering, he holds my hands tight. He doesn't let go, and we lay there for minutes. I love the feel of him. We are still connected and I hear his breathing slow just as my heart rate starts to stabilize. As he shifts off me, he pulls out and the feel of him leaving me is excruciating.

I roll over, bare-breasted and sweat-covered and Cade is smiling at me. The soft morning light just highlights his glistening skin. He's so beautiful when he's happy.

"Morning, pretty girl." He kisses me gently on the lips. "I could get used to waking up like this every day."

"Me too." I never want to leave this bed.

"What are your plans today?"

I'm still distracted by his nakedness and my body coming down from being with him. "Oh nothing. Can I just skip class and stay here with you all day?"

"Skip class? You've got those perfect grades to keep up."

"I don't have perfect grades."

He raises his eyebrows at me in disbelief.

"I have two Bs right now." See.

His expression immediately grows to one of complete shock and horror. "What!"

I just smile and roll my eyes at his mockery.

He leans in and kisses me again. "Still sounds pretty perfect to me. Now, what do you want for breakfast?"

"Hmmm. Something delicious."

"Lucky for you, that happens to be my specialty." He slides out of bed and squeezes my thigh. "Now, you go get in the shower and I'll make us something delicious." He has a big grin on his face and I watch his perfect little ass as he walks out of the room.

* * *

Cade has the whole day off but, alas, I begrudgingly go to classes. I can't concentrate. I'm itching in my seat and staring at the clock the whole time. Of course, this makes time feel like molasses, oozing out every second with great difficulty. Coming to school today was pointless. I cannot recall anything any of my professors say and I jump out of my seat as soon as time is up. Normally, I would have books and paper and pens to organize and pack away after a lecture, but by my last class, I don't even unzip my bag or take off my coat.

I race home as fast as I can and literally almost get hit by a car twice while doing so. I step into the house, all out of breath and cheeks burning, a grin ear-to-ear and am greeted by Cade in the kitchen.

"Hey, we have basically no food in the house. What should we do for dinner?"

"How about I make you dinner tonight?"

He crooks a smile, looking me up and down. "Oh yeah? All right. What are we having?"

"I don't know. Let's go to the store and see what looks good."

His eyes light up when I mention getting groceries. Cade seriously is the most enthusiastic grocery shopper I've ever met.

"Just let me go put my stuff away." I head toward the hall when two fingers hook around my elbow and spin me around.

"Okay, but you have to give me a kiss first."

I love his kisses.

Then he smacks my butt with just the right amount of sting. "Now let's get going."

Of course, grocery shopping is a whole production when you go with a chef.

I tell him I want to make salmon and risotto. Amused, he labels this "ambitious." Apparently, my menu merits a trip to no less than three different specialty shops. First a meat market for the freshest salmon in town, a health food store for the perfect Arborio rice for risotto, and a specialty cheese shop for the best Parmigiano-Reggiano to make the creamiest risotto. I watch Cade as he mulls through the aisles and chats with the artisans, all of whom he knows by name. He gives me his most stoic, blank stare—to hide his disgust, I'm sure—when I mention something about buying the pre-grated parmesan. Maybe this is too ambitious for me.

As we walk to the car, I am carrying the cheese and rice while Cade holds the freshly filleted fish and a huge loaf of crusty bread. Even with his hands full, he somehow manages to keep an arm around my shoulders.

"I wish we could stop by that little wine shop on Placer Street in the city. They have this Sauvignon Blanc that is perfect with salmon." He gives a little grr face as we reach his car parked at the curb. He would shop at all the little delicatessens and fine food and wine shops every day if he lived in the city. We have just enough hippie professors in this small college town to warrant some specialty food markets, but not nearly as many as elsewhere.

"Why don't you live in the city, Cade?"

He looks a little surprised as he places the bread loaf in the back seat. "I don't know. I mean I grew up there. I guess I always imagined I'd move back." We slide in the front seats, the black leather squeaking. "I went to school here for a couple of years until I decided to go to culinary school back in the city, but when I graduated I had no job, and nowhere to live. Tuck offered me a room and I found a job at *La Mer*.

"It was a blessing, really. I would never have been able to promote as fast anywhere else. It's pretty rare for someone my age to be a Sous Chef already. I'm getting experience and waiting for the right opportunity." He looks off into the distance. "I mean, it is a dream of mine to be an executive chef at a big restaurant, but for now"—he turns to look at me—"I like right where I am."

RAE KENNEDY

He gives me a wink as he pushes the clutch. I watch him slide the gear shift, just the tips of the scrolly script on his wrist peeking out from his jacket cuff.

* * *

I add another ladle of chicken stock to the rice and continue to stir. Cade is sitting across from me at the counter. He keeps fidgeting with his hands, opening them then balling them back up into fists before finally hiding them under the counter. I pretend not to notice. I just keep stirring.

Out of the corner of my eye, I see him open his mouth then promptly shut it. I look up at him. He gives me a big smile, still not saying anything. I season the fillets with salt and pepper and place them in the sizzling pan while still trying to give the rice the attention it demands. This time when he opens his mouth, a little breath comes out before he pins his lips shut between his teeth.

"Anything you'd like to share with the class?"

He shakes his head. Still smiling. "Nope."

I raise my eyebrow at him. The sizzling pan alerts me from my stirring and I flip the salmon. It's maybe a little darker than I would have liked. Oops. Now the rice is boiling. I turn the burner down and start stirring again. I can feel Cade squirming on his stool.

Stop distracting me, Cade! And you, rice, simmer dammit, simmer.

"You sure you don't need any help?" he asks. I look up from the traitor rice and glare at him. "You're pretty?" he offers, hands up in a protective position. My face cracks just barely.

He helps me finish the risotto. It's delicious, but he gives me all the credit. The salmon is a bit overcooked, but he doesn't mention it.

CHAPTER 17

Class is even blander than usual on Thursday. Everything seems duller without Cade in it. Professor Trobaugh is droning on and on, most of the class appears to be asleep or in some other trance-like state.

Except for the group of guys in the back. I tried not to notice them when I came in, but what can I say, I'm very observant—Adam.

He and a bunch a douche-baggy guys have been snickering amongst themselves ever since I walked past them. I'm assuming they're guys from his frat. I guess he never did introduce me to any of his friends. That's weird, right? But I'm kind of grateful I didn't have to spend time with any of them now. One guy even has his polo shirt collar popped. That went out of style like ten years ago, didn't it? Didn't it? Seriously.

I'm already squeezing my notebook into my bag when Professor Trobaugh finally stops talking and scribbling nonsense on the board. I have to walk past the group of assholes on my way out. I ignore them, but by the increase in volume of the laughter as I pass, I'm obviously their object of amusement. Adam's plaything. Or ex-plaything.

I hear them shuffling behind me. I can feel them looking at me. I try to walk as steadily as I can, even as heat rises to my ears. They are still behind me when I exit into the chilly November air.

It only takes me a second to spot him.

Across the small strip of lawn, Cade leans up against his black GTO, arms folded, the sleeves of his jacket pulled up just enough to show his tats peeking past the cuffs. The most gorgeous white smile spreads across his face when he sees me and I have never been so happy in my life. I practically sprint toward him and he squeezes me up into his arms when I reach him.

"Hey gorgeous," he whispers in my ear. The gentle brush of his lips gives me goosebumps. "You ready to go?" He puts me down and I look up at his boyishly excited face.

"Go? Where are we going?"

"It's kind of a surprise. You don't have any plans for tonight, do you?"

I shake my head at him. "Nope."

His gorgeous smile grows even wider.

* * *

I look at the clothes Cade packed for me to wear. An old Zeppelin concert T-Shirt (of his, I'm assuming) with several holes in it and a tiny black skirt I didn't even realize I still had. He must have really dug through my closet to find this. Leave it to a man to pack a miniskirt to wear in the middle of November.

"Can't I just wear what I have on?"

"Trust me." He glances back at me in his rearview mirror, still all excited about this surprise.

"Those will be perfect."

I am scrunched up in Cade's backseat, trying to change discreetly. Impossible. It takes me ten minutes to get my shoes and pants off back here. I literally have to lie on my back with my feet on the roof of the car to wiggle out of them, wobbling side to side like a destitute turtle. It doesn't help that Cade keeps chortling at me from the front seat.

"Hey! Eyes on the road, sir."

"Of course. Safety first." His eyes are on me the whole time he says this.

I roll my eyes and lift my shirt. Cade changes lanes abruptly as I am mid-undress, shirt covering my face, arms up over my head and I fall face-first to the slippery seat. Sonofabitch.

I sit up and just as I get my shirt up past my nose, he switches back unexpectedly and I fall to my right, smacking my temple against the door handle.

I cry out in exasperation.

"Sorry, babe."

He thinks I can't hear him chuckle. I can. I finally rip off my shirt to give him my best glare when we pass a large semi-truck and the driver honks. At me. I'm in just my bra and underwear. Dear God.

I snatch the shirt hurriedly and plunge in my head and arms. I can see Cade's eyes flickering back at me in his mirror every few seconds. I guess I'm being distracting. I inch the skirt up my thighs and over my rear. Whoa. I was definitely a few pounds lighter the last time I wore this.

Okay, girl dilemma: this skirt is a little snug around the hips and I am not wearing a thong. Do I chance looking a little frumpy with panty lines or risk being a little skanky with no underwear whatsoever? Both potentially embarrassing.

RAE KENNEDY

I shimmy my panties down stealthily so Cade won't see. Maybe it will be a surprise for later. Or sooner.

* * *

It takes over an hour to get into the city. We drive through downtown, and then past it. Where are we going? We seem to be in a sort of industrial warehouse district. The buildings all look a bit neglected with soot-stained stacks emerging from patched roofs, busted windows, and layers of graffiti. It's eerily dark—the streetlights are sporadic and dim. There are absolutely no people around. I can't help but feel a little nervous. I have to tell myself that Cade is not an ax-murderer who has taken me to his secret hide-out to dismember my body. Still, this would be a good place to do it.

He pulls into a gravel lot. I didn't know the city could get so dark. The headlights shine over several other cars parked in the lot. That's good. Murder seems to be off the table, at least.

"Ready?" Cade looks at me. I can barely see his face after he turns off the car, but I can just make out his beautiful smile and I realize as long as I am with him, I'm ready for anything.

I step out of the car and it is crazy cold. I hurry around the front and Cade meets me there. He throws his jacket over my shoulders and takes my hand as he looks at my bare legs.

"Let's get inside, huh?"

Um, thank you.

We walk briskly to a large warehouse, its sheet metal siding dingy and curling at the seams. It looks abandoned but the heavy duty chains and lock on the door suggest otherwise. I'm a little confused—I could do without a B and E on my record. But he guides me around the corner to the back of the building. There's a muscular guy standing in front of a very small propped open door, a faint yellow light radiating out of it.

We walk up to the man, who looks even more intimidating up close, by the way. He could be Filipino or Tongan, maybe. His mouth is set in a straight line. He stares out ahead, not focused on anything in particular. As we come to a stop in front of him, his eyes shift to Cade. His stony expression does not alter, but he gives Cade the slightest of nods and takes a step to the left. Cade places his hand around my waist as we step inside.

He guides me around large machinery to a hallway where caged halogen lights are stapled by their cords to the walls. They give off a peculiar weak orange light. Cade's touch is constant on me. At the end of the hall is an open metal cargo elevator.

"You're not taking me to some weird orgy or something, right?" I grimace at the rickety-looking contraption.

He tosses his head up and laughs playfully but when he looks back at me, he bites his lower lip. "No, Hale. Promise."

The elevator descends very slowly, screeching as it goes. It reaches the bottom with a thud and a thick wave of heat hits me. I slide off the jacket as we step out. Those same dim orange lights glow on one side of the hallway in front of us.

On the other side of the hallway are huge boiler units with giant knobs and pipes everywhere. It is so hot and humid I immediately feel sweaty. One of the boilers whistles and steams as we walk past and I almost jump.

Cade tightens his arm around me. "We are almost there."

The hallway opens to a massive open space full of people. Everything is lit by more of the large orange lights. At the far end of the room, a stage is set up with a shiny black drum set.

"A concert?"

"Yeah." He turns back toward me as we reach the crowd. "Some of my buddies from high school are playing tonight. It's their first gig back here for almost a year, so I had to come see them. Is it okay?"

"Yeah, it's cool."

The crowd starts whooping and clapping and stomping their feet. As I turn to look, four guys with increasing degrees of rock-ness come out onstage. The first two look like brothers dressed in all black—the same long lean builds and bare muscular arms. The only difference I can see from this far away is one has 'I just rolled out of bed' hair and the other one has short, slicked-back hair. They each pick up their instruments—the guitar and bass.

The next guy to come on-stage is short and stocky. He has a white mohawk that stands out against his fair skin almost as much as the red and orange tattoos that color his arms. He sits behind the drums, inspecting the sticks and touching all of the drum surfaces.

The last one is the singer. His dark brown hair is short and thick. He's got gauges and gorgeous pouty lips, an angular jaw, and steely blue eyes framed with dark lashes. He's all covered up with jeans and a long-sleeved charcoal gray Henley but I can still make out black tattoos on his neck and hands.

He gets even sexier when he starts to sing. His voice is

deeper than I expected and the band is amazing. The songs are raw with heavy drums but very catchy guitar riffs.

The whole time they play, Cade stands behind me, his arms wrapped across my chest. He rests his chin on my shoulder, occasionally kissing my neck or cheek. I can feel him humming against my skin. He is so into the music I don't think he notices the girls eye-fucking him from everywhere.

Seriously? It's very clear we are together but girls keep walking by batting their eyelashes toward him and puffing up their cleavage. It's kind of like watching peacocks. But sad, very sad peacocks.

It's crowded and hot. Extremely hot, like I-can-smell-the-moisture-coming-out-of-everyone's-pores hot. The music is loud and high energy. The crowd seems to know all the words and they jump and sway at the right points. I can feel the damp body heat of all the people in the room and my skin is sticky all over. But I can also smell Cade—clean yet musky.

The lead singer rips off his shirt and throws it into the crowd—much to the pleasure of several female fans. He is all lean muscle and covered in black tattoos. The only one I can clearly make out is the large pair of wings spanning his entire chest.

Cade's stubble softly pricks across my cheek as he moves his lips to my throat. His hands have slid to my hips and are firmly planted there. His whole rigid body is pressed up to mine and I suddenly realize I'm slick between my bare thighs. I don't know if it's sweat or arousal but I suddenly want nothing more than for him to touch me. Right there. No one is paying attention to us—he could just slide his finger right up my thigh…

Okay, it's not just sweat.

RAE KENNEDY

I'm starting to throb between my legs and I'm trying to send Cade telepathic messages: *touch me. I need you. I want you. Dear God, fuck me now.* Nothing. I arch my back slightly and push my rear right into his groin. He squeezes my hips tighter, but nothing more.

The music stops and now the lead singer is addressing the crowd, thanking them for coming out, and supporting them, blah blah blah. The concert was awesome, but I'm ready for the after-party—the one where Cade and I get naked.

The band exits the stage and Cade whispers in my ear. "What do you say we beat the crowd out of here?"

"I'm on it." I grab the front of his shirt and drag him behind me. Being short has given me an unusual talent for navigating through large crowds quite stealthily.

"Whoa, okay!" A little chuckle in his voice, Cade keeps his hand on the small of my back and follows me quite nimbly through the crowd, down the tight corridor, up the creaky elevator, and outside.

The cold bites at my cheeks as we leave the boiling building. Cade and I make a quick dash to the car. When we get inside, he roars on the engine and blasts the heat. He looks at me, just a faint light from outside hitting the edge of his jaw and the most gorgeous smile on his face. We are both a little winded from running in the cold and I can see our breath in the air. The windows are fogging up and I want to jump him right now, right here in the car. In fact, I'm just about to lunge for him when he asks if I'm ready to go to the next place.

Really? Then my stomach grumbles. Okay, I guess.

"Where to?"

"You'll see." He smiles confidently and gives me a wink

as he looks over his shoulder and rolls the car into reverse.

* * *

Cade's fingers intertwine with mine as we enter the bar.

I think it is more packed than the concert.

My view is mostly blocked, an endless number of human torsos at my face as we weave toward the back. I can make out the walls clad in rough-sawn wood planks, glimpses of bright red dart boards and beer signs, and a couple framed black and white photographs of what might be firefighter companies. The booths along the back are tall and carved out of dark solid wood, smooth and shiny. All the tables are full and the bar is barely visible beyond the pack of mostly male patrons. There appears to be standing-room only and I can't even hear the music over the steady drone of voices.

A pack of men part as we pass through them to a dimly lit booth in the back. Sitting there are four guys, six pitchers, and two bottles. I instantly recognize them. The band. Of course.

"Renner!" The guy with the disheveled hair stands and gives Cade a hug, practically knocking him over. "Where the hell have you been all my life?" he says, hitting Cade on the back unexpectedly hard.

"You know, just living the dream."

Bed-head guy looks me up and down, lingers at the boobs, as usual, but lands squarely on my eyes. I swear his dark brown eyes twinkle at me. "Who's this?" He doesn't even wait for Cade's response. He takes my hand and pulls me into the booth with him. I slide in rather clumsily, trying to use my free hand to hold my short skirt down. Cade is grinning as he scoots in after us, sitting hip-to-hip with me.

"Guys, this is Haley," Cade tells me bed-head guy is Logan. He plays the guitar. Logan winks at me when Cade says this.

Next is the drummer. He has the fairest skin and faint red freckles all over his face and hands. I suspect they are all over his arms as well, but they're covered up by tattoos. His eyes are super pale, framed by blond eyelashes and red eyebrows. His hair is also likely red but bleached to almost white. He gives me a shy smile and a nod when Cade introduces him as Joey.

The bassist, Dean, is studying my face and though his expression is much more serious than Logan's, and he has more piercings, his dark brown eyes are the same. His whole face is eerily the same actually, yet different. Logan and Dean are twins—identical twins. I don't think I would have known if Logan hadn't mentioned it.

Lastly, sitting directly across from me is the lead singer, Colin. He is all covered up again in long sleeves but I can see his hands are tattooed as well as the sides of his neck. Everything about him seems sort of dark—his dark buzzed hair, black tattoos, black eyebrows, black gauges, thick lashes. But then these bright blue eyes. They are mesmerizing. And looking right through me. I see his lips start to creep into a smile when I realize I'm totally staring at him. Cade puts his arm around my shoulders and my trance instantly breaks as I turn to him.

He smiles at me with his perfect white teeth. "Can I get you something to eat? Drink?"

"Yeah." I'm starving.

I have a couple of beers and some chicken strips. I notice Cade doesn't have more than a few sips of his beer, but the rest of the guys make up for that. They don't take shots, just swigs straight from the bottle in between chugging their huge frothed glasses.

Dean and Logan are arguing over whether there is ever a need for two guitarists in a band. Dean has some very verbose and philosophical responses, but Logan yells the loudest and is pronounced the winner by default as he slams down the bottle of whiskey and gets the last word in. Dean grabs the bottle and tosses back a huge gulp as he flips his brother off.

Meanwhile, Joey's gone from pale-white to bright-red with drink. His cheeks are glowing like they've been slapped, repeatedly. He has become very giggly and is starting to talk much louder than is necessary for us to reasonably hear him. Cade is laughing over my head with Logan about some roadie stalker they finally got to stop inviting herself on tour. His arm has been wrapped around me all night, his thumb constantly stroking my shoulder.

"She was convinced that she and Colin were in love and going to get married or some shit."

"It probably wouldn't have gotten to that level," Dean chimes in, "if she hadn't been led on."

"I never said a fucking word to her," Colin says, leaning back.

"Not you! Joey. He screwed her."

"What!" Joey practically screams it. "That was like three years ago."

I can't tell if he's blushing because he's embarrassed or if he's so hot he's going to pass out. Either way, his face looks like a fire hydrant.

"Don't lie. Gingers don't get laid. You wouldn't know what to do with a pussy if it put itself around your cock."

Joey throws his empty beer bottle at Colin, who doesn't

even flinch. It misses him by at least a foot.

"That kind of comes with the territory because of the whole no soul thing, right?" Logan asks Joey, looking very concerned. Joey, I can tell, is used to this ribbing and while flustered, gives up the argument.

"So, Haley..."

I turn my gaze from Joey's flaming cheeks to the electric blue eyes across from me. Colin asks, "Are you Cade's girlfriend or what?"

My immediate reaction is to say no. I don't know what we are, but girlfriend? That doesn't seem—

"Yes," Cade answers, as he softly strokes my arm. Colin seems surprised. Not as much as I am.

My boyfriend? It's too weird to say it like that. But he is mine. His sexy ass is mine. His perfect lips are mine. His beautiful smile is mine. I suddenly want to kiss every inch of his smooth skin, from the little bump in his nose right down across his sculpted abs...and now I realize I have my hand on his upper thigh. I squeeze it and he looks at me, his crystal blue eyes the happiest I've seen them.

"Never thought it'd happen, Renner. I'm glad," Colin says approvingly.

Logan and Cade start busting each other's chops about something. All I can think about is Cade's hard thigh as I slide my hand up it. I squeeze it again, not realizing that I'm squeezing my legs together too. Dammit, the leather seat under me is totally wet.

The guys are all laughing and pounding more drinks. I inch my fingers up to Cade's hip and over just a little and I can feel it. He's fully erect under my hand. I bite my lip to keep from sighing heavily as I tighten my hand around his cock. I wish we were alone right now. Cade lets his hand fall to my bare knee. I watch his angular jaw as he talks. I spread my legs apart just a little, and he takes the hint instantly.

His demeanor never changes. He just continues talking tattoos with Dean as his fingers graze the inside of my thigh. My fingers are still around his erection. He's taking his time, giving me goosebumps and making my tummy flutter. My clitoris is literally buzzing. Like, I wonder if Logan can hear it. I'm still just watching Cade's face though.

He finally reaches my wetness, his fingers slipping in it. A huge smile hits his face as he realizes I'm panty-less, but his conversation doesn't skip a beat. I don't think I'm as concealing as I'm pretty sure I let out a little "oh" when he promptly shoves his middle finger all the way inside my soaked pussy. It knocks the air out of me and I reach for my beer. I take a long sip, closing my eyes as Cade's slick finger circles around my bud, hoping that the bottle hides my face.

"Don't you think so, Haley?" Logan is looking at me expectantly, grabbing a fistful of fries from my plate and eating them casually. As though we were BFFs who had shared food on many an occasion. Cade now has two fingers moving parallel between my burning folds.

I try to snap out of it. "I'm sorry. I must have totally spaced out."

"Don't you think Cade should move back to the city? I mean, at least we'd get to see him more than once every two years like we have since he quit the band."

His finger presses right into my clit and I almost choke on my last sip. I try to cover it up with a cough. I think it was pretty smooth. "Cade was in the band?"

"Oh what! This guy? He never told you he was in our

band?"

I shake my head.

"He and Colin started it when we were like fourteen."

I'm trying not to be distracted as Cade rubs me faster. Then slower. Then faster. I try to stay engaged in the conversation. I look around the table.

"So, you've got a bassist, singer, drummer, and guitarist." I land on Cade, who looks cool and calm. "What did you play?"

His fingers slow considerably, barely touching me at all. "It's not a big deal—"

"No! Give it up, dude!" Joey yells from the end of the table, still as red as a beet and definitely the drunkest at the table.

I look right into Cade's eyes. I think this is the first time I've seen him even a little embarrassed. He eyes me, tongue pressed against his teeth, looking devilish. Then he sinks two fingers inside me.

"He played the keyboard." Dean rats him out.

I start giggling much louder than I ought to at that. Cade finger-fucks me even harder. I'm still laughing, but to be honest, it's to keep myself from moaning or screaming.

"You think that's funny?" Cade's being coy with me.

I stifle my laughs and shake my head.

"Yeah, his grandma had him take piano lessons since he was like five or some shit, right?"

"Yeah," Cade answers Joey, but he's looking at me. I don't know how he knows when I'm about to come, but that's when he stops.

"Since you were five? That's adorable."

All the guys immediately start making exaggerated "aww" sounds and Cade rolls his eyes.

"Seriously, man, you were seriously skilled. We'd take you back any day," Colin says.

"Sorry, guys." His hot fingers start rubbing me again. "I'm using these talented fingers for cooking now…among other things." He smirks just for me.

As he pushes his fingers inside me quickly I gasp out, "Yes!" and, thinking fast, follow it up with, "Very talented indeed."

Colin smiles at me.

I have been on the verge of coming for the last ten minutes. But he hasn't let me. It's been torture. The guys get sloppier. Logan finishes eating my cold fries. Joey tries to get anyone to partake in an arm-wrestling match with him (even me), Dean looks like he is about to pass out, and Cade stops touching me altogether while getting into an animated discussion with Colin, who is trying to convince us to go to an after-hours party.

Cade insists that we need to get home and we get up to leave.

"Bye. It was nice meeting you all."

"I'm a hugger." Logan gets up and, yep, gives me a hug. Cade too.

* * *

Cade shuts the car door and I attack before he can even put the keys in the ignition. I can't quite reach his face so my lips settle for kissing and sucking on his neck. I'm clumsily trying to get to him over the center console, almost getting a gear shift up my butt and definitely getting an emergency brake jabbed in my knee cap. I finally get to him as he lifts my hips and helps me over. Our lips are instantly devouring one another.

My hands are in his hair. It's soft and long enough on top for me to wrap my fingers in it. His breath tastes like peppermint and I feel like I haven't kissed him in days instead of hours. He grips my hips tight and then he pulls up my short skirt. His hands move to my behind, squeezing me against him.

I can feel the huge bulge through his jeans and rub up against it. He meets each one of my thrusts while digging his fingers deeper into my bare ass. It sends tingles all down through my inner legs to my toes and back up to just behind my ears. I'm panting.

Every time he turns his tongue into my mouth, I imagine another of his body parts sinking in and out of me. I'm pretty sure I'm making the crotch of his pants embarrassingly wet. Let's just get those out of the way. I put my fingers on his top button.

"Fuck." He's breathing erratically and hard.

"Cade, I can't wait until we get home. I want you now."

"Okay." He kisses me harder and slides his hand over my bum and up to my opening that's dripping with need. He moans deep in his throat. "Let's go somewhere more private."

I reluctantly fall to the passenger seat so that he can drive. My pulse is rapid. The car smells like Cade and sex. I watch him as he drives (extra aggressively) through the city.

He looks good in black. He looks good driving a stick.

I watch his leg flex as he depresses the clutch and his tattooed arm as it effortlessly shifts. I watch his eyes as he flicks them to and from the rearview mirror—I can't tell they're blue in this light but they're beautiful. As he turns his head, I look at his square jaw and sinewy neck muscles.

He throws me a smile as we turn off the main road. I don't care where we are going. As long as I am with him. Always.

The road becomes gravel and dirt, bumpy. It twists and turns. As we climb some serious elevation, I catch glimpses of the city lights in the distance. Finally, he turns out to an even rockier road and we come to a secluded clearing. The entire city is laid out before us, twinkling against the black.

"Wow. It's beautiful."

He sits and smiles at me. "This is one of my favorite places."

I'm like a little kid seeing a Christmas tree for the first time. In awe. "Yeah? Did you come up here often when you lived here?"

"I did."

"This would be amazing to photograph."

"You should take up photography."

"Yeah?" I like that idea. I don't know why I haven't considered it much before. "Maybe I will." He takes my hand and we just look at the view for a little while. "My dad used to have this old Nikon F from the seventies he would let me experiment with. I was in love with that camera. That's what a picture like this needs. A manual SLR. Automatic cameras can never get it just right." I'm babbling.

"You and your dad were close." It wasn't a question really. I look at him and he looks like he's thinking about something.

"What about you? What about your parents?" I hope I didn't just ruin the mood.

He looks at me, contemplating. "I didn't know them." He says it matter-of-factly. "My mother was young and an addict. She dropped me off with my grandma one day when I was three and left."

I'm not sure how to respond. I'm never good in these kinds of situations. So I just squeeze his hand a little. He looks at me, lovingly.

"It's all fine, Hale. I'm well past it. She would visit every once in a while until I was about nine, I think? Never met my dad. He probably doesn't even know I exist. I'm not mad about it anymore. I had a good childhood. My grandmother was a great lady..." He sort of trails off and looks out over the city. I want to ask him more but I don't think I should pry.

He changes the subject quickly, climbing into the backseat. "Now get your ass over here already!" He says with a huge grin on his face.

I crawl between the front bucket seats and into his lap. He's got his jeans pulled down to his knees and I have to hike my skirt up to my waist in order to straddle him. He's got both hands on my thighs, rubbing them softly up and down. I'm aching for him.

My hands are on either side of his face and we are looking right at each other. I kiss his nose, then his cheeks and his forehead. A low growl comes from his chest as he searches for my mouth with his. When our lips connect, it is soft and pure. Warm and perfect. I am sitting on him, skin-to-skin and I can feel his shaft between my slipperiness. I slide against it slowly, its head rubbing my clit just right as we both moan quietly through our kisses. He lifts my hips up and gets a condom out of his pocket. He has it on quickly.

"Whenever you're ready." He whispers against my lips.

I kiss him for a few more moments, clinging to his neck. His hands firmly grasp my hips and as I make a move toward him, he helps guide me down.

I sink onto him. Slow and deep.

He stretches me. It aches.

Our foreheads touching, mouths just an inch apart, he lets his breath out completely, his eyelids hooding as I take his full length inside of me. He is looking right into my eyes with his perfect blue ones.

"Hale...I..." His breath hitches as I raise myself up and plunge back down again. He throws his head back and I love how powerful I feel. How vulnerable he is to me right now.

"I love...this," he whispers. He wraps his arms around my waist and kisses my neck. He holds me to him the whole time, letting me set the pace. His hair tickles at my cheek and I can smell that fresh scent. I would be happy if this is the only scent I ever smell again.

CHAPTER 18

I must have fallen asleep in the car. I am awoken by the light in my eyes when Cade opens the door and a cold rush of air hits my bare legs. I whine in protest. Just let me stay here—I'll sleep half hunched over on this leather seat with a crook in my neck all night, I swear. But he insists I go inside. So he helps me up the front steps and takes me to his bed. I take off my shirt as he undresses to his navy boxer briefs. He rips my skirt straight down the ass when he tries to pull it off for me.

"Damn, I really liked this skirt."

I yawn. "It was too small, anyway."

"That was a major factor in its appeal."

I try to slap his shoulder but miss by a good margin.

"You're so sleepy," he says.

"I am! You kept me up way too late."

He pulls the covers up over both of us and I settle onto his chest.

"And on a school night, too," I add.

He chuckles softly and kisses my forehead. It relaxes every muscle in my body and I let myself go to sleep again.

* * *

There is a rustle of trees outside. A single trickle of light falls out beyond the curtain and I can see that it is just barely morning. I stretch my legs, taking a deep breath and reach for Cade but his side of the bed is empty. I roll to his pillow and bury my face in the smell of him. Pots and pans clank in the kitchen and I don't want to get up but the promise of watching Cade in the kitchen is enough.

I go to the bathroom. Whoa, my hair is out of control. Did Cade see it like that? Sure as shit he did. I tie it up on top of my head and throw on my most comfortable, albeit least attractive, pair of sweatpants.

He is shirtless, just in his little boxer briefs, cracking an egg into a skillet when he looks up to me. "Morning, Sleeping Beauty."

I rub my left eye. "Don't know about the beauty part, but morning."

"I hate when hot girls are all self-deprecating. You're sexy, own it."

I roll my eyes. "Come on, look at these." I point to my sweats. I've had them for five years—they're worn out, washed out (I am no longer confident of what color they originally were), baggy, and have a hole in the knee.

"Are you serious? Those fucking sweatpants! Drove me nuts the whole first month you lived here wearing those. Every time you'd come walking out in those, I'd lose it. I'd have to go jerk off to get rid of my hard-on."

I stare at him for a minute. "Um, what?" Disbelief.

He walks over to me. "It's because they are so loose, they just hang off your hips." He puts his hands on my bare skin just above the waistband. "Every time I would think if I just pulled on them a little bit"—he pulls the waistband away from my hips—"they would just fall off." And they do. Right to the floor go my pants and we are just standing there in our underwear.

As if choreographed, I wrap my arms around his neck in the exact moment he lifts me by my hips to the counter. We are kissing frantically. I'm already out of breath. The counter is cold under my ass but I don't notice after a second. Cade drops his boxer briefs and I wrap my legs around him. Guess those sweatpants really do get him stiff.

Our mouths are hot and I am sucking on his bottom lip as he fumbles in the drawer next to us. I want to ask why he has a condom in a kitchen drawer, but he currently has my tongue hostage and I don't really care about the answer right now. Before I know it, he pulls my panties to the side and slips a finger deep inside of me. I'm already wide open for him. His finger is gone and suddenly his huge cock is plunging inside of me, filling me so completely I scream out.

I dig my fingers into his naked butt as he pounds into me. And he is pounding. Hard. But not too fast. Each time seems to go deeper and I am getting louder. He stills inside of me for a moment, giving me a deep kiss. We are both trying to catch our breath. My heart beats so rapidly I feel like it is trying to get out.

Our eyes meet. He grins then silently pulls out of me, sets me down on the floor, spins me around and bends me over the counter. He pushes my drenched panties to my ankles and then I can feel his hot breath at my clenching pussy. He starts to eat me out from behind, his tongue twirling on my clit and then poking inside of me. His nose is totally in my butt and this would normally make me self-conscious but right now I like it. I like how dirty it is. I like how dirty he is.

"Fuck me hard."

And he does. His cock is as hard as steel as he enters me from behind. I cry out but he doesn't let up. All I can hear is the smacking of his hips to my ass, his grunts, and my screams. When I yell that I'm coming, he shudders inside me instantly, his arms clinging around me.

It's the only time I've seen Cade burn food.

* * *

Cade is working late tonight. So when Court asks if I want to hang out at her place this afternoon, I am extremely grateful.

She drives us in her Jeep, taking corners so fast I have to hold on to the handle. She tells me how excited she is to be graduating in May but her thesis is sort of kicking her butt.

"I might have to shut myself in my room over the entire Christmas break just to get the proposal done." She scrunches her nose. "Boring. Enough about me. How are you?"

I can't help but break into, I'm sure, the biggest, stupidest grin ever grinned.

She smiles at me from the side. "Cade?"

"Yeah."

She pulls into a spot right in front of her building. "Oh my gosh!" Her mouth is wide open in a giddy smile that's still not as goofy as mine probably is. "You looove him!"

"I don't know…"

"Yes. Yes, you do."

"It's only been a week…"

"Haley." She looks at me seriously.

"Okay, maybe..."

She lifts an eyebrow at me.

"Maybe yes?"

She practically screams in glee and hugs me. I'm not a hugger. But her happiness for me feels wonderful, so I allow it.

We scurry in the biting cold up the stairs. Of course, she lives on the top floor.

"How is he in bed?"

"Court!"

"Oh, you know you're going to tell me anyway."

"Fu...you're right. He's...amazing."

She does a little victory dance in front of her door before getting out her keys. "Damn right. You get it, girl."

She opens the door and simultaneously four male heads turn to look at us. The guys are watching a college basketball game.

She introduces me. There's her roommate, Caleb, and their friend Jake, whom I vaguely remember meeting before. Her other roommate is named Nick. He has light brown hair, dark eyes, and a lopsided smile that is weirdly cute.

Last is another friend named Josh, who gives me a quick wave and a "hey" but doesn't take his eyes off the game.

They are all in love with Court. I can tell by how they watch as she goes into the kitchen to get me a drink. And how they are all trying discreetly to sit next to her on the couch. Nick looks smug that he lands a spot next to her and Jake is visibly annoyed when she makes him move so I can sit down on her other side.

I look at her as she is arguing with Josh over the ref's last call on an offensive foul. Her legs are long and toned in skinny jeans and she's wearing a soft cream sweater that hangs off her shoulder. Her perfectly thick blonde hair is just up in a ponytail (it probably took her all of thirty seconds but looks better than my hair after twenty minutes of attention) and then she has this beautifully angelic face with her big round blue eyes and cute little nose that has been kissed by the faintest of freckles.

Fuck. I'd be in love with her too if I were a guy. Actually, I might have a major girl crush on her, the more I think about it.

"So, Tuck's getting back into town tomorrow?" Court asks me.

"Yeah." Shit, that means I need to tell him about me and Cade.

"You gonna tell him or what?"

"That's the plan."

Court pops the tops off a couple of bottles of beer and sits back down on the couch. She hands one to Nick and takes a swig of the other.

"Well, let me know how it goes or if I can help in any way."

Court is way too nice for me. I don't deserve her.

The guys order pizza and we finish watching the game. Court and the guys are immersed in the television, yelling at the refs' bad calls and giving each other high fives after particularly flawless plays. Meanwhile, I'm stewing about how I'm going to talk to Tuck.

When I get home, it's after dinnertime and I hope Cade will be home soon. I haven't been keeping up with my homework this week, so I decide to get some much needed studying in before he does.

My dilemma is that there is only one place I want to be right now: Cade's bed. Preferably naked. So I haul my books into his room and strip. I lay stomach-down on his navy comforter and spread the books around me in a circle.

I am literally like the hands of a clock—after twenty minutes on one book, I rotate to the next one on my right and so on. I plan on continuing this until either A: I finish all of my reading (good luck) B: Cade gets home or C: I fall asleep from boredom (seems most likely).

* * *

I wake up with my face in a book and I am cold. The clock says 12:42. Then I see Cade. He's standing in the doorway, leaning up against the thick white door molding with his white dress sleeves rolled up and a smile on his face.

"Hey, babe." He walks over to me and starts moving the books off the bed.

"Hey." My voice cracks with sleep. I wipe my mouth to check for drool. All clear.

He kisses my forehead as he reaches for his collar. I watch as he unbuttons his shirt all the way down and removes it. My eyes roam over his smooth pecs and ink-covered shoulders, then down to his tight abs and the shelf-cut into his sides over his hip bones that disappear into his pants… The pants that he is currently unzipping and dropping to the floor.

"How was your day?" I yawn at him.

"Fucking sucked. I just wanted to come home to you all day." He comes and lies with me, sweeping some hair off my face behind an ear. All I can do is smile sleepily up at him. I'm in the tiniest of panties and a lace bra, but he is only looking at my face as he traces my arm down to my hand to intertwine our fingers. He kisses me on the nose. "Let's get ready for bed, yeah?"

"Yeah." And we do. In tandem. In our underwear. Can this be forever, please?

We slide under the covers and it is warm and soft all I want to do is curl up and never leave. I cozy up to Cade's side and he squeezes me tightly to him. I feel so close to him, like nothing could ever separate us from where we are now. I have wanted to ask him all day but don't know if I should. I just want to be as close to him as possible. Closer.

"Tell me about your grandma." I realize after it comes out that it was more of a demand than a question. I listen to him breathe for a few seconds. The silence feels much longer.

"What is there to tell? She raised me. She was my mother. She gave me my own apron so I could help her in the kitchen. My first memory is when I was four, helping her roll out biscuits and I got flour everywhere. Like on the ceiling everywhere."

I can't see his face, but his chest bounces under my head like he is laughing to himself. Then he goes quiet.

"Why does talking about her make you so sad?"

He lets out a hard sigh. I'm afraid I've pushed him too much. He shifts me off him and rolls on his side, facing me. We are eye-to-eye. I can barely make out the details of his face in the dark but I can tell he is looking directly into me.

"I failed her."

I lay still. Noiseless. When he starts talking again, I realize I've been holding my breath.

"All she wanted was for me to be happy, successful,

educated. To turn out better than her daughter had. I was nineteen and I didn't give a shit. I had barely graduated high school and had done nothing but get into trouble since. She wanted to pay for me to go to college but I wouldn't even consider it. I was in the band at the time and I was sure we were going to make it big. Don't know why I ever thought that. We never rehearsed. I spent my time drinking and being with girls, and I started getting tattoos. I would stay out all night. I know I worried her." He hesitates for a minute. I don't know if he's going to continue. He clears his throat. "I started doing drugs. I was becoming just like my mother and it killed her to see it."

I put both of his hands in mine and squeeze them.

"One night, I came home late. Almost four in the morning, and I found her." His voice cracks and he pauses, taking a measured breath. "She was lying on the dining room floor. Cold tea in a cup on the table, next to the crossword from the daily newspaper." I want to wrap him up in my arms but I'm too afraid to move, as if I'll startle him like a wild animal and he'll run away. "I was out. High. And she died alone. I should have been there. She deserved better."

I lunge for him and cradle his head to my chest. He wraps himself around me and all I can smell is his hair like rain and all I can feel is him. His legs are woven with mine, arms around my waist, his warm breath softly at my collarbone.

"It's not your fault, Cade."

He slides his nose up my neck and kisses my cheek. "I know that now. But I don't think the guilt will ever leave."

"Life's not fair. Sometimes a healthy thirty-seven-year-old man drops dead from a brain tumor and his nine-year-old daughter is furious with him because she thinks he forgot to come to her school play." I can't hold back the tear that has been welling up in the corner of my eye. I don't know how he sees it but Cade wipes it away almost immediately. "She would be so proud of you now, Cade."

He hugs me close, his lips right at my ear, "So would he."

* * *

A whistling wind hits the window panes, rattling them slightly. The room is still dark. The clock says 4:37. Other than the wind, it is silent. Cade's chest rises and falls under my cheek. His heart beats against my temple and his skin is warm and smooth. It smells clean and sweet and I can't help but run my fingertips across his torso, up over his shoulders and down his stomach to the band of his boxers. He stirs under me.

"Come here." His voice is gravelly with sleep.

I slide up to him and he holds my face in both of his hands.

"Do you realize what you just started?" A mischievous turn at the corner of his mouth.

I give him my most innocent look, batting my lashes. "Whatever do you mean?"

His smirk turns into a snarl as he grabs me by the arms and rolls me under him, practically throwing me against the mattress. He settles his hips right between my thighs and I squeeze them around him. I can feel his rather large erection pressing against my inner thigh and it sends electricity up my spine, down to my toes, and fingertips. He already has me needy, but when he kisses me, he is slow and tender. His lips are soft and not too eager. His hand slides through my hair and rests to cup the back of my neck. I want him.

I pull him to me. I want him closer. I suck hard on his bottom lip as I dig my fingers into his perfect ass, pressing his ridge harder against me. My clit zings and I can already feel the slickness inside my panties.

He smiles against my mouth. "Easy, babe. I just want to enjoy you."

I'm aching for him but how can I argue when he's being all romantic and shit? He presses kisses all along my jaw and down my neck. I'm trying to massage his back in soft circles to match his indulgent pace, but I can't help but rock against him, rutting my vee against the head of his cock.

"Christ, Hale." He is starting to sound out of breath.

"I just want you already." I'm practically begging him. I slip my hand down between us, into his shorts and when I cup his balls, a deep rumble comes from his chest. He rips off my shirt and tears my panties down to my knees as he descends on my breasts. He sucks one pink nipple into his mouth, teasing it with his glorious tongue while he rubs the other with his thumb. I am overcome by him. I still have him in my hand—he is hard but as I stroke his length he keeps growing and becomes even more rigid. I push his boxer briefs down. I am panting. He lifts his head from my breast, his lips are shiny red and swollen, his eyes filled with lust.

He kisses me firmly, our wet tongues intertwining. He gasps for air. "I need you now."

I nod back, my lips tingling.

He leans across me to get a condom out of the nightstand and I slide under him. I grab him tightly at the base of his cock. His tip is already wet with his arousal and I lick it off him. He steadies himself over me, hands on the mattress. I take his full length into my hot mouth.

"Fuuuck." He is breathless, powerless, as I suck him.

The second I let him fully out of my mouth he backs away. I'm about to protest but then he is putting on the condom and laying back over me. Our chests are heaving against one another. He caresses the side of my face with his hand, holding my chin as he kisses my lips. Then he kisses the tip of my nose and my forehead. I look into his steady blue eyes as he is looking into mine. The room is again silent except for pounding in my ribs and echoing in my ears. His hips are snug between my legs and he seems to barely move but he is entering me. My legs fall to the side and he pushes even deeper into me. Filling me. I let out a soft moan and I hug him to me. Full body contact, skin on skin.

And he makes love to me. Really makes love.

* * *

A door slams. Urgent footsteps. Then another door cracks.

"HALE!"

Yelling. I'm groggy.

"HALE!" Again with the yelling. A deep voice. "HALEY!" He's scared. What? I think I yell back in response, but I am actually still asleep. Still unable to speak, or move, or process what is happening.

"HALEY!" The voice is louder. Closer.

I recognize it.

Then my eyes explode open.

Cade is face-down asleep next to me. Peaceful.

"HALEEEY!" The yelling is right outside the door.

It's Tuck.

I glance at the clock. As the numbers come into focus, so does the realization of what is happening. A sickening fear sinks through my body like when you know you're about to crash—you can see it happening perfectly in slow motion but can't do anything to stop it. I shake Cade awake. He forces one eye open, cringing against the morning light.

I'm frantic. "It's Tuck! I was supposed to pick him up from the airport an hour ago."

It takes a second for my words to register but when they do, Cade shoots out of bed, pulling his boxers on. I sit up, looking around for my clothes.

The door bursts open. "Cade! Haley hasn't been answering her ph—"

I'm paralyzed as Tuck's eyes lock instantly with mine.

Crash.

CHAPTER 19

Tuck looks at me, then to Cade. At first he is silent, but I can see it building in him. His chest puffs up and his hands become fists at his sides. Clenched. Shaking.

"Tuck—" I start to say, but he doesn't hear me. His eyes are fixed on Cade in a stare meant to murder. He takes a menacing step toward him.

"My sister!" He looks like he is searching for a punching bag. "You fucking promised me!"

"Man, it's not like that—"

"Don't say a fucking word." Tuck backs Cade against the wall. He towers over him, arms tensed.

"Tuck, just listen!" I am yelling but he doesn't notice. I want to run up to them and stop this. I want to calm Tuck down. I want to protect Cade. But I'm sitting here, trapped in the bed, covers clinging to my chest. Completely naked and helpless.

"That's my baby sister in your bed!" Tuck is flushed, neck strained, veins throbbing. Cade has his hands up, trying to mollify him but Tuck is inconsolable. He shoves Cade hard into the wall.

"You don't understand. I lo—"

Tuck grabs Cade by the neck and raises his fist to Cade's face.

"NO!" My scream is deafening.

Tuck stops his fist just in front of Cade's nose. "I trusted you." Tuck looks as though he is going to break into tears. He doesn't look at me, but he finally addresses me through gritted teeth. "Haley. Get out. Now."

"No." No fucking way.

Cade is up against the wall, he and Tuck are eye-to-eye. Tuck is fuming, and Cade looks like he is preparing to take a serious beating. I can feel Tuck's wrath. He's radiating hatred and the whole room is pulsating red.

Cade's eyes lock with mine. Soft blue. Sad. "Haley," he says to me calmly, "go."

He gives me a reassuring nod but I don't want to obey. His eyes are pleading with me. I wrap the comforter around myself and walk past them in silence, never breaking eye contact with Cade. His eyes follow me to the door, the most lost look on his beautiful face. Tuck has his back to me. I don't know what to say.

* * *

I have been sitting on my bed for what seems like hours. Maybe it has only been minutes. I don't know. When I came in here, I put on the first thing laying on top of my hamper, pacing my floor like a lunatic. Frantic thoughts filling my head.

What are they doing?

Is Tuck going to hurt Cade?

Oh my god, this is all my fault. I should have told Tuck earlier. Explained. I can still explain. He will understand. I will make him understand. It will be okay. Everything will be okay.

But now, I don't know. I don't know anything. At first, there was yelling. Then muffled voices. Now, silence. It's been quiet for a while. I have been staring at the same imaginary spot on the back of my door since the stillness came. Sitting with Cade's comforter around me. Waiting.

The door opens.

Cade appears in the doorway. He is dressed.

I have never felt so relieved in my life. I jump off the bed and run to him, arms open. I just want to hold him against me, apologize for Tuck's awful behavior, and feel his warmth.

But as I reach him and try to throw my arms around him, he catches them in both of his hands, holding them firmly at my sides—and away from him.

He barely looks at me. "We need to talk."

A wave of ice-cold dread falls through my body from the center of my skull to the heels of my feet.

We sit across from each other on my bed. Cade keeps his distance.

"Haley." He looks right at me. His perfect pink lips in a pout, almost quiver. A little line forms between his eyebrows. He swallows like his throat is constricted. "It's over."

What? I want to respond but I can't. I can't speak. I can't move. I can't think. What does he mean 'it's over?'

I don't know if it's the way I'm looking at him or if he's trying to hide his own face, but he looks away. "It was never going to work between us. I'm sorry I put you through this."

What. The. Fuck. Is. Happening?

I snap out of my stupor.

"No." I shake my head. I do not accept this. This is not over. "I will talk to Tuck. It will be fine. I promise."

"It doesn't matter. He's right. I'm not good enough for you."

"He said that?"

Cade doesn't respond. He just looks down. "He knows who I really am."

"The fuck he does. If he knew you like I do, he wouldn't think that. Ever."

Cade is quiet for a minute. Studying something on the wall before he looks back at me. His eyes wrench my stomach. "Do you know why I've never kept a girlfriend?"

"Cade, I don't care—"

"Because I've never been faithful." He face has become like stone. Jaw clenched. But his eyes might as well be bleeding.

"Your past doesn't matter to me, Cade. I know who you are, now."

"I'm a selfish prick. I am no good for you." He says it with such conviction. He truly believes what he is saying. "It's better this way. I only ever hurt the people I love." He gets up to leave, turning for the door. I grab his hand before he is out of reach. He is still turned away from me, but he grasps my hand, tightly.

"I know you've screwed up, but you're not that guy anymore."

He runs his other hand through his hair, gripping his fingers in it like he is going to rip his scalp off. He squeezes my hand. It shakes as he speaks. "I meant it when I said I hoped you would be with a guy who would treat you the way you deserve. That guy just isn't me."

"Why? Who says it's not?"

"It's just not."

We stand there, holding hands, desperately, for another minute. Then he lets go. And leaves. He doesn't look back. My eyesight starts to blur and I can feel the tears trembling in my lids.

I am stunned. I am looking through my open door. Where he just...left.

Cade left. He left me. I still don't understand what happened. This can't be real.

I hear the front door slam. Then it sinks in—Cade is leaving. Right now he is leaving. No! I won't let this happen. I need to fight.

I run out of my room and around to the front door. I can see the back of Cade's black leather jacket through the window outside on the porch. He's right there. Just on the other side of the door. He's still so close to me. I need to get to him. I grab the door handle just as two large hands fasten around my waist. Tuck pulls me away from the door. I twist and writhe away from him, prying his fingers off me and this time I get a good grip on the lever. I can see Cade walking down the front path toward his car parked on the street.

"Cade!" I scream at him. "Wait!"
This time Tuck wraps both of his arms around my waist and pulls me. My whole body is up in the air as he tries to take me away from the door, but I have the handle and I'm not letting go. Tuck yanks me hard. I am kicking at him, twisting and thrashing so he will let me go.

"Stop!" I push down on the lever and when Tuck pulls me again the door swings open. Cade is at his car. "Cade, please!" The tears are streaming down like a faucet. The cold air hits the wetness on my face. I can't breathe. I kick

Tuck in the shins, scratch his arms, elbow his ribs, twist, scream. I am screaming. "Don't go!" I am sobbing. I know he can hear me. He doesn't turn around. "Please, come back."

He gets in his car.

The sobs wrack my body. I can't see him anymore. I try to cry out to him again, but the sounds that come out are undecipherable. Primal. His brake lights turn on. I am no longer fighting Tuck. Cade's shiny black car rolls forward. At first it seems to move in slow motion but then I hear the engine groan and he is gone.

I go limp. Tuck lets me go and I almost fall to the floor. I feel like crumbling in on myself, like becoming nothing but a heap of dust.

I barely register Tuck's deep voice behind me. "You'll thank me one day."

Everything that just happened condenses into a little ball in my stomach and then sets itself on fire. A white-hot rage burns in my cheeks. I turn and punch Tuck right in the neck. He doesn't move. His expression is set. I hit him again in the arm. The chest. His stomach. I punch him with both hands. I hit him as hard as I can. He doesn't move. He doesn't say anything. I don't seem to be hurting him which only frustrates me more. I want him to hurt. I want him to know what I'm feeling. That I'm breaking and he did this to me. I start screaming as I punch him.

"You had no right to do that! I HATE YOU!" Tears still streak my face and my eyes are so wet and puffy I can barely see. Tuck is a blurry punching bag. "I. HATE. YOU." I say each word with as much force as I can muster. He just takes it in silence. I am bawling and exhausted. I am weak. My hits barely make contact. Tuck picks me up and carries me to my room. I can't fight or speak. Only cry.

He lays me on my bed. I don't look at him. He leaves me alone and shuts the door behind him.

My cries have turned silent but they still wrack my body. I pull the comforter up over my face.

Cade's comforter. It smells like him.

* * *

I've been sitting here for hours. I only know this because the hazy gray sky out my window has started to dissolve into a charcoal one. My tears have stopped. I am empty. Maybe more will come tomorrow. I stare out the window. I am wrapped in his comforter. My skin feels tight where the tears have dried.

A large white tuft of snow meanders down to the ground. It glows against the black sky. Another white fluff floats down and lands on my window sill. I watch as the snow wisps across my window. It falls slowly. Silently. Peacefully.

The snow has stopped. The dusting of white on the ground reflects the light from the moon. Beyond the white, there is only black. Only black.

I have not slept. Have I even blinked? Surely I have. I cannot recall.

I look away from the window for the first time all day. My neck is tight and aches when I turn. The clock says 3:22. It's 3:22 in the fucking morning. Less than twenty-four hours ago Cade and I were in his bed, making love. My eyes are sore. My back is stiff and my ass is asleep. Good for it. Maybe I should try to get some sleep too.

The idea of sleep, of going away for a while sounds wonderful. But I can't. I lay down and instantly the aloneness hits me. I close my eyes and I see him. I wonder where he is. What he's doing. What he's thinking, how he's feeling. I have to open my eyes again to get the thoughts to go away. I sit up. I need to focus on something else.

I am staring out the window again.

The clock says 5:19.

I get up and go to the bathroom. I don't look at myself in the mirror.

When I step out into the hall, I am face-to-face with his door. I open it. There is his bed, stripped of the comforter, everything else is the same. Nothing out of place.

I drag his comforter from my room and crawl onto his bed. I curl in a ball and cocoon the comforter around me. It smells like body wash and running water and his skin... And I sleep.

CHAPTER 20

My eyelids flutter against the bright sunlight on my pillow. I inhale deeply. Cade. Cade's pillow. It's soft and wraps my face in his glorious scent. I stretch across the bed, expecting to feel him next to me. The bed is empty, but I hear a noise coming from the kitchen. He is making us food, of course. I smile into the mattress and open my eyes.

Then it hits me. It's two in the afternoon because I've slept all day. Because I didn't sleep all night. Because he's gone. I'm alone. And he's not coming back.

* * *

I only sleep with that comforter for the next two weeks. I don't do much of anything else.

The mornings are the worst. That second when I first wake up and I don't feel the hurt. Then it comes back all at once.

The smell of him all around me, as I lie in his bed, is simultaneously soothing and devastating.

The thought of food makes me want to vomit.

I don't go to classes. I might have missed a quiz. I don't

care.

I manage to finish and email in two papers that are due before the break. They are terrible. I get Cs on both.

I don't talk to Tuck.

The comforter doesn't smell like him anymore.

I miss him. Both of them.

* * *

The drive to Grandma Netty's house for Thanksgiving is long and silent. I stare out the window and Tuck keeps his eyes straight ahead, jaw set, one hand on the steering wheel and the other resting lightly on his knee.

Grandma Netty is our dad's mom. I call her Nenee. She insisted we come to her house. It will be the first time the whole family is together since I started college. And since Mom started dating Gary.

Ugh. Gary. He's not a bad guy or anything, he's just… so…blah. His personality is beige. And his two kids are so weird. God, I hope they won't be there. Mom's oblivious to my feelings about him, just as she is oblivious to most of my feelings or anything going on in my life. Not that she asks.

The only person I am here for is Nenee. She reminds me of Dad. Always smiling and willing to throw in her opinion—asked for or not. She smells like coffee and cinnamon and face powder.

When we arrive, I hop out of the truck and Grandma Netty is already hugging Tuck around the waist tightly. She barely comes up past his bellybutton. She makes him bend down so she can smack a kiss on both of his cheeks. When I come around the truck, she pulls me in with her. There's no use protesting, even though I do not want to hug Tuck.

TO BE YOUR GIRL

My face is smashed against his side and he puts his arm around me. It's the first time we've touched since I literally tried to beat the shit out of him.

When we go inside, the most wonderful smells of turkey and butter and gravy fill the house and I wish the smells could take me back in time. Back to the memories they evoke of me running around in my new polka dot dress, hair a jungle of curls, one shoe missing to who-knows-where.

"Oh, hey, guys." Mom acknowledges us but she doesn't get up from her seat next to Gary.

Gary pushes his glasses up his long, straight nose. "Hello." Then he turns back toward Mom. I don't know how he manages to be so boring and get on my nerves just sitting there. Thankfully, it appears his kids are staying with their mother.

Nenee asks me to help her finish the pies while the others watch football. I try to roll out some dough, but I feel lethargic. And it's so stiff and hard to roll. Nenee takes over and I sit down at the counter, but not before she clicks her tongue at me, her light gray curls staying unnaturally still atop her head as she charges her large rolling pin forth.

"What's going on, young lady?"

"Nothing, Nenee. I'm just burned out from school."

She transfers the dough to a pie plate and then places one flour-covered hand on her hip. "Like hell. You never have trouble with school." She points at me. "And you have never not gotten along with your brother."

I rear my head back. "How did you know?"

"Oh, I could tell the second you two arrived something wasn't right. Now, spill it."

So I tell her. I tell her about Cade. And I tell her about Tuck.

RAE KENNEDY

She listens to me quietly as she fills the pies to the brim, covers them with more dough, crimps, the edges, and cuts three slits into each top.

It takes me three pies worth to finish talking.

She shakes her head slowly. "You're a grown-ass woman. Don't let your brother interfere with your love life. If you want this young man, go get him. But make up with your brother. Family is family."

She's right. Like always. As I sit and think about it, I realize how exhausting it has been being mad at Tuck. And I can't ignore the thought that has been a constant sting in my head the last two weeks—Tuck told Cade to leave, but Cade is the one who left.

* * *

Just before dinner, I sneak into the bathroom. I call Cade. It goes to voicemail. I hang up. I text him instead. I sit on the edge of the tub bouncing my knee erratically waiting for a response. Nothing. I keep waiting. Staring at my phone. I have now been in the bathroom an unusually long amount of time and I am risking drawing attention to myself. I half expect Grandma Netty to come knocking on the door any second to see if I need any Dulcolax. Still no reply.

So I go downstairs to the table just as everyone else sits and Nenee places the steaming bowl of mashed potatoes next to the turkey.

As Tuck carves the huge bird, a little buzz vibrates against my leg. I slide my phone out of my pocket, keeping it hidden under the tablecloth and try to discreetly look at the screen.

Cade: *I just can't*

It's like a bowling ball smashes my chest.

The food gets passed around and I fill my plate with the standard expectation. I move the food around a bit, finally taking a bite of turkey. I know it is delicious and juicy but it might as well be sandpaper in my mouth. I push my plate away. Nenee notices.

My mother hasn't stopped talking about her and Gary's upcoming cruise. "The kids are so excited about the Bahamas but it will be weird to be somewhere tropical for Christmas—"

"You're going to be gone for Christmas?" I hadn't been paying attention.

"Mmhmm." She nods happily and keeps talking about their off-ship excursion plans.

Another soft buzz resonates in my lap. I take a deep breath and look down.

Cade: *I miss you too*

I'm lightheaded and there's a stinging in my eyelids that I need to get a hold of.

"May I be excused?"

Mom stops rambling to glance over at me. "Oh, don't be silly, Haley. We just barely started eating—"

"Yes, you may," Nenee chirps in, giving me a sharp nod.

* * *

The ride home so far has been just as silent as before. I'm trying to think of what to say. I don't think I owe him an apology. An explanation? Probably. Everything I think feels weird in my mouth and I can't get the words out.

Tuck lets out a long sigh. I look over at him. He looks tired. I realize he's hurting too. However misguided, he loves me. And I told him I hated him.

"You know I don't hate you, right?" Those are the first words I've spoken to him in twelve days.

He turns his head toward me. A small, relieved smile turns at the corners of his mouth and suddenly some tension in his forehead that I hadn't noticed was there disappears.

"I know, sis."

"I still don't think you had any right to do what you did. You're not Dad."

His face hardens. I know that jab was low. But he stays calm.

"Hale, don't get me started on Cade. You don't know the half of it."

"I know all I need to. Anyway, that doesn't matter when you care about someone."

Tuck is still for a minute.

"You two weren't just screwing?" His face twists as he says it.

My eyes bulge wide at his words. "Yeah, because that sounds like me, right?"

"No, I guess it doesn't."

"You guess?"

"But he's still not good enough for you."

"That is not your decision to make," I snap back.

"You're probably right, but that's not how I felt in the moment." He sighs heavily. "I'm sorry for how I handled it."

I stare at the phone in my lap. Only a black screen since Cade's last text.

* * *

When we get home, I go to crawl into Cade's bed. I open his door and I'm blindsided. His bed is gone. His desk, his dresser, his pictures...all gone. The emptiness of the room rivals how I feel inside. Just when I thought I couldn't get any hollower.

I sleep in his room on the floor all the same.

When I wake up in the morning, my shoulder is stiff and there's a crick in my neck but I don't care. I grab my phone and then I see it.

A missed call. From Cade.

He called me last night at 2:06 am. My heart is racing, and my cheeks are hot. My fingers are shaking and feel like they are not attached to my brain as I hit the return call button on the third try. I bring my phone to my ear, holding my breath.

CHAPTER 21

Sitting alone on the floor in Cade's room, I am keenly aware of the sound of my breathing as I wait for the phone to connect.

Why did he call? What is he going to say? What am I going to say?

A high-pitched tone sounds in my ear followed by a pleasant robotic female voice stating that the number dialed is no longer in service. I'm confused. I recheck the number. It's correct. I send Cade a text asking if he reconsidered my request to talk. I get an error message back. It didn't go through either.

I officially no longer have Cade's number.

* * *

Monday rolls around and I tell myself I only have two weeks left in the semester. I can power through. Focus. On anything but Cade. Finals will suffice. I go to every class and take diligent notes. I am now a robot. When I get home, Tuck is there already. With Court. This is new.

They are sitting on the couch and she jumps up and

runs over to me. She gives me the biggest, tightest hug ever.

"How are you doing?"

Ah, the dreaded question. The very reason I refused any visitors during my two-week pity party with Cade's comforter. But she has the most sincere look of concern in her eyes that she instantly melts my guard. That's the thing with Court, she truly cares. When she listens, she's not just waiting for her turn to speak. She is a true friend and suddenly I am overwhelmed by her support. Tears bubble up.

"Let's go sit." She ushers me over to the couch.

Tuck stands. "I'm going to go get us some food. What do you want?"

"Oh." Court scrunches up her nose and bites her lip. "I could go for some chow mein right about now."

"Chinese? Does that sound good to you, Hale?"

It doesn't.

"Sure."

Tuck leaves and Court and I talk. About nothing in particular. It feels good.

Tuck comes back with the food and we all sit and talk. Well, Tuck and Court seem to be doing most of the talking but it is still keeping my mind preoccupied and I'm thankful. I manage to take a few bites of sweet and sour pork and even steal a piece of Tuck's beef and broccoli. He must have said or done something hilarious that I missed because Court is rolling around in a fit on the floor, laughing hysterically.

Tuck is laughing too. I'm glad they amuse each other, at least. Then Court, laughing so hard, snorts. Like really loud. This makes Tuck bust up and she is still unable to stop her fit, silently shaking her head and holding her hand to her tummy. I'll admit the scene makes me a chuckle a bit too.

In the morning, I actually wake up feeling starved. As I rummage through the kitchen, Tuck comes out, dressed in his suit and tie. Since I haven't been eating much lately, and Cade usually did the grocery shopping, we have next to nothing to eat. Also, our cookware (or should I say, Cade's cookware) is now severely depleted. There's not even a frying pan. This is what I'm lamenting to Tuck when he hands me his credit card and tells me to get anything we need for the kitchen.

That afternoon, after class, I buy the cheapest, most non-Cade-like cookware I can find.

* * *

Over the next week, things slowly start to feel a little more normal. I go to classes. I study and try not to stress about finals coming up next week. Tuck is home all the time. Court comes over almost every evening for dinner and stays until bedtime. Each morning when I wake up the day feels a little less heavy than the one before, like I can stand straighter, and it's okay to smile and not be sad. It helps that the gray skies have miraculously given way to bright blue and rays of sunshine to lift my mood as well. Court has even succeeded in getting me to agree to attend the end-of-semester party at her place.

I wake up Sunday night with a prickly throat. I better not be getting fucking sick right before finals week. I sleepily pad down the hallway to get a glass of water, but before I turn from the hall, I hear Tuck and Court whispering. She's here late.

I halt when I hear his name.

"Is it true that Cade is dating Mary Thompson?"

I peek around the corner.

Tuck sort of shrugs. "Is that what she's saying?"

"Yeah, she told everyone in our study group this weekend."

"I know he's gone out with her a couple of times in the last week, which is…unusual for him."

There is a sudden pang in my chest. Cade's dating someone? Actually dating? Was it that easy for him to move on? To forget about me?

"I've already invited her to our party on Friday. I just got Haley to agree to go."

"We're not on the best terms right now, but I'll see what I can do."

"Thanks."

I go back to bed but I only seem to be able to toss and turn.

* * *

I try my best to push thoughts of Cade and his new girlfriend out of my head and focus on school. I've never been so grateful for such challenging exams—they are graciously taking up most of my brain-power. But as the week comes to a close and I turn in the last test to my professor Friday morning all of the bad thoughts come right back to the forefront.

What if he is at the party tonight? Will he acknowledge me? Ignore me? Be so crazy infatuated with this new girl to even care?

My nerves are getting the best of me as I get ready

at Court's place. The boys are busy setting up the keg and tables and shot glasses while Court does my makeup and insists I wear one of her super tight dresses. By the time the first partygoers start trickling in the door, I look gorgeous (toot, toot) and Court hands me a shot of tequila to calm my nerves.

I look in the mirror. Court put me in a deep plum dress that hits me at mid-thigh—she's so much taller than me I wonder how the dress even manages to cover her bum. My hair twists into soft curls past my shoulders and the dark liner makes the glints of gold stand out in my light brown eyes. Ready or not, here we go.

We down our second shots together and start coughing, which kind of turns into giggling.

"Hey!" Court has to speak loudly over the speakers that have just been blasted on. "Are you excited this damn semester is finally over?"

"Hell yes."

"Then let's go celebrate!"

And with that, we step out of Court's room and into the party. The living room is already starting to fill up and Nick meets us with two more shots.

* * *

Court, eternally the social butterfly with an endless list of friends (not-to-mention the ever-hopeful males on her dance card), is understandably busy through the evening. I see her mingling through the groups of people and getting swept up into endless conversations.

Nick has been entertaining me and a couple of other people with stories of the many ways he and his brother got in trouble growing up. He is very animated, especially a bit inebriated. Jake hands me another drink and I realize I am having a pretty good time.

Court runs up to me, a little flushed, huge grin on her beautiful face.

"How are you doing? Having fun?"

Nick steps over, putting his arm around my shoulders. "Of course she's having fun. She's been hanging out with me."

He gives me a nudge and Court nods. "Good." And she's back to entertaining her throng of admirers.

Nick still has his arm around me. He finishes the beer in his other hand and sets it hard on the counter. "Hey, you wanna dance or what?"

"Sure."

We dance to a few songs—the blaring hip-hop beats overpowering and shaking the floor. We are dancing close but he doesn't try any grab-ass shenanigans, which I appreciate. He has a huge smile and is making me laugh by mouthing all the lyrics to songs and busting out some seriously old-school dance moves that weren't even cool when they were cool. I finally need some air so we make our way back to the kitchen.

"You want another drink? A shot?"

"No, thanks." I'm plenty tipsy as it is. "I'm good."

"Okay." Nick goes about making himself a drink as Caleb and a few other guys come in. They all start talking about guy stuff—sports and cars and boring. So I step out. I notice out the window that it has begun to snow. I'm suddenly reminded of the last time it snowed—the day Cade left. That was almost a month ago.

It's almost midnight and I'm thinking about calling it a

night. Then I hear it. Just a little chuckle. It's from across the room and I can't see its owner, but I would recognize it anywhere, even covered and distorted by loud music and forty other voices.

It's Cade's deep little laugh.

It's like I'm in a trance being pulled toward it. A bug flying into the blue light that will zap the life out of it. And even though, unlike the bug, I realize it might kill me, I can't stop it. I wander through the crowd searching for him.

And then I see him and stop. He is sitting in the corner, very cozy with a cute blonde, big tits. And they are laughing. She has her hand on his thigh, really high up on his thigh.

A sharp pain jabs in my stomach. I can't stop staring. I can see his perfect profile, the bump in his nose, soft lips, hard jaw as he lowers his face to hers and whispers something in her ear. She closes her eyes and giggles, bringing her hand up to his cheek. And then she kisses him. Right on the lips they are kissing and he is kissing her and I am not breathing.

I can't breathe.

I feel like I am gasping for air, my throat is closing up. My chest is heaving. All around me are drunk people having fun, dancing, and laughing while my world is coming apart.

Cade is kissing her. *My Cade.*

I need to get out of here.

I don't even think. I just turn to run in the opposite direction to get away from him as fast as I can. Right now there is no one I want to see less than Cade Renner.

I run right smack into a firm chest and almost fall back on my ass. I look up. Correction—there is someone I want to see less than Cade and it is the person standing in front of me. Adam.

"Well, looky here." His breath smells like cheap beer. I definitely need to go home. "Hi."

"You look hot."

I know. Thanks. Bye.

I roll my eyes and step around him to leave but he grabs my arm. "I've missed those pouty lips of yours."

Oh God, fuck off.

"Please let go of me, Adam."

He doesn't. "Hey, you know I'd be willing to throw you another bone, for old time's sake if you want." His eyes are a little glassy and they dart down to my mouth and then my cleavage as he licks his lips.

"Um, no. Now let go."

His grasp on my arm starts to get a little tighter—it's on the verge of hurting and I look around for someone I know through the crowd.

"Oh, come on. You owe me a round two considering how lousy last time was."

Then I don't see or hear him, but I feel him behind me. Cade grabs Adam's wrist and applies pressure with his thumb, Adam immediately lets go of my arm and rubs his wrist with his other hand, obviously in pain.

"What the hell, man?"

"Fucking leave. And never touch or speak to her again." Cade's face is hard, but he puts a gentle hand on my arm and steps between me and Adam. He whispers the next part. "And I don't know about your problems in the bedroom, but they must be coming from your end because she's the best I've ever had."

"Oh, you had her?" Adam's smirk is wicked. "The repressed ones are the best, aren't they?" He looks over Cade's shoulder to me. "Thanks for that text practically begging me to come do you. It earned me an extra grand."

"You better stop talking right fucking now," Cade says through clenched teeth. His body is rigid.

Adam doesn't seem affected by Cade's tone and says, louder than he needs to, "Did she moan pretty for you too?"

Cade punches him square in the jaw, sending him to the floor.

"Whoa!" Nick calls out. He and Caleb are instantly between them.

"You stay out of it," Cade spits at Nick. What's that about?

Nick and Caleb have to hold Adam at bay as he is desperately trying to get back at Cade. Cade just stands still. Eyes fixed on Adam, hands ready in fists at his sides. Steady.

Court runs up to us, and her eyes go wide as she looks between Adam and Cade. "What the hell? Who even invited you?" She gives me a horrified look. "Get out of my house. Both of you!"

Cade turns to leave. Our eyes meet for a second, his mouth twitches like he wants to say something, but he doesn't. He walks past me toward the door as Adam shakes off Nick and Caleb.

"Fucking fine with me," Adam says as he leaves after Cade, but his face is still twisted. In a fraction of a second, he thrashes his almost empty beer bottle against the wall and lunges at Cade's back with the mangled glass weapon.

It happens in slow motion. I scream out and dive toward Cade. I reach for him just as the broken bottle makes contact with my arm. I don't feel it but I can see it slice my skin. The room is silent. I look at my arm—the white line goes from wrist to elbow. Then the white line turns red. Red starts to ooze from the cut.

"Oh shit, I'm sorry, Haley!" Adam actually sounds sincere. The look on his face is panicked.

The blood starts to gush. Cade turns around, realizing what happened.

I'm feeling a little queasy watching my arm covered in surging blood. Cade rips off his shirt and wraps my arm with it. I can see the dark crimson starting to seep through his white shirt already and my head feels like it's floating away from my body.

I almost don't notice when he scoops me up in his arms. Then we are outside. I'm starting to feel fuzzy. I can remember a shirtless Cade, carrying me in the snow, only the streetlights shining off his bare chest as the snowflakes melt against his skin.

Then I remember being in his front seat. He looks upset. He says something I can't make out.

It's dark in the car. I remember the knobs on his radio, the glow of the green lights in his dashboard.

The snow outside is heavy.

A bright light in my eyes.

Screeching.

Being jarred and jerked.

Cade screaming my name.

CHAPTER 22

My eyes try to open but they feel glued shut. I hear shuffling around me, a steady beeping near my head. I feel a thin blanket over me and a pain in my hand when it twitches. There's a metallic taste in my mouth. I can't move. I fall back asleep.

* * *

My eyelashes flutter again. This time I can sense light behind my eyelids, off-white, and shadows moving. I can hear them. They sound like they are far away or under water.

"...she's very lucky...Mr. Renner is in room 305... He won't be there much longer..."

Mr. Renner? Cade? I try to shoot up. I want to jump out of this bed. But I can't. I think I manage to move a leg and groan a little.

* * *

Cade? It's the first thing I remember thinking before my

eyes finally open. I am in a hospital bed. The room is all beige and yellowed, bumpy ceiling tiles. I turn my head and see gauzy tan curtains over the window, letting in a hazy, filtered light. Then I see Tuck, sitting by my side, his eyes tired and anxious.

"Hi, sis." He smiles the sweetest, most relieved smile at me. He looks like he just let out a breath he had been holding in for a week.

"What happened?" My voice comes out all weird and foreign to me. It sounds like I've smoked a pack a day for the last forty years.

"You and Cade were in a car accident—"

I sit up stalk-straight. My heart is a heavy thud in my chest. "Where's Cade? Is he okay?" My breath is shallow and my head hurts and I'm starting to feel dizzy again.

"Lie down." Tuck tries to calm me, his hands on my shoulders but I can't lie back down.

Where is Cade? What happened? I can't get enough air in my lungs. Get me out of here.

"Hale, relax." Tuck is up, physically restraining me. "Cade is fine." I feel my heart start to beat slower, but still on high alert. "The accident itself was actually pretty minor, thank God. But the front axle was dented. Cade couldn't drive it and you lost a lot of blood while waiting for the emergency responders."

"Oh."

I am trying to put together the events of the evening, but it is so slippery at the end—the details keep disintegrating as I try to recall them.

A doctor walks in, takes out my chart and flips through a couple of pages, looking up over his glasses at me. He has kind, light gray eyes with lots of laugh crinkles around their edges.

"I'm glad to see you're awake. How are you feeling?"

"A little lightheaded."

"That's to be expected. You lost a lot of blood, and it looks like you're also a bit anemic so your reaction was even more severe than anticipated." He writes a few things down on my chart, then smiles as he puts it away. "Your vitals are looking good. We will probably keep you here one more night for observation, but if things continue to go well, you'll be discharged in the morning."

"Okay, thank you."

"No need. You should thank that young Mr. Renner. It sure is a good thing he was here." And with that, he turns and leaves the room.

"What did he mean by that?"

Tuck looks like he is deciding what to say when we hear muffled voices outside the door. There is a quiet knock. It cracks open and Cade is there—holding a small bouquet of orange tulips.

My chest tightens.

He and Tuck make eye contact, giving each other the slightest of nods. Tuck stands, clears his throat, and goes toward the door as Cade walks in. He gives Cade a solid clap on the shoulder as they pass, exchanging another look but not saying a word.

My eyes follow him as he places the flowers on the small table next to the window and sits. He puts his elbows on his knees, resting his chin on his knuckles. I can't stop staring at him. He is looking at me too, with his heavenly blue eyes. My pulse quickens and I can hear the beeping behind me pick up slightly. I wonder if he notices it too.

After an awkwardly long few seconds of just looking at

one another, Cade says, "Hi."

"Hi." I return. I don't know what to say. "Um...thank you...for..." For...I'm not sure how to finish that. For taking me to the hospital? But we got into the accident and he didn't actually take me to the hospital...

"It was no big deal. Really, I've done it so many times."

"Take bleeding girls to the hospital?" Now, I'm confused.

"Oh, no. Uh, I mean donating blood."

"You donated blood? For me?"

"Yeah." He waves it off. "Like I said, it was no big deal." He gives me a tight smile and looks away, clearing his throat.

"Cade?"

He turns back to me.

I almost startle to see the sorrow so clearly pouring out of his eyes. "What happened?"

He takes a long breath.

"The roads were icy. As we passed through an intersection, a car coming from the other side couldn't stop. They slid right into the front of my car, on the driver's side." He's looking past me as if he is seeing it happen again. "It wasn't that bad, but...then we were stuck. And you were losing so much blood. You were so white. I've never felt so helpless." He swallows hard, his eyebrows furrowing into a pained expression. "I've never been so terrified in my life."

I smile at him, trying to relax him a little. I can't tell if it works.

"We finally made it here and then, ha!" He throws his head back and rakes his hands through his hair. "They call this a hospital? It's a glorified doc-in-the-box. They have no trauma ward and with the shortages, they didn't have enough blood!"

"They didn't?"

He shakes his head. "Did you know your blood type is O-negative?"

"No." Then I remember. "Just like yours, right? The universal donor."

"Yeah, that's the good thing about O-negative. The bad part is O-negative's can only receive other O-negative blood. They didn't have very much on hand. They gave you what they had but were going to have to life-flight you into the city. But then…" He chokes up a bit but then waves it off, putting on a smile for me again. "You know what, never mind. You're here and you are going to be fine and that's all that matters."

"Cade. Tell me."

His jaw clenches and his foot taps quickly on the floor. He gulps and clears his throat but his voice still comes out a little shaky. "I heard a nurse say she didn't think you'd be able to make the flight." He blinks rapidly and lets out a heavy breath.

I'm frozen. Eyes wide. Mouth open.

"It was a no-brainer. I made them take my blood."

All of my breath exits my lungs. It comes out sounding like a whimper. Cade takes my unencumbered hand in both of his.

"I'm so sorry." His face contorts as he tries to find words. "I'm sorry I was such a coward when I broke it off. I just want to be with you." He's searching my face for my reaction.

I want to reach for him, feel him in my arms, yell hallelujah, and take him back instantly. But then I get the flashback of him walking out my door. Not turning back. Then of him kissing that girl at the party.

I'm tired of not being in control of my life. He doesn't get to suddenly decide when it's okay to be together. And neither does Tuck.

"No."

His entire face and shoulders fall. Broken. "What?"

"You left. You just left me. I wasn't worth fighting for."

"You are. I just didn't know how."

I'm fighting back tears. "I don't buy it."

"I...it's hard to ex... I don't know how to make you understand." He looks lost. "Tuck is the brother I never had. I was still trying to figure things out when we met. Then he took me in, kept me straight. He's just always been so...put together. Honest. Loyal. And the one thing he asked when you moved in was to not fuck with you."

"Were you just fucking with me?"

He winces at my words, but says resolutely, "No."

"What about that girl at the party. Aren't you dating her?"

He looks a little confused and then straightens. "No. I mean she keeps inviting me to things, but no."

"You were kissing her."

He nods, his jaw clenching again. "I saw you hanging all over Court's roommate and I got pissed. I'm sorry."

"It's not good enough, Cade." I feel a tear hit my cheek and I am so mad at my stupid body for betraying me.

"I know. Fuck. I know I don't deserve another chance. But I need it. I promise I'll never let you down again." He's practically begging and I feel another tear fall. I have to stay strong. I will not be mistreated. Not by him, or any man. Ever again.

"Cade, I...I was just starting to feel normal again." I am nowhere close to normal yet. He's looking at me and I can see his eyelids start to quiver as his eyes become glossy. I wipe two more tears from my cheek. "You were right before. You'll only hurt me in the end."

A single tear spills over from his crystal blue eye and hits his smooth cheek. "Haley, please."

I pull my hand away from him and cover my eyes. It's all I can do to hold it together. The tears start to become uncontrollable.

"Please leave." I can't do this anymore. I can't see him, hear him, be near him. It hurts too much.

He whispers, "I love you."

I smash my hands over my eyes and roll away from him on the bed. There is a sharp pinch in my hand from the IV. I can barely push out my breath to say, "Go. Please."

And he does. It takes him a minute to get up from the chair. I can feel him stand over me. I'm grateful he doesn't say anything. I can't bear any more. His footsteps retreat to the door and as soon as it closes behind him, I let out the wail I've been holding in.

CHAPTER 23

Tuck helps me up to the house, even though I've told him I can manage. My arm has twenty-eight stitches, not my legs, I told him. But I didn't want to admit that my head is still a bit fuzzy and I feel like passing out every time I stand up too fast. So he has his arm around my middle and I don't protest too much as he helps me up the uneven steps.

"Do you need anything to eat? Drink?" Tuck asks as we step inside.

Everything looks the same, but somehow the feeling in here is different. Like I've been gone years instead of days.

"No, I just want to rest."

"Sure."

In my room, I change into my most comfortable sweats and get lost under the fluffy blankets and the smell of the freshly cleaned sheets. Tuck brings me a tall glass of water with my pain meds and watches as I take them down. I love mother-hen Tuck. Even when she hovers.

I sleep all day. And all night. I wake up and it is black outside. I pull the covers up over my cold ears and nose and roll over to continue my slumber when I hear muffled voices in the hall. Deep, male ones. It's a little late for Tuck to have someone over, especially when he has work in the morning. I'm too tired to think any more of it before drifting back to sleep.

When I wake up, the glass of water is full. Two pain pills sit beside it and a little note,

Take your pills. No arguments. – Tuck.

I roll my eyes and take the damn pills. I'm starving and I need to pee. I take care of the latter then shuffle to the kitchen, still drowsy.

The fridge is open. All I can see is his hand on the handle. I didn't realize Tuck was still here. Maybe he's going in late so he can keep an eye on me. Then I see a little of the arm attached to that hand. And the myriad of black and gray tattoos covering it.

Cade closes the fridge just as I step into the kitchen, his arms full of eggs, milk, butter, and a bunch of fresh herbs.

"Mornin,' sunshine." He flashes me a huge grin, showing off his perfectly straight white smile. "Eggs?"

I'm pretty sure I have been standing here staring at him like an idiot for an hour. Okay, maybe two minutes. And apparently, he is very amused, chuckling at me as he gets a skillet out of the drawer.

I finally clear the giant lump in my throat. "What are you doing here?"

"Right now? I'm making us some eggs." He points across the counter. "Sit."

Being so used to following his commands in the kitchen, I find myself sitting before I even realize I have obeyed.

"This"—he shakes the new skillet at me—"is a fucking piece of shit. Like, I'm going to throw it away." But he turns on the burner and cracks the eggs into the shit skillet nonetheless.

"No. I mean what are you doing here? In my house."

He looks at me, cocking his head. "What do you mean? I live here." He gives me his devilish sexy smirk and continues making us eggs.

They are fucking delicious.

When we are done, Cade stands, takes my plate and heads to the sink.

"I'll help." I go to stand but he stops me.

"I've got these. You should stay off your feet."

"Oh my gosh, boys. I'm fine." But then I buckle a little as I stand up, bracing myself with the table. Cade rushes over and steadies me.

"Come on, you should go rest."

"That's all I've been doing for the last three days. I don't want to go back to bed."

His face is close to mine, studying me. His eyes are light and clear. "Fine. But if you're staying up, you need to go change."

"Why?"

He leans in close, his warm breath at my cheek. His lips barely graze my earlobe as he speaks.

"Because. You know what these fucking sweatpants do to me."

* * *

"What the hell Tuck?" I whisper-yell at him, huddled in my room.

He chuckles at me from the other end of the phone. "So, you're not happy about Cade moving back in?"

"No! You didn't even tell me!"

"Sorry. I thought it would be a good thing."

"No, I told him at the hospital we aren't getting back together. You were right. Even though it still makes me furious, what you did. He doesn't know how to be in a relationship"

"Are you sure? I'm not so sure."

"What? Are you kidding me?"

"I think you should give him another chance."

I don't know how to respond. It's like I'm in the Twilight Zone. Tuck wants me and Cade together now?

"Gaahhh!" I hang up on him just as a knock comes at my door.

"Haley." Cade's deep voice rolls through my walls. "I'm leaving for work. Do you need anything before I go?"

I'm about to have a breakdown. "No." The floor squeaks as he shifts his weight. I hold my breath so I can hear him. After a few seconds, he walks away and then I hear the front door close.

* * *

Waking up the next morning, I need a shower. Bad.

I run the water hot and when I see steam emerging past the curtain I step in, letting the heat soak over my body and relax all of my muscles.

The bathroom door opens. I hear him walk across the floor and the ting of the toilet lid being lifted. Really? I stick my head out of the curtain and, yep. There is Cade, barebacked and all lean muscle under his tattooed skin, his ass in tight charcoal gray boxer briefs and nothing else. Goddamn his perfect little ass.

"Still trying to sneak a peek, huh?" He says over his

shoulder as he starts to pee.

Embarrassed, I retreat back into the shower. "Shut up!"

"Does that mean I get to look as well?" I can hear the devilish grin in his voice.

"No!" I don't know why my heart is beating so fast. As he leaves, he stops at the door. "Let me know if you need any help in there."

"Get out!" I know he's just being facetious but the thought does cross my mind for a second that with only one good arm, I could use some help washing my hair. But I'm not admitting that to him.

I shampoo my hair, albeit slow and inefficiently, and definitely much better on one side than the other, but I do it. See, I knew I could. But when I lean my head back to rinse out my hair, I feel like I'm spinning. My eyes can't focus and before I realize it, my tail bone hits the bottom of the tub hard with a thud and then I land on my back. Fucking ouch. It's so slippery and the water is spraying my face. I'm disoriented and not sure which way is up. My arm aches and I double-check that I didn't tear any stitches.

Cade rips the shower curtain open. "Hale! Are you okay?"

I'm lying in the shower, naked. I feel more embarrassed than injured. I meet his eyes. They are filled with worry.

"I just got a little dizzy."

He is still wearing only his tight tiny boxer briefs but he steps in quickly, and without me asking, he lifts me up. "Let me help you."

Then, without any of the cockiness or teasing he displayed just a few minutes ago, he steadies my hands on his shoulders and starts rinsing my hair. I watch his face as he massages his fingers into my scalp and then runs his fingers through my hair, wringing my long locks out under the water. He is focused on his task, keeping his eyes on top of my head, not once glancing down to my bare breasts, heaving and slippery wet just inches away from his naked chest. My nipples are hard and needy, so close to him, yearning to feel the pressure of his palms against them. My heart is racing and I can feel the blood pulsating to all of my extremities.

Why does my body respond so easily to his presence?

Next, he kneads in my conditioner and when my hair is thoroughly rinsed, and his gaze returns to mine. He gives me a little smile. He reaches for the washcloth and squeezes a good amount of my peach vanilla body wash over it. He's going to wash me. I'm thankful the water is so warm it has turned all of my skin pink so he won't notice me flush.

My lips part and I try to steady my breath as he brings the cloth across my shoulders and down my arms. The cloth tickles as it brushes the insides of my elbows and wrists. His eyes are on my body, going over every inch of skin as the washcloth follows, across my chest and down between my breasts.

A small whimper escapes my lips as he brings the cloth up over my breast, cupping it with his hand and caressing over my nipple. He can surely feel my heart thumping behind it. He doesn't linger but I can tell he is affected too. He bites his plump bottom lip as he moves to wash my other breast. He sweeps the cloth down my sides and across my quivering tummy before putting more body wash on the towel. He turns the water up and it is almost too hot against my sensitive skin.

Then he drops to his knees in front of me, his face at my navel. I'm glad my hands are on his shoulders because

I'm not sure I can stand on my own. He has to notice my legs shaking as he washes the outside of my thighs, calves, and both feet. He brings the washcloth up the inside of my leg slowly. When he reaches my knee, I spread my feet just a little wider, allowing him farther up. Cade pauses for a moment but then continues, dragging his hand up the inside of my thigh.

My whole body throbs, but nothing more so than the hyperactive pulsating between my legs. My clit aches—it's almost painful. My insides are clenching as he reaches the apex of my thigh, desperate for some pressure, hoping he'll provide it. The water has soaked his boxers so they cling to his body like a second skin and I can clearly see his excruciatingly large erection between his legs. Fuck. He skims the cloth over my sex briefly on the way to the other leg, and the roughness of the terrycloth over my swollen clitoris makes me gasp and my fingers dig into Cade's shoulders.

"Sorry," he whispers.

Doesn't he know I liked it? Can't he tell I want more? Need it, even. But I know it's not right to ask him for it.

He washes the rest of me carefully, gently. When he's done, he turns off the water and wraps me in a large soft towel, drying me off quickly.

"Thank you," I mouth to him.

I hold on to his arm as I step out of the shower. He stays inside.

"Are you okay to get dressed on your own?" His face looks pained.

I nod.

"Good." His smile is tight. "I'm going to take a shower then."

I can't keep my eyes from dropping, looking at his gigantic and obviously very uncomfortable hard-on. He sees me staring and I don't do anything to mask my fascination.

"Yeah," he says, clearly addressing the elephant in his shorts. "And I'm going to take care of this."

I imagine him masturbating. Because of me. For me. His hand stroking up and down his length. The throb between my legs constricts tightly. He moves to close the curtain but I don't want him to.

"Can I watch?"

His face falls, desperate, and he clutches his stomach in agony. "Fuck, Hale." It comes out guttural.

He seems conflicted but he rips off his shorts, not being able to take it anymore. His erection springs free. He is bent over, one arm straight out, leaning against the shower wall while his other hand is firmly around the base of his engorged cock. He grunts and gasps for unsteady breath as he drives his fist up and down his erection, squeezing, pulling, rocking his hips. His arms flex under all of his black ink.

The tip of his penis is red and swollen, the skin shiny and taut—I want to touch it. But I don't. Watching him, raw, vulnerable, and so intensely overcome with sexual desire sends electric shocks up my spine and makes me lusty. I can feel my little pebble, hard and beating waves of pleasure back through my entire body. My towel drops to the floor as I touch my most sensitive spot, applying the pressure I need.

I'm openly moaning with Cade and I think I might come with him. I can tell he is getting close as his speed becomes more frantic.

He grabs the knob and turns the hot water on over his

body, and I watch him come, expelling into the water, his abs contracting as he whimpers. My release comes too. I'm barely able to stand as the sizzle under my skin starts to subside.

Then he looks at me. He's panting and spent. His eyes are so beautiful but empty. He's not embarrassed, ashamed? The hot water is streaming down his face and torso. He closes his eyes and shuts the curtain.

* * *

I've been sitting on the couch for almost an hour. I'm not sure what just happened, or what's going to happen next when Cade comes out of his room. My stomach is in a bundle.

Cade comes around the corner, dressed in a fitted black cotton shirt and gray worn-out jeans. His hair is perfectly coiffed, skin clean and glowing, and eyes bright. He looks sexier than ever.

"Hey, you," he says, smiling at me and giving my shoulder a quick squeeze as he passes me on the way to the kitchen. He smells divine.

"Hey."

He shuffles around in the kitchen, much happier after having unpacked his pots and pans.

"Are you hungry?"

I get up and walk cautiously to the counter. "I guess yeah."

He busies himself mixing up some batter for French toast. I watch as he whisks.

"Are we going to talk about what just happened?" I ask.

"Do we need to?" He's humming softly to himself as he

submerges the bread.

"Um...I think so."

"Okay."

"Okay?"

"Are you upset about it? I'm not."

"I...I just think...I don't know. It's too much. Can we just be friends?"

He puts a few pieces of the soaked bread on the hot skillet. There's a loud hiss as each slice hits the pan. Not looking up from the stove, he says flatly, "No."

"No?"

"No. I don't want to be your friend, Haley."

I reel back. The room fills with the scent of warm cinnamon.

He meets my gaze steadily. "I want to be your everything."

I have to remind myself of how he walked out of my life a month ago. Not putting up a fight when Tuck asked him to leave, not caring when I begged him to stay. I have to strengthen my wall against him. I won't let him do that to me again. "Cade, I can't..."

He flips two pieces of French toast onto the plate in front of me with a sexy smile.

"Don't worry. I can wait."

CHAPTER 24

"Get your cute little ass in here."

The contents of three sacks of groceries Cade just carried in are now strewn about the countertop as he unearths various cutting boards and cooking utensils.

"For what?" I say as I walk into the kitchen, knowing very well what he wants.

"You're going to cook with me, duh."

I scoff at him. "You are so bossy in the kitchen, you know that?"

He shrugs. "I have experience." He raises his eyebrows at me. "You've never complained about it before."

I bite the inside of my cheek. I feel us falling into our old habits again, something I've dreamt about and longed for over the last month of our separation, but now that it's happening… I just can't let it. I don't know why but my gut is telling me I have to protect myself. My brain is telling me he never actually loved me, or he wouldn't have abandoned me. But my heart is fluttering like a fucking tween with braces getting noticed by her big crush.

"Please?" he asks so genuinely I almost melt.

I slink over to where he is, and he puts me on chopping

duty with a huge grin. As he gets the rest of the dinner put together, he keeps close to me—our arms just brushing against one another. It makes the hair on the back of my neck stand on end. I know I should stop it, not lead him on. But I like it. So I don't.

After I finish chopping, he bumps me playfully with his hip and tells me to go set the table. I prepare for his customary ass-slap as I leave the kitchen, but he doesn't do it. I'm more than a little disappointed, and even more annoyed with myself for being so.

The chili needs to simmer for a while so we go to the couch to watch some television. A Christmas movie I've seen a few times. Cade leans toward me on the couch. I should probably scoot a little farther away but I don't know how to do it without being completely obvious. I don't want to hurt his feelings or give him a complex—like he smells or something. Because he actually smells really, really good.

Oh God, I've actually leaned a bit into him—you know, so I can smell him better. And then I feel his soft, warm hand lightly set on top of mine.

Shit! I pull it away quickly. *Don't lead him on, Haley. You are not getting back together.* I look over at his face and, double shit! He looks completely rejected, big blue puppy-dog eyes.

"Sorry," he whispers as he stands, rubbing the back of his neck. He goes to the kitchen and stays there until dinner is ready.

The steaming chili is hearty and thick and the cornbread smothered in butter and honey is perfectly sweet. We eat in silence.

He insists I go sit down while he does the dishes. I'm trying to think of a way to fix this. Whatever is still between us. I want desperately to either go back to just being friends or go back to being lovers. Neither is possible because we never were just friends. And I can't trust him with my heart. He comes to sit next to me again and I make sure to curl up on the opposite side of the couch.

"Give me your feet so you can lie down."

My feet? My face turns red as I think about what he did with my feet on this couch.

"Come on, Hale. No funny business, I swear." He puts his hands up in a show of good faith.

Hmm. Still not a good idea to lie down with him.

"I think I'm just going to stay over here."

"Dammit, Haley, put your fucking smelly feet in my lap. I went crazy without you for a month. At least let me have you in this way."

I'm stunned with no clue how to respond. So I put my (not) smelly feet on his lap and lie across the couch. He pulls a blanket down over me and true to his word, he does none of his hand magic. His hands are folded, resting gently on my shins as we watch the end of the movie we started earlier.

* * *

The next afternoon, Tuck calls me unexpectedly early.

"Hey, come out here and give me a hand."

The phone goes silent. Okay...

I step out the front door. There is a light dusting of white over everything from the night before, just barely sparkling as the sun peeks in and out of the clouds. Tuck's truck is parked along the sidewalk and he has his tailgate lowered. I walk down to him, the cold nipping at my ears. I pull my sweater tighter around me, wishing I had grabbed my coat.

As I reach him, Tuck is all rosy-cheeked and red-nosed in his blue beanie, pulling out a huge tree from the bed.

"Here, you take this end," he says, directing me to the tip of the evergreen, "and I'll get the trunk."

He follows me up the steps but he's probably carrying ninety percent of the weight of the tree by the time we reach the door.

Tuck gets the tree set up in the living room after moving the chair so it's awkwardly smashed in the corner. The tree is tall—almost touches the ceiling—and it has a couple of barren patches, but it is a beautiful deep hunter's green and smells like magic. I haven't had a real, live Christmas tree since I was in elementary school.

We probably spend an hour just untangling lights and giggling. Tuck makes us some spiked eggnog and I drink like half a liter even though I don't particularly care for eggnog.

We happily sift through Tuck's Christmas ornaments, all haphazardly thrown in a big cardboard box. Some I recognize from when we were growing up, but most are newer. To say the mix is eclectic is putting it lightly.

"Oh! Let me go get Cade's ornaments." Tuck retreats down the hallway and comes back with a considerably smaller box. We open it up and there are a half-dozen or so ornaments in it, all nicely wrapped in tissue paper.

I unwrap them as Tuck places them on the tree. There are a few metallic orbs, a glass reindeer, and a beautiful white ceramic angel. The last one I open is handmade in a little round metal frame with frilly red and green ribbon woven around it. In the frame is a picture of a little boy with wild blond hair and a big toothy grin. Even though he has a more rounded face, he has the same light blue eyes—bright and alive. I turn it over and on the back. Scribbled in black marker is: Cade, age 7. I find myself stroking the picture along his nose and chin, then I notice Tuck is watching me. I quickly hand him the ornament and he places it right in the front.

The front door opens, letting a crisp gust into the house.

"Hey, you guys finish without me?" Cade calls as he strides in, throwing off his coat and shoes.

"Just about," Tuck says.

Cade looks at the tree, his face wide open. "Well, the star is not on the top, so can't be done yet."

"That's all that's left."

I remember decorating the tree every year when I was little. My dad would always lift me up high so I could place the star on top of the tree. In the pictures, the star is always askew, tilted and looking like it might fall off at any second, but my parents never fixed it. They left it however I placed it and I felt so proud.

"Haley, you want to put the star on?" Cade asks me. It's like he is literally in my head.

"Uh, sure."

He hands me the glittery golden star. I definitely can't reach the top of the seven-foot tree. I look around for a chair or something I can stand on.

"Hop on." Cade hunches over, offering me a piggy-back. He doesn't wait for me to respond—he just hikes me up on his back and stands.

I can barely reach the top branch and I have to steady myself on his shoulders. I'm pressed up against his back, all strong and muscle-y, and he grips my thighs. Put the damn star on already! I place it quickly and he sets me down.

We all step back and look at the big, beautiful, mismatched tree. I'm much more particular about the star being level and plumb than I was at age six. It is decidedly leaning to the left, and it makes my eye twitch a little bit, but Cade turns to me, smiling with pure happiness.

"It's perfect," he says.

* * *

Cade is on his best behavior over the next week. He doesn't come into the bathroom while I am showering and I don't see those tight little boxer briefs again. I'm grateful not to have the temptation but also a bit disappointed. I miss our old innocent flirting and easy back-and-forth. We smile as we pass each other in the hall. We say good morning and good night. But he has been working the night shift so we don't cook dinner together and he has been going almost directly to bed when he gets home.

I find myself looking at seven-year-old Cade on the Christmas tree more often than I would admit to anyone.

But the separation is good. I hurt a little less when I think about him. When I do see him, it feels less awkward, if maybe more formal. My wall has been fortified and I know I will be okay...eventually.

Then something happens, like we shuffle past one another as he leaves the bathroom and I enter. He gives me his drop-dead gorgeous smile and his arm brushes against me as we pass. I get a hint of his clean, musky scent and I am knocked on my ass again.

* * *

On Christmas eve, I shower so I can be ready when Tuck wants to leave bum-fuck early tomorrow for Grandma Netty's house. It's already getting pretty late so I get ready for bed and head out to the kitchen for a glass of water.

Cade is in the kitchen, studying a piece of paper.

"Whatchya doin'?"

He looks up as if I startled him, then smiles. "Making cookies. You want to help?"

"Why are you making cookies?"

"For Santa, duh."

"You make cookies for Santa?"

"Every year."

"What kind are we making?"

"Sugar cookies. That's what my grandma and I always made."

"All right. What's that there?" I ask, nodding at the paper in his hand.

"My recipes. Never had Grandma's. I tweak it every year, trying to get them just right."

I look at the paper as he takes down the mixing bowls and gets out the ingredients. Indeed there are at least six different sugar cookie recipes, all with little notes scribbled around them: *too flat, needs more baking soda, too dense, less flour, too crispy, lower baking temp?* I read over all of his little notes and it makes me smile.

"Have you ever tried adding some milk? That's what my Grandma Nenee does. Just a couple of tablespoons, I think."

He looks at me thoughtfully. "I haven't. Let's give it a shot." I am impressed at how well Cade creams the butter and sugar together by hand and he compliments me on my egg-cracking skills. No shell when this lady is involved.

When Cade preps the counter to roll out the dough, flour goes everywhere. I've never seen him let the kitchen get so messy but he loves it. He lets me roll out the dough, inspecting and letting me know when it's at the perfect thickness. I have flour on my hands, elbows, pants, and hair.

I am going to need another shower.

As we are cutting the dough out with various cookie cutters—a bell, a tree, a snowman—I catch Cade watching me from the corner of my eye.

"What?"

He chuckles at me. "You have some flour"—he licks his thumb and brings it to my face—"right there." He wipes his thumb from the side of my nose across my cheek down to my jaw. He leaves it there for just a moment. My pulse is beating in my throat and I realize we are staring into each other's eyes. I break the contact and start placing cookies on the sheet.

We can't wait for them to cool completely before we each take a bite. They are heavenly, buttery and soft.

"So, how'd we do?"

Cade closes his eyes as he finishes his bite. "Pretty damn good. Not quite exactly like Grandma's." He looks at me with his handsome smile and happy eyes. "But it's the closest I've come yet."

* * *

It's already dark as we drive back home from Grandma Netty's. Everything outside is black and blue, blurring past in the periphery all around the bright glowing moon. I find myself nodding off against the window.

The truck rolls to a stop, the tires grinding in the pebbly gutter as the overhead light pings on. I shuffle up to the door, new snowflakes falling on my cheeks. When we get inside, I shrug off my coat and wet boots. Tuck sets down our gifts from Nenee: hand-crocheted dishcloths, matching blue sweatshirts with snowmen cross-stitched on the fronts, and cards each with a crisp ten-dollar bill inside.

"Okay, I'm going out. Merry Christmas."

"You're going out? Where? It's Christmas."

"I have other friends, sis." He smiles at me, his dimples deep and adorable. He kisses me on the forehead then heads out the front door, a few flurries making their way onto the tile floor.

No lights are on—only the array of tree lights shining from behind the pine needles and reflecting off the shiny gold ornaments light the living room. Cade is sitting cross-legged on the floor, in front of the tree with a huge mug in his hands. We had asked if he wanted to come with us today but he had declined. Seeing him now, sitting there alone, I wish we had insisted.

"Hey." I sit on the floor next to him.

"Hi, you. Hot chocolate?" He offers his mug to me, a hopeful smile on his lips. The way the lights throw a gentle glow on his face makes me want to reach out and touch him.

"Sure." I take the warm cup from his hands and sip the rich chocolaty drink, watching the almost-melted mini marshmallows swirl around. A satisfied hum comes from my chest as it flows down my throat and warms me from inside my belly. I take another drink as I breathe in the sweet steam. When I open my eyes, Cade's face is closer to mine.

"You going to drink all of my hot chocolate or what?"

"This isn't for me?"

"Fuck no. I was just being nice."

I hand it back to him. "Oh. Sorry."

He chuckles at me, big-ass mug in one hand as he reaches under the tree with the other. "Here. I have a present for you."

The small box is heavier than I expected. The wrapping paper is a little wrinkly and there is about three times as much tape as required holding it together. With some effort, I unwrap it only to find another fortress of tape across the box. I have to use my teeth to rip it open and Cade laughs under his breath.

Inside the box, packed in clear squishy plastic I pull out a perfectly used Nikon F SLR camera. It is just like my dad's. I turn it over in my hands, remembering the weight of it and the feel of the textured black case. It's an original and it is beautiful. And pricey.

"Wow." I stare at it a little more. "Cade, I...I can't accept this."

"What? Of course, you can. I want you to have it."

"No, it's too expensive. Too...it's just too much.

He looks offended. "Hale, if it's about money, don't –"

"No. It's...this isn't a gift just friends give."

Then he goes off. "Well, good! Because I don't want to be just friends."

I practically shove the camera into his arms as I stand up. "Please, Cade, just take it back."

He shoots up to his feet, fuming. He looks like he wants to scream, but he closes his eyes before he speaks, his jaw ticking under his skin.

"Why must you reject everything I try to give you?"

I can't respond because I am afraid my voice will crack

and tears will spill when I do.

His eyebrows furrow. "Why can't you give me another chance?"

I take a deep breath. "You. Just. Left me! I don't matter enough to you. I can't trust you." I'm barely holding it together.

"What can I do to prove to you I won't leave again? Hale, please, tell me."

I think about it for a minute. He looks heartbroken and I desperately want to give him an answer—to figure out how this can be made right, this...thing between us. I want it too, but I can't think of anything. I've built my wall tall and strong. He's made it to the top, but there's no way he's getting over.

"There isn't anything you can do."

Any hope on his face dies. I might as well have just slapped him. We stare at each other silently for a moment.

"There has to be someth—"

"No, Cade. You were right. You can't do the boyfriend thing."

His face crumbles. Just for a second. Then his jaw sets and his eyes narrow.

"Fuck it." He heads for the front door.

"See," I say over my shoulder, feet frozen, holding back the tears welling in my eyelids, "just proved me right."

The door slams shut so violently it shakes the walls and I can feel it reverberate through the floor.

I leave the camera under the tree and go right to bed. I'm so sick of this crying-myself-to-sleep bullshit.

My eyes are sore when they open in the darkness. It's 2:37. Then I hear what woke me up. An unmistakable female giggle in the hall. A rustle of clothing. Then they shut the door loudly to Cade's room.

CHAPTER 25

I didn't know it would hurt so badly. I feel like Cade has ripped all the organs out from my body one by one. I don't want to hear them. I press my face so hard into my pillow I can barely breathe.

It's 2:54. They are still in his room. Normally, I would be hearing the headboard hit the wall by now. But nothing. Then one loud hit bangs against the wall. I hold still, preparing for what will come next. I don't expect to hear the girl yanking the door open and yelling, "Thanks for the awful evening, asshole," then stomp down the hall and slam the front door.

The house is silent again.

I hear the quiet creak of my door as it swings open. Cade's silhouette leans in my doorway. I'm a mess. I want him to go away.

"Hale?" It's just a whisper.

I hold very still. Maybe if he thinks I'm asleep he will leave.

Footsteps pad across the carpet.

The bed dips behind me as he lies on top of the covers, his body molding tightly against mine. He puts his arm around my shoulder and I can feel his breath at my neck. His body is solid and warm and I love the feel of him against me. I need to ask him to leave.

I can't.

I focus on my breath, trying to keep it steady and quiet but I'm sure I'm trembling.

"I miss you so much," he whispers into my neck, so softly I can barely make it out. I'm frozen. "I haven't been with anyone since you. Fuck, I've tried. I can't. You're the only one I want."

My chest compresses. I hold my breath to keep quiet.

"If I had known the last time we were together was the last time I would get to hold you, to have you, in my bed..." He swallows hard and nuzzles into my neck. His closeness sends prickles down my spine and makes my tummy twist and flutter.

I can smell him, feel his breath, the weight of his arm around me, the heat of his body against mine. I didn't even realize how much I've wanted it. Needed it.

"I would give anything to have you like before, even for just one night," he whispers.

I'm still holding my breath.

Finally, when I need air, I blurt out, "Okay."

It comes out of my mouth so faintly, I'm not even sure I said it.

He stiffens next to me and sits up abruptly. "Sorry, I didn't mean to wake you—" He starts to scoot off the bed when he stills. "What?"

I can't turn around to face him, afraid I'll lose my nerve, but I want it as much as he does.

"I said okay. Just for tonight."

He is silent for a minute. "Are you sure?" he breathes.

"Yes," I whisper.

He stands and moves toward the door. "I'm just going to go get a—"

"No, just stay."

"What do you mean?"

Less than two weeks ago I had his blood inside of me—I'm not worried about contracting a disease. "I'm on the pill," I whisper to him. I still can't see him but I can feel him here. In the dark. His energy. His nerves. His heat.

"Oh." There's a sharp intake of breath. He shuts the door and walks back over to the side of the bed behind me. I hear him undo his belt and it hit the ground with his jeans. A couple more articles of clothing fall to the floor. Then he lifts the covers and I feel him slide in. The weight of him pulls my body back against his as he wraps his limbs around me. I'm stock still. Rigid and holding my breath. Anxious, waiting. But he just holds me there. He holds me for what feels like an hour. I start to breathe normally again.

I feel the lightest touch of his lips to the back of my neck and it makes me sigh. He gently rubs my arm as he traces soft kisses down my neck to my shoulder. Then he kisses right behind my ear, the warmth of his sweet breath giving me goosebumps. He closes his arms around me and pulls me tight to him. His skin is burning through my thin sleepwear and I feel myself sink into him.

I let go of the tension in my body and tilt my head, opening up for him and he kisses my neck with more intent. He trails his hand across my stomach to my hip, leaving a path of fire. Every inch of my skin is humming. He tastes my neck as he kisses it. His hand firmly cups my breast and I arch into his touch, needy. His thumb presses a circle around my nipple. It stiffens instantly for him and when he grazes over the tip, a moan escapes my lips. I can feel his breath quicken as he lifts my shirt up and off me.

I reach behind, feeling his strong thighs pressed against mine. My hands glide up his smooth skin to his round behind. He is completely naked behind me and my heart is racing inside my ribs. Gripping his butt, I pull him even closer to me. I can feel his rigid member dig into my rear as his hands at my tender breasts and his lips at my neck become more frantic.

I slide my hand between us, to feel him. The hum between my legs responds with a sharp zing to my toes. I grip him at the base and he growls against the back of my ear. He clutches at my hip as I rub my palm against his throbbing cock. My clit is aching and I squeeze my legs together to dull the tingling.

Cade releases my hip to slide my panties down. I have no control over my body. My hips are shaking and my tummy is quivering with the overwhelming need between my thighs.

Cade reaches around between my legs, finding my slippery wetness, "Is this what you need, baby?" Just as he places the most excruciating firm touch to my engorged little bead, I cry out. He continues touching me, his two fingers sliding between my swollen folds. "You're so beautiful," he says. Then his fingers plunge inside of me with no effort and I moan as I grind on his hand. His fingers spread, stretching me. A deep pressure builds inside me and I can't control my breathing.

"Cade. Please. Now."

With his fingers still inside me, I feel the large blunt head of his prick at my entrance. He pauses there for a moment. Cade lets out a deep breath and I feel him enter me, just barely. Just an inch more he slips in between his fingers. I now have him and two of his fingers in me and I am panting. I've never been so stretched. It is new and intense. He moves deeper into me as he slides his fingers out slowly. I can feel every bulge and knuckle of his fingers rub along my sensitive opening as they exit and I groan with the sensation.

He rests his head on mine, cheek to cheek as he wraps one arm across my ribs just under my breasts and holds my hip steady with the other. Slowly, he fills me. I gasp as I try to steady my breath.

"Wow." He shudders behind me. "I've never done this before. You feel amazing."

I think he is all the way in but then, somehow, he pushes in deeper. Deeper. "Christ." His voice is hoarse, shaky. He clutches me to him as we focus on the feel of each other. Skin to skin. Heat in heat.

Holding my hip firmly, he eases out almost all of the way. We breathe in together. He rocks in and out of me again, rubbing perfectly against my inner sensitive spot and heady pleasure rolls up into my belly.

I'm trying not to think about what this means. About us. It's just for tonight. But, God I love this. Being with him.

His lips are at my cheek and I can feel him start to breathe erratically. I let out more gasps and *ohs* as he continues to drag up and down along that sweet spot, slowly but directly. Electric shocks zap into my hip bones and shoot down my legs. My lips are swollen and tingling. My clit is painfully erect, throbbing and desperate for more. I push back against him as he enters me, forcing him in faster, harder. He takes the hint and meets my pace. I arch my back to push our pelvises deeper together, squeezing his steel inside of me at the apex of the motion.

"Fuck." His whisper is ragged and there's a deep rumble in his chest when I tighten around his cock again.

He releases his vise-grip on my hip, reaches down my front and lifts my leg over his. I am spread wide and this allows him deeper inside me. He slides his fingers to my aching bud and I cry out when he touches it. My whole body is on fire and it's concentrated in the little button under his fingers that are massaging and circling it. He thrusts into me with more force and I'm getting dizzy from the feel of him and my screaming. Then he rolls my clit between his two fingers and I buck with the severe jolt of pure sensation it sends through my body. I'm about to explode.

"Look at me," he says.

I turn to look into his eyes. They are an inch from me but I can barely make them out.

"I need to see you when you come." He is still entering me from behind powerfully and the buildup is agonizing, just below the surface, growing.

I don't think I can contain it anymore. His hand is entirely slick with my wetness as he presses against my swollen bead. He rubs it fast and gives it a little tug. I break around him. He covers my lips with his as I scream into his mouth. Waves crashing around us, our mouths are swollen and burning as his tongue penetrates me as I come. I feel myself contract around his cock inside of me.

"Ahh," he gasps out, panting against my lips. I can only moan and cry as another wave breaks in me and I feel it burst, hot and wet all over us. Cade is in pain, his eyes are shut and he is biting his lip, hard, as I start to come down.

He pulls out of me. I am gasping for air and quivering all over with aftershocks and spasms multiplying under my skin.

I still feel like I am floating when Cade rolls me onto my back. He brings me solidly back to earth as he lies over top of me, his weight pressing me to the mattress. My legs spread to allow his hips to settle against mine. He is still hard.

"Did you come?" I ask.

"It took everything in my power not to." He holds my face in his hands. I can feel our hearts beating rapidly together. "I'm going to make this last all night." His eyes are heavy with lust and he smiles a small crooked grin at me. "If that's all right with you."

Yes, it is all right. I kiss him in response. He caresses my jaw with his hands as we kiss. Our lips are tender yet firm against one another, massaging, pulling, sucking, nipping. I part my lips so he can slip inside and our tongues dance together, rolling and twisting around, slowly. I can taste just a hint of blood from his bitten lip.

My hands are fisted in his hair and I wrap my legs instinctively around his waist. Our bodies are pressed together—slick with sweat, they slip together easily. His stiff erection enters me again. We don't break the kiss as he presses in and out of me, slowly and rhythmically. His fullness inside of me is wonderful. His hands at my face are gentle. I love his touch. I love feeling the weight of his body against mine. I love his lips, kissing mine. I love him inside of me.

I love him. I love Cade.

We are completely wrapped in each other. Every inch of skin touching more skin. His deliberate pace gradually picks up and each time he fills me to the hilt, the air knocks out of me. He keeps me in his embrace and his lips on mine, even as I start moaning under the pressure building again in my stomach and his thrusts come quicker, stronger. I can't catch my breath. I am overcome with sensation. Cade's mouth, his weight, his heat, his scent. I feel myself going.

"Come with me?" I barely pant out.

He nods, sweat glistening on his brow. "Yes."

I let go as it overtakes me. Cade holds me tighter, keeping me together as he falls apart over me, grunting and shuddering, emptying himself in me.

He is looking right into my eyes, his voice raspy. "I love you."

"I love you, too." I don't even think before I say it, still coming down from my high. His smile is the most gorgeous I've ever seen, blissful.

He holds me to his chest as he rolls on to his back. I nestle into the space just below his shoulder. I can feel his heartbeat. He pulls the covers up over us and kisses my forehead. His breathing slows and I watch his chest rise and fall as I listen to his soft exhale of air.

It's 5:47 and my mind is racing. Being here, with him, like this is…perfect. I'm exactly where I want to be, but the idea of being with Cade scares me more than anything. It's like when you break a bone—after it heals that spot is even stronger, but the rest of the bone is weaker, more vulnerable to breaking than before. Then, if it does break again, it will never break as cleanly as before. The second break is ugly. A mess. It will never heal as fully either. I'm scared that he's going to break me again, and this time I won't be able to take it.

I listen to him sleep a bit longer. After this, I can't imagine ever telling him no again, but I'm not ready to say yes.

RAE KENNEDY

I slip out of the covers. I miss his warmth as soon as my feet touch the floor. I throw on some jeans and a sweatshirt. Before I leave, I look at him in my bed. He is peaceful. Beautiful. I want to give in to him, but I don't know how.

I go for a long, freezing bike ride to clear my head.

CHAPTER 26

I needed the air. The ride succeeds in giving me a runny nose, purple ears, and in dulling my anxiety. Exercise always makes me feel better. I realize that it is okay to listen to my head, but it is also all right to listen to my heart, that whatever decision I make will be the right one. I also realize that I don't need to make the decision right now. I feel better taking the pressure off of myself. Cade said he can wait. That's all I need—time.

The house is still quiet when I get back.

I don't think Cade has moved even an inch. He is in the same position as when I left him. As I undress, he starts to stir, and with a big stretch, peeks his eyes open.

"Where've you been?" He yawns.

"Couldn't sleep."

He looks at the clock as he sits up, the covers falling to reveal all of his sexy, taught pecs and abs and his intricate sleeves. "I have to go into the restaurant in a bit. You want breakfast?"

"No, I think I'm going to try and go back to bed."

He smiles at me goofily, still half asleep, his hair all mussed from the pillow. It reminds me of seven-year-old

Cade. His smile grows wide and I can tell he is thinking about last night.

"You love me."

I can't help but smile at him and nod. His eyes light up and it tears me apart.

"That was never the issue between us," I remind him.

A crease appears above his nose and it kills me to see his grin dissolve. He stands and the sight of his gloriously naked body makes my knees shake a little. He walks over to me, smoothes my hair with his hand, and kisses my forehead.

"Get some rest, Haley." Then he leaves, closing the door behind him and I feel just as lost as I did last night.

* * *

I end up sleeping until late in the afternoon. When I wake up, the house is empty and I'm still confused about last night. About everything. I need to talk it out with someone, but I'm certainly not going to divulge details about my sex life with Tuck, or my mom, or Nenee. I text Court.

Me: *Are you still home for break or have you come back in town yet?*

Court: *Still here at home, everything okay?*

Me: *I could just use a friend to talk to...Cade.*

Court: *I was going to head back in a couple of days but I'll leave in the morning.*

Now I feel bad. I wasn't trying to get her to cut her vacation time short.

Me: *It can wait. Don't change your plans for me.*

Court: *Too late, already packing. If I leave by 8 I can meet you at the Bistro on 3rd St by 10. Brunch?*

Me: *Sure.*

* * *

I take a sip of my bubbly, sweet mimosa when I spot Court at the door. Her stunning face lights up and she waves at me, the sunlight glowing off her blonde hair.

She gives me a hug and sits across from me, immediately waving the server over to us. Addressing him by name, she orders us two more mimosas, requesting hers with grapefruit instead of orange juice. She gives him the sweetest smile and he hurries off, then returns amazingly fast with our drinks, a plate of fruit on the house and takes our order attentively. I guess I should dine with Court more often.

I tell her everything about what's happened since the accident. She listens closely while tearing pieces of cinnamon roll off and eating them with her fingers.

"I thought you were crazy about him."

"I am."

"Then what's the problem?"

"I don't know."

Court sits back and raises her eyebrows. She's not buying it. "Well, I've got all day for you to figure it out."

I stare at my eggs benedict for a moment. It's not as good as Cade's. I look up at Court, all of her attention focused on me. "I'm scared, okay? He left me. He hurt me so much I don't know if I can trust him. What if he hurts me again? I don't think I can take it."

She considers my words as she finishes her second mimosa. "Maybe he will. But what if he doesn't? Wouldn't that be worth the risk?"

Yes. "It's the risk that's scary. I can't love him without being completely vulnerable to him again."

She is smiling at me. Her eyes are round, like glass marbles reflecting a brilliant blue sky. "Isn't that the only way to love?"

* * *

On the walk home, my heart is pounding. Buterflies flutter in my stomach, the whole gamut. I am going to tell Cade I want to be together. Together. For real. Cade and me. Tuck approved. My feet start to speed up. A little skip and a hop are thrown in here and there. I can't get home fast enough. My cheeks are starting to hurt from the grin spread across my face.

I burst through the door and run straight for the kitchen, knowing he will be there. But when I land in the kitchen, breathless, Cade is sitting at the table, staring at a steaming cup of coffee with a somber look on his face.

"Cade!"

He looks up at me, but the hard look on his face doesn't ease.

"What's wrong?" I ask.

"We need to talk."

That sounds...menacing. I sit across from him at our tiny table.

"What's going on?"

"I got a job offer."

"Oh yeah?"

"As an executive chef...in the city."

It's not bad news. Relief washes over me. "Cade, that's awesome! Congratulations."

TO BE YOUR GIRL

His smile is tight. "It's at a new restaurant that hasn't opened yet. It's going to be fresh and cool." His eyes light up as he talks about it. "And they want me to create the menu and help hire all of the staff..." He is smiling and it makes me so happy. This is his dream come true.

"Sounds amazing." I interlace our fingers across the table.

He squeezes my hands, but his smile fades. "I need to know, Haley." He looks at me intensely. "If there is any possibility, no matter how far in the future, of us ever being together."

Of course there is, dummy! Right now! I want to be with you right now! I'm just about to yell these words at him when the grave look on his face gives me pause. "Why?"

"They would basically need me to be available at a moment's notice. I would need to move there. They want me to start on the first so I would need to leave immediately to find a place to live there downtown."

I still don't understand. "Okay..."

I let his words sink in, not sure why he is being so grave.

"If there is even a chance to get you back, I'll stay. I won't take the job. I will wait here for you as long as it takes."

"Cade, whatever happens with you and me shouldn't affect this decision. It doesn't have to be either, or—"

"No," he says definitively. "If I'm with you, I'm with you. All the way. Not long distance. I will not leave you again. Ever."

I am screaming inside. At the top of my lungs for him to stay. My internal screams are reverberating in my skull, hammering at the bone. I WANT YOU. I LOVE YOU. BE WITH ME. I want to say this but nothing comes out. I am mute. I can't ask him to stay. In this little college town. Just for me. Not after seeing the glisten in his eyes as he spoke about this new opportunity.

This is what he has been waiting for. He deserves this. I won't let him give this up. I won't be the reason.

It breaks my heart to lie to him.

"No." My voice cracks, I can barely get the word out.

"What?" His blue eyes search mine, panic rising.

"There's no chance...for us." I have to bite my tongue to keep my expression steady and my jaw from quivering. I can feel the sting behind my eyes and I pray I can keep them in long enough for him to believe me.

His perfect face breaks. Shattered. I've smashed it. His eyes are still searching my face, still begging for a different answer. But I hold my expression steady.

He stands. His voice trembles a little as he says, "Okay then."

He turns his head away as he walks off but I can see him wipe his eye with his thumb.

I sit at the table, staring at Cade's coffee until I hear him leave.

As soon as the door shuts, I start sobbing. Sobs that hurt.

For the second time, Cade leaves the house with no intention of returning.

This time, he never comes back.

CHAPTER 27

18 MONTHS LATER

"No. Opening night is two weeks from Friday. It absolutely needs to be installed by Tuesday, at the latest."

I scroll through different flight itineraries as the man on the other end of the phone continues to be noncommittal about finalizing the install date for our newest exhibit.

"Hmm," I say, "you must be very busy. And you're right—two weeks is a tight timeline. If it is too short of notice for you, I am happy to discuss a finding a new company with Ms. Decker."

That gets him to perk right up. He backtracks and assures me his men will be here and the job completed on Monday.

It's already almost six o'clock and I should get going if I want to make it to dinner on time. The clicks of my high-heels echo down the marbled hallway. I knock on her door to announce my presence, even though it is already open.

Claire Decker, head curator at the museum, looks up from her desk. "Haley, come in."

She walks around to lean on her desk, the magnificent

city landscape through the wall-to-wall windows behind her. Her bangle bracelets chime as she takes off her glasses to look at me from under blunt-cut black bangs.

"Did you get the installation scheduled yet?"

"Yes, it is all taken care of."

"And it will be done by Wednesday?"

"It will be done by Tuesday."

Her face softens into a smile. "Have you booked flights for my meeting in London next month?"

"Not yet." Shit.

"Good. I was wondering… If you're available, if you'd like to join me. I'd love to have your opinion on some of the pieces for our next collection."

"That would be amazing, I'd love to."

"Terrific. You have a good eye. I loved the photography portfolio you sent with your resume."

"That means so much coming from you, thank you."

* * *

I practically skip down the sidewalk as I make my way to the restaurant. A notification dings in my purse and I check my phone.

Ben: *I had a great time on our date Saturday*

Me: M*e too*

Okay, maybe not great, but by first-date standards, it had been nice.

Ben: *I'd love to go out again. Are you free on Friday?*

Me: *I'm busy with a wedding this weekend, but next week sometime?*

Ben: *Great, I'll give you a call*

I always say yes to a second date, as first dates tend to

be awkward, as a rule. But in the last year, I've yet to accept a third. Something has always been...missing.

To be fair, I don't think any man will ever make me feel the way Cade did. I try not to think about him. About where he is, what he's doing, who he's with. Is he happy, is he sad, is he...in love? I can't go there. I've gotten through the last year and a half by pushing thoughts of Cade out of my head and focusing on things like school, finding a job, and now, helping Court with her wedding and finding a place to live. And it feels good. I've been taking care of myself. I'm responsible for my own success and my own happiness.

* * *

"Cheers to the bride!"

We all clank our wine glasses but before I can down the last of my Riesling, Court chimes in, "And to Haley! For finally effing graduating and getting a great job!"

I smile at her from over the rim of my glass as the rest of the girls toast to me as well. It still amazes me how Court is always the light in any room, the center of everyone's collective adoration and attention, yet she constantly puts her spotlight on those around her, making them feel important. Maybe that's why she has become my very best friend. Anyway, her spotlight-shedding attempt doesn't work. We are all here for her, to celebrate her wedding this weekend.

Court is positively glowing and I couldn't be happier for her. Truly I am. But seeing how blissfully happy she is and how truly in love she is, only serves to remind me of my own pathetic love life.

The server comes to retrieve our empty plates and to

refill our glasses. There is a clinking of dishes and silverware. The girls are all chatting, full from our glorious four-course feast. Court said she had been dying to go to this restaurant in the city for forever, so I made the reservations and surprised her.

The restaurant is in an old warehouse building—the space is huge. It has fifteen-foot-high ceilings with thick steel beams and old pipes and ductwork all painted black above the aged brick walls. The windows to the street are tall, floor-to-ceiling, framed in black with intricately carved moldings. The floors are old and beat-up wide plank wood with gouges, scrapes, scuffs, and screws all over. The space is moodily lit, with hundreds of single droplet pendants hanging at various heights from the ceiling, creating a sparkling cluster of stars above our heads. I love it. Almost as much as the food. It was so good I could not stop eating. Now I am stuffed.

I am telling Court this when she looks up over my shoulder and her eyes go wide. A feeling I can't describe cascades over me. It's like a chill that is prickly, but warm—familiar, even.

Then large warm hands are on my shoulders. Even after eighteen months, I know his scent, his touch. I can't believe how quickly my body reacts to him. My heart beating, my cheeks flushing. Cade.

I turn my head, and there he is.

He is wearing his head chef's uniform. This is his restaurant. My heart stops.

He looks right into my eyes and smiles. His big, breathtaking smile.

"Hey, you."

The knot in my throat is choking but I manage to get

out a small, "Hi."

"Cade! I thought we might see you tonight." Court beams. Cade smiles at us. She knew? Of course she did. "Hey, thanks for hooking us up with your friend's band for the wedding!"

"No problem." He still has his hands on my shoulders. "How did everyone enjoy their meal?"

All the girls moan at how great everything was. He absentmindedly rubs small circles into my back with his thumbs as the flock gushes and flirts with him. He steps away from me, his warm hands going with him as Court introduces him to everyone at the table—her little sister, Gracie, and a few coworkers. He shakes each of their hands.

He smiles at them and I swear each girl either giggles, bats her eyes at him, or just drops her panties and offers herself to him right there on the table.

Okay, I may have made that up. But, basically. I have no right to feel so possessive of him, but don't they know that he's mine? Or was. Which, in girl code, is the same fucking thing.

He is making conversation with Court and her coworkers and I can't help but stare at him. I'm watching the sharp angle of his jaw as he talks and the movements of his hands. It was much easier to push him out of my mind when he was just a memory. Now, with him standing here in front of me, I can't stop the flood of emotion that hits me. The connection I have to him—I can feel it, and I'm drawn to him. Hearing his voice, having his hands on me just for a minute, smelling the rainstorm on his skin, makes me realize how dull my life has been.

Cade turns his face toward me, and I think he catches

me staring at him.

"So, Haley, are you ladies just out for a night on the town or are you sticking around for a little while?"

Before I can answer, Court tells him, "Actually, she lives here now."

His eyebrows rise in surprise. His lips take a sharp downward turn before he recovers them into a nice smile. "Oh, really?"

"Well, technically I don't yet, I have to find a place to live first."

"That's great, Hale." His smile is genuine and it makes my insides melt. "Hey, do you still have the same number?" He says it sort of off-handedly and it takes me by surprise.

"Yeah."

"Cool. Well," Cade addresses the table, "it was nice meeting you ladies, but I should get back to work." The women collectively protest. He nods to Court and gives my shoulder a squeeze as he passes. "Really good to see you."

After he leaves, the girls resume their chatting. Court looks at me. Grinning mischievously.

"He is still crazy about you."

I roll my eyes at her, waving her off. "He is not."

Could he be?

* * *

The next morning I am still trying to sleep off my wine-induced headache, grateful I have the next few days off, when my phone rings. I don't recognize the number. It is my rule to never answer a number I don't know. If it is important, I am confident they will leave a message. Another rule of mine in regards to the phone is never to answer it before I am up out of bed. And it is, what the hell time is it? 10:42, holy fuck. The phone is still buzzing—then I have a panicked thought that it is someone at the HR department or Claire calling. I reach for my phone and hit the screen just before it goes to voicemail.

"Hello?" I sound like a frog—hence why I don't freaking answer the phone while I'm still in bed.

On the other end, I hear chuckling. "I thought I waited late enough, sorry." His deep, amused voice slaps me the fuck awake.

"Cade?"

"Morning." More laughter.

"I'm totally up."

"Hale. C'mon. I know your morning voice." When he says it, it hits me like a truck. He still knows me more intimately than anyone.

"Fine. I'm still in bed, but I'm awake. Swear."

"Good. Wanna get your ass out of bed and meet me for lunch? Catch up a little?"

I remember Court's words from last night and I am suddenly sweating in my sheets. Never mind hearing Cade's voice while I am mostly naked has my whole body on alert.

"Sure."

* * *

I take advantage of the warm weather and wear a cute little skirt and my nude heels that make my legs look longer. As I walk toward the café, I feel like I am going to throw up.

I spot him already seated at one of the tiny outdoor tables, sunglasses on his head, reading a menu. Just as he looks up toward me, I stumble over a crack in the sidewalk. *Dammit heels! Get it together.*

"Hey!" His face lights up and he stands as I reach the table. He brings me in, wrapping his arms around my shoulders. My arms encircle his waist, probably tighter than is appropriate. We hold the embrace just a second longer than a friendly hug and I take the opportunity to press against his solid chest and smell his great Cade smell.

We sit and order. I get the smoked ham, mozzarella, and apricot Panini after Cade tells me I'll love it.

"So, you're moving to the big, bad city, huh?"

"Yeah. I just started as the assistant to the head curator at the Museum of Natural History."

"Right out of school. That's great! Sounds exactly like what you always wanted."

"I'm pretty excited about it."

"Now you're apartment hunting?"

"Yep. I'm starting out at base salary, so I think I'm going to have to find a roommate. I can't afford anything I've looked at so far."

"Hmm." He looks a bit concerned, but then our food arrives and my stomach grumbles as the server sets my plate in front of me.

So we eat. The sandwich is amazing. The shoestring fries are also divine, the perfect amount of exterior crisp versus soft potato insides and all salty goodness. As we eat, we fall into easy conversation about Tuck's new job, Cade's new menu at the restaurant, and that I ended up minoring in photography. I don't tell him he was the reason.

Our plates are long gone and the check is on the table. But neither one of us makes a move. He looks like he wants to ask me something.

"So..." I say. I don't want our time to end, but there isn't much else to do.

"So." He nods. He takes a drink and pretty nonchalantly asks, "Are you seeing anyone right now?"

My heart starts pumping up into my ears. I don't know what I had been waiting to happen, but this is it. I shake my head, smiling shyly. "No."

He nods at me, contemplating. "I am."

Wait, what? My heart stops. Then I can feel it shattering inside of me. I try to keep a light look on my face. "Oh yeah?" I smile. I'm happy for him. So fucking happy.

"Yeah, I've been seeing her for a few months." A few months? "She's a great girl. Her name is Julia."

I hate the way he smiles when he talks about her.

He is telling me about her, but I am not listening. I am staring at him, just focusing on keeping this stupid ass smile on my face. But I can feel it slipping. I am no good at hiding emotion. I should have never gotten my hopes up. I shouldn't have come here. I feel a tickle in my throat and the pit of my stomach hurts.

He tilts his head at me. "What's wrong?"

I'm about to lie. Say nothing is wrong. I'm great. But I'm not. I'm dying inside and I can't hold it in.

"I lied."

"You lied?" He looks confused. "So you are seeing someone?"

"No. I lied a year and a half ago. When I told you there was no chance for us to be together, I lied." I can tell he's still processing what I'm saying. So I continue. "I came home that very day with the intention of getting back together with you. I wanted to be with you more than anything. But it would have been selfish to hold you back. Moving here, this job, was your dream. So I lied."

He sits back in his chair as my words sink in. "Selfish?" He runs his hands through his hair, distraught. "You murdered me that day." The look on his face stabs me right in the chest. He's overwhelmed. He stands, rubbing the back of his neck. "My…fuck… My dream? Don't you know?" His light blue eyes plead with me. "My dream was you. You." He pulls out his wallet and lays enough cash for both of our meals on the table. "I'm sorry."

He doesn't look at me. Then he turns and walks away. I sit there, numb, watching as his figure, hands in his pockets, gets smaller and smaller until he is lost with the other pedestrians on the street.

CHAPTER 28

"He's seeing someone."

"What? Oh no, Haley, I'm so sorry." Court steps out from behind the partition. She is breathtaking in her dress. It is soft white with a deep V-neckline that's tight to her waist then flows to the floor. She already had her final fitting, but she couldn't resist trying it on again when we came to pick it up from the shop.

"It's okay."

She tilts her head, a little crease forming between her brows. "Hale..."

"Really. I'm fine. I'm glad he's happy." I do wish him happiness. "Anyway, enough about me. It's your special time. You look beautiful."

"Thank you. I can't believe the wedding is only days away."

"Are you nervous?"

She smooths out the bodice of her dress in the mirror, her angelic face completely serene. "Not even a little." She turns to me, tall and elegant. "I better change and get this dress home. It's a long drive. Are you sure you don't want to come with me? You can stay with us—it'll be better than the hotel."

"I'm sure. I'm going to do some apartment hunting tomorrow."

"Okay. I'll see you in a couple of days for the rehearsal dinner?"

"Wouldn't miss it."

* * *

Apartment hunting today is, again, a bust. I'm going to have to figure that shit out soon.

I finish inputting the company credit card number and close my laptop. Two hotel rooms and flights to London booked. First class.

I sit on the floor in my hotel room. Television off. Window open, I listen to the sounds of the street outside. I love the city—the opportunity, the anonymity, all the possibilities for the future. My mind drifts to the wedding... then to Cade... I should probably just go to bed. I probably should have gone a couple of hours ago.

The high-pitched rattle of my phone startles me. This time I recognize the number on the screen. Cade.

"Hello?"

"Haley?" His voice is low. "Can we talk?"

Deep breath. "Sure."

"...in person?"

"Okay."

"I'll send a car."

* * *

The driver is super chatty. Luckily, he doesn't seem to

notice I'm not taking part in the conversation. He drops me at a dark brick building. Cade already paid him and now I'm alone. I don't see any lights on through the windows. It's later than I realized. The sky is a dark hazy gray with no stars. There is no one else on the street. It is eerie. The tall trees that line the sidewalk rustle softly as a light warm breeze meanders its way to the east.

I walk up the front steps. Next to the door, I scan the names until I reach the very bottom. C. Renner is on the top floor, apartment 6A. I feel kind of like throwing up. I can feel my heartbeat through my whole body. After a couple of slow breaths, I ring the button next to his name with a shaky finger. He doesn't say anything to me, but I immediately hear the buzz and click of the front door unlocking.

Of course, there's no elevator in this building. I walk up to the sixth floor and to his door, standing there for a moment to let my heart-rate normalize. To prepare. For what? No fucking clue. Then I knock.

"It's open." I hear Cade call from inside. His voice sounds decades away.

I open the door slowly. It is heavy. I step inside and it swings closed loudly behind me. The room is huge. It's dark, the only light coming from the impressively large arched windows at the front of the apartment. It's a studio loft with the kitchen in the far corner, the living and dining areas in the center and the bed at the other end of the space. Cade is sitting on the deep sill, looking out one of the windows. He turns to look at me, no smile on his lips. The putrid feeling in my stomach grows.

"Sorry to call you so late."

"I was up."

He motions me over to where he is and I cross the

expanse of wood floors to the large window seat. I sit across from him, leaning into the corner of the window.

He looks at me seriously. "What did you do today?"

Are we doing small talk? I don't know what I expected him to say, but it wasn't that.

"I looked at some apartments."

"Find anything?"

"I saw one that I could actually afford the rent."

He nods and smiles politely. I can't tell what he's thinking.

"Of course, I couldn't afford to put food in the fridge… or pay the electricity to keep the fridge running."

I get a bigger smile out of him with that.

"The city is expensive," he says as he looks out the window again. I don't know what to say or do. I can't read him. We sit for a minute before he takes a big breath.

I don't like the silence.

"What did you want to talk with me about, Cade?"

The light from the street highlights the contours of his face, smooth forehead, angled cheek, strong chin, and his beautiful eyes. His expression is earnest.

"I broke up with my girlfriend."

"What! Why?" My heart is racing.

"You know why."

"But you told me the other day how wonderful she is."

"She is." He furrows his brows as he gathers his thoughts. "Being with you made me realize that I could do the relationship thing. That I actually wanted to. I've had a few relationships since then. I kept trying to find something like I had with you. But nothing was. None of them were you. That's the problem with every other girl."

I am trying to take in his words, decipher what he means,

but the blood pounding in my ears keeps interrupting my thoughts. He clears his throat.

"When I met Jules"—him using a familiar nickname makes me jealous—"it was easy, like it was with you." That stings a little. "We got along great. She's awesome, and I thought this might be it. But about a month into the relationship, I knew I wasn't falling in love with her. I was going to break it off, but I realized that no matter how long I searched, I was never going to feel the same about anyone else."

I am paralyzed.

"After our lunch together, I just walked. I had so many thoughts, I couldn't get them straight. I walked around the city for hours. Then I ended up in front of her building. I hadn't even consciously made any decisions but once I got there, I knew exactly what I was there to do." He turns his gaze from the window back to me. "When I saw you at my restaurant... Fuck. I thought as long as I made her happy it was okay, but now I understand that being with her wasn't fair. It was a lie. She deserves to have a guy whose heart stops whenever he sees her, who can sense her the moment she enters the room. She deserves to have someone feel about her the way I feel about you."

I exhale the breath I didn't realize I'd been holding in. I spring toward him, throwing my arms around his neck. But he doesn't hug me back.

I pull away. Why is he still being so distant? I'm looking directly into his blue eyes and they look directly into me.

"I'm scared shitless here," he says.

My face is just inches from his. I can smell his intoxicating stormy scent. His lips are parted and his eyes flick quickly down to my lips and back. My breathing quickens.

"The last time I poured my heart out to you, you ripped it out," he continues.

I had. I recognize now in his eyes the look I took before as indifference, is guarded fear.

"You didn't say you still felt the same, but my feelings for you haven't changed. Haley..." He takes a slow breath. "Do you still want me?"

My heart explodes. "Yes!"

"Yes?" He is still incredulous.

I nod vigorously and his perfect smile is heartbreakingly beautiful. He sweeps me into his arms, his lips crashing into mine instantly. Even in my most vivid dreams, his kisses are never this good. I devour him. His taste. I take in the sensation of his strong hands on me, one gripping at my lower back, the other cupping my neck. I hold on tight to his muscular shoulders. I don't want to let go of him. Ever.

Our mouths keep constant contact as he slides his hands down to my rear and lifts us up. My legs wrap around his waist as he walks and I'm overwhelmed by the feeling of him against me. I have him. I have Cade back.

He leans down and I feel the soft bed under us. Our kiss breaks for the first time as he climbs over me. He touches his forehead to mine, our eyes locked, chests heaving. His hot hand slides up my thigh, bunching up my skirt and the touch makes my skin ignite.

"Haley," he breathes, "I need you."

I'm already lifting off his shirt. "Yes," I whisper. He throws his shirt to the floor, revealing all of the lean, hard muscle under his black ink. He makes quick work of my skirt and top while I undo the button of his jeans. The head of his glorious erection has swelled past his waistband and the sight of it has me needy. I suddenly feel so empty and the tugging inside of me has me squeezing his hips between my thighs.

Cade drags his kisses across my jaw then behind my ear, sending shivers down the whole right side of my body. His soft lips brush along my neck, across my collarbone and then down to the swell of my breasts. My nipples tighten under the fabric of my bra, heaving with desire. With one finger, he pulls the cup of my bra down and surrounds my pink tip with his wet mouth. I am overcome by the sensation of his sharp suck, tingling everywhere. My eyes roll back and I moan uncontrollably. He kisses the delicate skin between my breasts, then down my stomach, down to my belly button. My little bead buzzes as he gets closer. My whole body is quivering with anticipation.

He looks up at me, head tilted. "Hale, are you all right?"

I gasp out, "Uh huh."

"You haven't shaken this much since the first time."

I try to steady my breath as he moves up the bed toward me.

"Just go easy on me, okay? It's been a while."

He kisses my lips gently. "How long's a while?"

"A year and a half."

He looks right into my eyes. "Really?"

"No one even came close to you."

"I don't deserve you."

"You have me."

He smiles against my lips as he unhooks my bra and removes it effortlessly. "I just need to taste you and be inside you. I'll be as easy as I can."

He moves down to my knee, kissing the inside of it and up my inner thigh until he reaches my underwear. He kisses the outside of the silky fabric as my ache builds beneath it. The throb of my clit is voracious, wanting him there, needing pressure. He slips one finger under the fabric, my slickness immediately apparent.

"Christ, I forgot how ready you always are for me." He slowly slides my panties down and kisses me firmly against my trembling bud. I let out a loud gasp. "You taste so good, babe." And then his tongue flicks my little bundle of nerves, sending me into oblivion. His mouth explores every inch of my wetness and I can't hold still under him as each lick pulses shocks into my bones. The tension in my body rises and when I hit the top and crash down I scream out his name.

Still shaking, lips numb and tingling, I pull him up to me. I kiss him deeply, tasting myself in his mouth and he holds me tightly as I come back from the edge. His cock is stiff and digging into my thigh, hard. I yank his boxer briefs down to free it. Feeling its weight in my hands, I grip him at the base, making him groan.

He kicks off his briefs and reaches for his nightstand.

He comes back to settle between my legs and I pull him into me. His rigid length penetrates my wetness effortlessly and his breath catches. He takes a moment to steady himself then shoves all the way inside me, jolting me with pleasure. Every time he thrusts into me, I cry out, pushing back against him as hard as I can. All I can feel is him—there is nothing else in the world at this moment. I dig my fingers into his back and he slows his pace.

"I want you to know, it's never been like this with anybody else. Only you."

I know what he means.

He pulls me up to him, sitting so I am straddling him, still connected. He holds me as I rise and sink onto him, slowly. He watches me, in awe. "Move in with me."

"What?"

"I've wasted too much time not being with you. I don't want to ever be without you again."

It seems fast, but we've lived together before. Nothing would make me happier.

"Okay." The smiles that overtake our faces are ridiculous. Obnoxious, probably.

"I love you so much." He grips my hip and lifts me up and down on him, a little faster, a little harder until all I can do is hold on to him as I come around him again. I have his face in my hands, watching as he shudders into me, trembling.

We stay wrapped in each other all night. His bed is warm and perfect. Our bed.

I wake to the steady sound of Cade's breath, his chest rising and falling slowly under my cheek. His arm is draped across me and as the early morning misty light soars in through the enormous windows, I trace my finger along the black lines of his tattoos. Down through the tentacles and then over to the little bag of flour by his elbow. As I slide my finger down along the blade of the knife. There is a new one—a tiny Nikon F. It's just above the script that scrolls around his wrist and I twist my head to finally read it.

Learn from yesterday, live for today, hope for tomorrow.

***

Keep reading for a preview of the next book in the series, Court's story, TO BE YOUR WIFE.

ABOUT THE AUTHOR

Rae has always been a creator. She has degrees in Architecture and Interior Design but also loves to draw, paint, bake, and, of course, write. A hopeless romantic, she's been married to her high school sweetheart for ten years. Together they have three children and live in the Pacific Northwest.

For more info and a complete list of books, visit www.raekennedyauthor.com

TO BE YOUR WIFE

CHAPTER 1

At least the food is delicious, because this guy is fucking awful.

The first words out of his mouth were: "Whoa. You're, like, really tall."

No shit Sherlock.

I am tall. And I'm wearing heels, which make me taller. I won't apologize or stop wearing them.

The evening has spiraled gracefully to shit since that moment.

"So, Chip, do you have any brothers or sisters?" I ask.

"One brother."

Okay... I sit for a moment, smiling, hoping maybe he'll ask me a question in return. Why, yes, I have four siblings, Chip. Three older brothers and one younger sister. But no. He does not ask me anything.

Our server comes to refill my water.

"Thank you, Henry," I say with my sweetest smile. He has literally been the best part of my evening thus far. He's been my hero, keeping those bread baskets coming during that awkward time after ordering. When there were no menus to pretend to read, just the two of us, sitting across from each other—staring—he brought me carbs and butter and I will be forever grateful.

"You're welcome. Can I get you anything else?" Henry asks.

"No, thank you."

He walks off and I have an urge to call him back and order myself a drink. A strong one.

I look back at Chip in his polo shirt and tousled blond hair that many girls might find attractive. You know what I find attractive? A guy who can hold a conversation.

"You're a communications major, right?"

"Yeah."

That's it. That's all he says. Ironic, actually. I'd laugh if I weren't so bored. Luckily I couldn't give two shits about this blind date. I agreed to go because I'm always up for meeting new people but I'm not actually interested in making a love match right now. I'm too busy with my last year of school for anything serious and after graduation, I'm moving back home where I already have a job lined up.

Without a word, Chip gets up and heads toward the bathroom.

I can't.

I need to get out. I text Haley to call me in five.

Shortly after he sits back down, my phone rings.

"Oh, my gosh! I can't believe I forgot to silence my phone, I'm so sorry!"

He shrugs and takes a bite of his now cold spaghetti.

Why am I even bothering? Because you're nice, dammit. I answer the phone, "Hello?"

"How's the date going?" Haley's voice is friendly with almost a chuckle in it. There is laughter and noise in the background and I immediately want to be wherever she is—

TO BE YOUR WIFE

having fun and maybe getting an effing drink. Yes.

"Oh my god! That's terrible!" I feign my best shocked and concerned reaction. Chip isn't paying any attention.

"That good, huh?"

"Where are you?" I really want to know.

"We're at Flanagan's downtown." Fuck. Yes.

"I'll be right there!" I hang up the phone and give Chip an apologetic look. I start to explain there's an emergency, but I give up. "I've got to go." I get up and lay forty dollars on the table. That should cover my meal and most of his, but I feel bad making him pay when I'm ditching.

* * *

I step out into the crisp November night and am invigorated. The breeze nips at my cheeks and when I take a deep breath, the fresh air fills me. It smells like fall. I wrap my chunky scarf around my neck, glad my long blonde hair is tied in a knot on top of my head.

As I walk down the sidewalk toward Flanagan's the street is alive with other people ambling to their destinations, laughing and slapping each other on the backs. Mostly other college students but some older folks too. Cars line the street and wait at intersections as the slow-moving pedestrians cross well past the "no walking" sign. The streetlights and headlights make a beautiful painting of light—red, yellow, and green, against the black sky.

Voices get louder and more jovial as I get closer to the bar. The air smells faintly of cigarettes and hotdog vendors set up for the late-night crowd.

I get to the front doors, manned by a large guy named

Francis. Of course, most people don't know his name—they might be less intimidated otherwise.

"Evening, Fran."

He scowls at me. But I smile at him as I hand him my ID and he nods me in with a small smile creeping to the corner of his mouth. Francis doesn't talk much while he's working. Mostly grunts. I've only got six more months in this college town, but I think I can still crack a full smile out of him one of these days.

The bar is much warmer than outside. It's almost humid in here, packed with bodies. Drunk and rowdy twenty-somethings playing pool and dancing and shooting darts and yelling so they can be heard over the loud Irish rock music. I spot Haley right away, sitting at a tall table near the back, a huge foamy beer overflowing before her.

I tend to hang out with a lot of boys, and I've only known Haley a couple of months, but I adore her. She is practically my opposite in every way—petite and curvy with wavy dark hair and dark eyes. I'm surprised she's out, even though it's a Saturday night. She generally requires dragging, begging, or bribery to get her to come party.

"Hey!" I squeal, running up to her and flinging my arms around her shoulders. "Thanks for saving me Hale." Haley is not a hugger but she puts up with me.

"No problem." She looks way too sober for this late in the night at a place like this. As I take off my coat and nubby red scarf, revealing my short cream lace dress, I realize why. Across the table is a very drunk guy completely ogling my legs. Like, drool-out-of-the-mouth-and-not-even-ashamed-of-it drunk.

"Court, this is Cade." Haley directs me to the man to her right, not that he needs an introduction. Everyone in this town knows who Cade Renner is. Sex covered in tattoos. He shakes my hand across the table and I smile at him. I see what all the fuss is about. He is hot.

"Hi Cade, we've sort of met before."

"Uh yeah…" He nods at me. I can tell he is searching for a memory of me, probably in bed, but he won't find one. Cade gives women attention for a night, not long enough to remember a face or a name. Being someone he hasn't slept with makes me completely off the radar.

"And this is my brother, Tuck." Haley gestures across the table to the drunk one, her cheeks brighten as she admits her relation.

He straightens up a bit and stretches his hand out to me. As I take it, he says, "Hey gorgeous." Cheesy. But it makes my face open up and then he flashes me the most gorgeous smile ever, complete with deep dimples on each side. He has perfectly straight white teeth with a square chin and sharp jaw. His hair is dark, buzzed short and his ears stick out just a little too wide but as he takes my hand, our eyes lock.

His large hand envelopes mine and sends a wave of liquid warmth up my arm. His eyes are a beautiful mix of green and blue and gold. We have stopped shaking and are just now kind of holding hands. Entranced. His thumb barely brushes along my knuckles and I snap out of it, giggling.

"Nice to meet you, Tuck."

He looks a tad more devious as his grin widens, his left dimple getting deeper.

"You want to get out of here?" Haley calls to me, completely breaking the spell Tuck's eyes are casting on me and I turn to her as I let our hands fall.

"Are you kidding? I just got here. I'm ready to drink!"

"Oh, hell yes!" Tuck jumps up from his stool lightning-fast with a smack of his hand on the table. "What'll you have?" He looks at me with excitement. I'm excited too. I need to let out some steam before finals, and Chip certainly wasn't doing it for me.

"Anything with tequila."

Tuck looks as though he is about to faint as he crosses both hands over his chest. "I just fell in love." He actually does stumble a bit but recovers nicely and reaches for my hand again. "Let's go do this, girl."

He takes my hand and we walk over toward the bar. We weave through the crowd—Tuck is taking care to block me from flying elbows and other people getting crazy. I am impressed at how steady he is walking and even more impressed with how much taller than me he is. He must be about 6'5" because I'm over six feet in these heels and he still has a few inches on me.

When we finally make it to the bar, there is no bartender. I step up on the foot rail and lean over the counter. As I do this, I realize with my short dress I very well may be giving Tuck a prime view of my ass, but that thought doesn't bother me enough to jump down. The bartender is at the far end and I wave to get his attention, which is futile. I turn around to face Tuck, who quickly tries to look like he wasn't just checking out my butt, failing.

"He's down at the other end." Even two inches away, I must raise my voice two octaves to be heard.

Tuck nods. "I'll try to get him. You stay here."

He melts into the crowd and I lean over the bar again. It is at times like these I wish I had any sort of cleavage to offer. But alas, this tall, thin frame only comes with boobs that can't even fill out an A cup on a good day. The bartender turns his head my way for a second and I manage to catch his eye.

"Joaquin!" I recognize him from our English class sophomore year. He smiles and heads my way.

"What'll it be, pretty girl?"

"Four tequila shots, top shelf."

He gives me a nod and starts grabbing glasses.

"Can I buy your drinks?" The smarmy guy next to me—where did he come from?—asks with a skinny smile.

"Oh, thank you so much for the offer, but I've got it." I smile sweetly at him and then turn back to the bar. Hopefully he will get the message.

Nope. He moves a little closer to me. "You sure? Top shelf is pretty expensive." He has an abnormally small nose.

A large hand wraps around my waist from the other side and a strong arm ease me gently against a solid torso. I turn a bit startled right into Tuck's face. His bright green eyes just inches from mine. He's giving me his dimpled smile. "Hey darlin'," he says with a wink.

I crack up at this. Really? He bites his lip to keep from laughing too, our noses almost touch. He glances over my shoulder for a second, the twinkle in his eyes giving way to an intense glare. Whoa. That look could murder. The little man scuttles off.

Breaking away from Tuck's powerful grip, I raise my eyebrow at him.

"I didn't know if you wanted rescuing," Tuck says with a shrug. "But I figured if you did, I'd help. And if you didn't... well, that would have made me completely jealous." He only slurs his words a tiny bit.

"I could have handled it, but that was easier." I smile at him, giving him a playful punch in the arm.

Joaquin places the four shots down in front of us. He doesn't spill a drop of the clear liquid as he fills them to the brims. He tells me the price and I dig out some cash from my pocket.

"Put it on my tab," Tuck yells over, "and add four more."

"Hey, I can buy us a round."

Tuck looks at me with a goofy smile. "But darlin', I've got you." He hands me a shot and raises his to mine. With a clank and a couple drops spilled, we down them in a second. We take the next ones then slam them down on the bar right as Joaquin sets down the next four. We carry those back to the table.

Haley and Cade are clearly disappointed we've returned and interrupted their alone time. She tells me he is different with her, but I need to keep my eye out for her, especially since Tuck doesn't know they've been seeing each other. Judging from the look in his eyes at that random guy who hit on me, a girl he just met, I think he might actually murder Cade if he knew about him and his sister hooking up behind his back. Especially since the guy is his best friend and roommate. But Tuck is blissfully oblivious.

"Shots!" Tuck slides the little glasses around the table.

"Naw man, you take mine. I'm driving." Cade passes his back.

"And tequila makes me vomit." Haley hands hers to me.

Tuck has his eyes on me. When he looks at me it's like I can feel his stare on my skin. "They've been like this all night. Thank God you showed up." He raises his glass. "To you." He sinks it back.

"How about we pace ourselves a little, okay drunkey?" I pat his arm. Wow, that's a solid bicep.

He cocks his head to the side, a sly grin showing his

pearly whites. "Okay, I'll slow down. But I've been at it all night. What's your excuse?"

A lifetime in sports and I was never able to curb my competitive side.

"Touché." I touch the small glass to my lips and down the burning liquid in one smooth gulp, not letting its effect on me show. We are staring at each other as I reach for the next one and slide its contents down my throat as well. When I grab the shot sitting in front of him, his eyes widen in surprise. I sip that one down too, never breaking eye contact.

"Fuck. Me." He is impressed.

"Was that a proposition?"

He gets a little flushed up through his cheeks but then smiles, stunned. "Will you marry me?"

"Not a chance."

"I'll ask again when I'm sober. I'm much more charming."

"Oh yeah?"

"Yeah. You'll definitely say yes the next time I ask."

"I guess we'll have to wait and see."

"Yup." He hiccups. "Wanna dance?" He holds his hand out to me.

"Sure."

Tuck has surprisingly good rhythm for his level of inebriation. He wiggles his booty and shimmies his shoulders. At one point I think he throws in some jazz hands. He has that big, silly smile on the whole time. The one that's completely carefree and fun. He can't moonwalk or do the worm, but that doesn't stop him from trying. The best part is he doesn't care. We laugh at how horrible he is.

"Your turn, girl. Show me your badass moves."

I pull out a couple classics—the sprinkler and the shopping

cart. Tuck claps for me and joins in, laughing the whole time. His smile is so genuine and beautiful, it's disarming. As we dance, my elbows and hips keep bumping into him. We seem to be drifting closer together.

The next time we make contact, the full length of my arm brushes against his side and neither of us are in a rush to pull away. He's dancing even closer now. He smells like fresh laundry and a mix of beer and tequila. His eyes are laser focused on me while we dance, still smiling.

He is watching me and I'm aware of how warm my entire body is and how fast my heart is beating. As the music picks up speed, his fingers touch lightly to my back, encouraging me to step closer. I do. Tuck's hand slides slowly down to my hip.

My pulse quickens. When's the last time a guy did that to me?

With a little pressure on my hip I move with him and we sway to the music. Our bodies are almost touching and his body heat is overwhelming. He's still looking at me intently, his lips parted. He's leaning in toward me. Am I holding my breath? But then the song ends.

"Whew, it's hot in here," I pant.

He chuckles, flashing his big smile and deep dimples as his hands leave my sides. "Yeah. Let's go."

Tuck wraps his solid arm around my shoulder as we walk back to our table. He leans down to me, his lips brushing at my earlobe. "Do you want another drink before I close my tab? I think I'm done celebrating for the night."

"No thanks. Maybe just a water?"

He smiles and gives my shoulder two quick squeezes, "Sure thing, darlin'."

It looks like Haley and Cade have left to the dance floor

when I get to the table, their beers still mostly intact.

The crowd has started to thin a little and Tuck returns shortly with a glass of ice water for me. He sees the two mostly full beers and sighs.

"Guess it's all up to me." He slides one in front of him and takes a swig. His eyelids are getting heavy and his eyes are glazing over. I softly pat his knee and grab Haley's beer. Eff, this glass is big.

"I'll help."

He sleepily grins, his left dimple appearing as he lays his hand over mine, pressing it around his thigh, just above his knee. I didn't realize how intimately I was touching him and now I'm a little embarrassed. Let's change the subject.

"So, what are you celebrating?"

He looks at me dazedly. "You're gorgeous."

I roll my eyes but can't keep a serious face. "I asked you a question."

He shrugs. "Being single."

"Oh?"

He nods, his head steadily lowering toward the table. "My girlfriend. Ali." His cheek is now resting on the shiny surface. "Just dumped me."

Damn. "I'm so sorry, Tuck. That sucks."

His eyes are now closed, mouth open. "Broke my heart."

Well, shit.

Made in the
USA
Monee, IL